House of Christmas Secrets

Lynda Stacey

Where heroes are like chocolate – irresistible!

Published 2018 by Choc Lit Limited
Penrose House, Crawley Drive, Camberley, Surrey GU15 2AB, UK
www.choc-lit.com

A CIP catalogue record for this book is available
from the British Library

ISBN: 978-1-78189-429-3

Printed and bound in Great Britain by Clays Ltd, Elcograf S.p.A.

To my brother, Stuart Thompson, who has been the one constant in my life.

Not only did he once buy me an Audi TT, for which I'll be forever grateful, but he also bought me my very first word processor, which he gave to me with the words:

'You keep saying you're going to write a novel … here you go, get on with it.'

Well, thank you, I finally did!

x

Acknowledgements

Many thanks go to Mr Gerald Aburrow and Dr Mark
Giles, the true owners of Wrea Head Hall. You've
both been so unbelievably supportive throughout
the publication of both *House of Secrets* and its
sequel, *House of Christmas Secrets* and for that
I thank you from the bottom of my heart.

Wrea Head Hall Hotel, your home is the most beautiful
and inspirational setting that I could have wished for.
I always feel very spoiled when get the opportunity
to stay at the Hall and I constantly encourage
everyone that I know to go and stay with you too.

As always a huge thank you goes to my husband, Haydn. I
couldn't write any of my books without your support. Our
brainstorming sessions over dinner are always fun, we tear
the books apart and put them back together and always
for the better. You really are the best husband I could
have ever wished for, you're the anchor in my life and the
one person in the world who I could not live without.

Many thanks to author Jane Lovering who critiques
all of my work. On some days you pull me along,
kicking and screaming and on other days we get to eat
afternoon tea and drink Prosecco, which is always fun.

To both Kathy Kilner and author Victoria Howard
who read my manuscripts over and over. You both
give me the valuable (honest) feedback that every
author needs and for that I thank you both.

To my cover designer: you are amazing.
Thank you. I love them all. x

To my editor: thank you for all your hard work. You add
the sparkle and the shine to each and every one of my
novels and I love every moment of working with you. x

To the Tasting Panel readers who passed this novel:
Melissa B, Sigi, Elena B, Jo O and Barbara P.

And finally to the team at Choc Lit: you're the best. Thank
you so much for all your support and encouragement.
You have no idea how much it's appreciated. xxx

Chapter One

Jess hovered in the hotel's grand hall and leaned against the huge inglenook fireplace. She brushed her dark, wild Afro hair away from her face, more out of habit than need, before allowing her hand to run across the stone mantel. Her fingertips traced the detail in the antique carved stone, and she tipped her head to one side in order to study it more closely. She had lived at Wrea Head Hall now for almost eighteen months, yet each and every day she found another thing of beauty that she hadn't previously noticed.

Kneeling down by the tiled hearth, she felt herself shiver as she plunged her fingers into the thick pile of the new carpet. Everything was new and had been replaced after the fire that had almost destroyed the whole hotel just over a year before and now, instead of the dark blues that had previously run throughout the grand hall, everything was decorated in warm reds and golds, giving the whole room a rich and luxurious finish. Jess looked up to the ceiling, thankful that the ornate plaster had survived, along with the carved bosses within it that were painted gold on the white background. So much had been lost, yet miraculously much had also been saved or repaired. Even the Wren oak panelling had been restored, and Jess smiled at its beauty, grateful that the insurance had covered the work, and relieved that skilled craftsmen had pulled out all the stops to bring the Hall back to its former glory.

Jess picked up the long, cast iron poker, and began to stab at the embers in the grate, before carefully choosing a log, lifting back the fireguard and throwing the wood into the flames that already danced up the chimney. The sudden addition of another log created new flames of gold, orange and blue that wrapped themselves around the wood. For Jess the flames held a mesmerising magic and comfort that she couldn't explain, and many a night she'd come down here with Jack after the guests had all gone to their beds. Together they'd sit on one of the settees, cuddling up, holding hands and simply staring into what remained of the embers.

'Never waste a log,' Jack often said to her; it was a saying he'd picked up from Madeleine's father shortly before his untimely death. The saying always made Jess sigh and she wondered what life at the hotel would have been like had Morris survived. Would she be living here? Would she have got to know Jack? Would they have fallen in love? And what if they hadn't, where would she be now and what would she be doing? She held a hand to her heart and acknowledged that she had so many reasons to be happy. Yet, she was fully aware that she was only happy because others, including herself, had previously suffered. She thought back to the year before, to how her sister Madeleine's former boyfriend had terrorised them all and every single day she wished that Liam had never existed, that Madeleine had never met him and that he'd never got involved with their precious family. After all, he'd killed many of the people they loved and had almost succeeded in killing the rest. His obsession with Madeleine had caused each and every one of them more pain and heartache than Jess could have ever imagined.

Feeling a little warmer, Jess moved back from the fire, sat on the upholstered fender seat within the inglenook and thought about the past. It was times like this, as she sat watching the flames, that she'd think of her mother, of Madeleine's father and of all the people that Liam had killed, while all the time feeling ridiculously overwhelmed and grateful to have survived his clutches.

'This year we're just going to have a nice, normal

Christmas,' she whispered to herself in full knowledge that the happenings of the year before had been somewhat extraordinary. In fact, she thought that this Christmas might end up being what most people would classify as boring. But she didn't care; after being kidnapped, after thinking that both she and Maddie might die, any kind of boring would be absolutely perfect. The only good part of the Christmas before had been Christmas Eve, the wonderful meal that Nomsa had cooked and the fact that both Bandit's grandmother, Emily, and his father, Arthur, had come back to live at the Hall, where they belonged. It still seemed such an amazing coincidence that Bandit, the former gamekeeper of the hotel and the man Madeleine had fallen in love with, was a direct descendant of the family who had owned Wrea Head Hall for generations, before Maddie's father had bought it and turned it into a hotel.

'Penny for them?' Madeleine asked as she walked into the grand hall and threw herself onto one of the red and gold settees. 'Come on, spill the beans.'

'What?'

'You're miles away. Are you okay?'

Jess knew that Madeleine was concerned for her, knew how many times she'd begged her to go for counselling after the trauma of being kidnapped, but Jess didn't want to talk about it, not to Madeleine and certainly not to a stranger. All she wanted was to be left alone. She watched as Maddie lifted a hand to pat the seat beside her.

'Come and sit with me for a while, you look completely done in,' Maddie said, moving up and making room. Jess stood up, moved across to where Madeleine sat, but then stopped and stared at the hundreds of sparkling lights that shone out from the Christmas tree. Even though it was only just after three o'clock, the early evening light was fading fast, making the tree lights shine out brighter, and Jess knew that before long the darkness would once again surround the Hall and the hotel's guests would gather for dinner, a time that always felt special.

'I know it's only just December, but I was dressing the tree and making it look beautiful while no one was around,' Jess began to explain. 'You know, making it symmetrical, just the way Emily likes it.' The tree stood twenty feet tall in the corner of the grand hall in full view of the grand staircase and next to the ceiling-high, stained glass mullion window, so it could be seen by everyone as they arrived at the hotel.

Jess stood staring at the tree with her cardigan pulled tightly around her. She then sighed, tutted, walked over to the tree and moved a bauble from one branch to another. 'It has to be perfect for her, Maddie.' She turned to face her sister. 'She's ninety-three and so very frail. I don't think she'll see another Christmas, not after this one and … What about the wedding? What if she isn't here for my wedding?' Tears began to drip down Jess's face. They glistened against her dark mocha skin and she wiped them away in haste, angry that she'd allowed herself to cry. 'I don't know why I'm crying, it's not like she's died already, is it?'

Madeleine stood up and tucked her shoulder length blonde hair behind her ears. 'You've done all you can for Emily, Jess. She knows how much you love her.' She put an arm round her sister's shoulders, pulling her into an embrace. 'You've been by her side every moment you could during the past year, as well as covering reception when I've needed you. I've seen you sitting in the garden with her, hour after hour, taking drinks and cakes to her room, and the hours you've spent pushing her round the shops, not that you ever bought anything, but you took her anyhow, because she liked to look.' Madeleine squeezed her shoulders. 'Honey, she couldn't have wished for a better homecoming, or a better companion. I know she loves and appreciates you.'

Jess cuddled into Maddie and closed her eyes. Was that what she'd been to Emily, a companion? She shook her head; it hadn't been like that at all. Emily had helped her come to terms with her own life, just as much as she'd helped Emily. What's more, she genuinely loved Emily. She loved spending time with her and it truly felt as though she were part of her own family rather than Bandit's.

'And it's not long now till your wedding, and I'm sure Emily will be here.' She kissed Jess's cheek. 'And talking of the wedding, is there anything you need doing? We're only a month away,' Madeleine questioned, and raised her eyebrows.

'No, everything's sorted. Nomsa is making the cake and you and Poppy and I have just one more dress fitting and then we're good to go.' Jess smiled at the thought. A week after New Year's Eve, when the hotel would be at its quietest, she and Jack would be married. She'd dreamed of this day and she closed her eyes to picture Jack's face, smiling down at her.

'Are you and Bandit ever going to tie the knot, Maddie?' Jess asked, opening her eyes again. 'I mean, you are engaged, and you do live together, so you might as well, right?'

Madeleine shrugged her shoulders. 'If I'm honest, I haven't really thought too much about it. We are both always so busy with the hotel, but I guess we will, someday soon. Maybe next year. Let's get your big day all sorted first.'

Jess felt Madeleine's hold loosen, felt her sigh and saw how she too stared unseeingly at the Christmas lights. 'Besides, it's been a very turbulent year, hasn't it?'

Once again Jess wiped at her eyes. 'Oh, Maddie, you came here looking for safety and security for you and for Poppy, but then, without warning, Liam tracked you down, and turned all our lives into a living nightmare. But we came through all that, together, and not only did you find love with Bandit, but you also found his long-lost grandmother, Emily, brought her home to the Hall and the true story of Bandit's heritage emerged through her diary.' She nodded. 'So, yep, to say you had quite a turbulent year is an understatement.'

Madeleine tipped her head to one side. 'It's quite a story, isn't it? Maybe I'll write about it one day.'

'I think Emily would love it if you found the time to write her story. After all, you are the author in the family.' It was true, before the events of last year Madeleine had written books that had all been bestsellers.

Jess thought of the many nights she and Emily had sat here before the fire together, Emily reminiscing about the past. Jack was the assistant manager at the hotel and regularly worked the evening shift as Madeleine had four-year-old Poppy to look after, leaving Jess with time to spend with Emily. Over the last year Emily had told her all about her life, about the many secrets she had kept and that there was one more secret to reveal. She had talked about the past, of how she'd grown up at Wrea Head Hall and fallen in love with the gardener, her Eddie. How they'd meet on the secret staircase, and the desperate time when she'd given birth in the tower room, afraid and alone. She'd told Jess about her father, who had dominated her mother and siblings, expecting them to live by his rules. But now at ninety-three years old, Emily was the only one left. She'd survived them all.

'There you both are, my lovelies,' Nomsa's deep Caribbean voice rang out like a melody as she walked from the bar and into the grand hall. 'I'm going to need some willing volunteers to come into my kitchen and taste the first of my Christmas cakes, and you two both look like you need feeding,' she joked. 'What's more, I've got extra brandy here to soak the others.' Nomsa waved a bottle of brandy in the air and laughed before heading to the oak door that led to the kitchen. 'I'll be cutting you both a huge slice, so you need to come quickly before Poppy eats it all, and I don't have to tell you what all that brandy will do to a four-year-old,' she cackled as the door swung to a close behind her.

The sisters looked at one another and began to laugh. 'Do you think for one moment that Nomsa will allow us to have a nice, quiet, or boring Christmas? Especially with a wedding to plan.'

Nomsa had worked in the hotel's kitchens long before Madeleine's father had bought the Hall and, although she had a home of her own nearby, she never seemed to be in it. She had loved both Madeleine and Jess as part of her family from the moment they had come to live at the hotel, taken them under her wing, and, like a mother hen, she'd clucked around them, looked after them, cared for them, hugged and fed them. In fact, it was Nomsa that turned the hotel into a home, not just for them but also for the hundreds of guests that stayed there every year.

'Well, for what it's worth, provided Poppy doesn't end up plastered on the Christmas cake, I'd be up for a quiet and normal Christmas,' Jess added as she saw Madeleine's eyes skim the room. 'If you ignore the fact that we have a hotel to run, and we're fully booked for the festive season, with all the guests wanting the perfect Christmas. I have no idea how many turkeys Nomsa will prepare and stuff, or how many mince pies she will bake before we get to New Year.' She sighed a happy sigh. 'What would we do without her, Maddie?'

Madeleine shook her head. 'I have no idea. But right now all I can think is if we don't get in that kitchen fast, my four-year-old daughter will be as drunk as a skunk on Christmas cake and it won't be Nomsa that has to sit up with her while she throws up, or sobers up.'

Chapter Two

Jess and Madeleine followed Nomsa into the kitchen, where Poppy was dressed up in a Spider-Man outfit. She jumped up and down giggling with excitement as she pointed at walls, pretending to cast her web.

'And you, Jack, you've got to hide under there, and pretend to be injured,' Poppy said to Jack who was sitting on the floor of the utility room, leaning against the freezers with a sleeping Buddy on his lap, the spaniel having made himself comfortable. 'Then ... then I can fly around the kitchen, like this, and make you all better and I can save you with my super powers, can't I, Mummy?' She directed the question at Maddie who had already picked up a slice of Christmas cake from the plate that Nomsa had eagerly held out.

Madeleine smiled and nodded. 'You sure can, but can you please tell me why my little girl is such a tomboy these days?' she asked as she pushed a small piece of cake into Poppy's mouth. 'I mean, come on, it isn't that long ago you were playing with dolls and teddy bears. But now ... now you dress up like a superhero, kick balls and climb trees.' She gave Poppy a hug and a kiss before allowing her to run back to where Jack was sitting.

'Because being a superhero is more fun, isn't it, Poppy?' Jack began to tickle Poppy. 'And climbing trees makes you look like a monkey, doesn't it?' Poppy squealed in delight, and Jack glanced up to where both Madeleine and Jess stood. 'Jess, Jess. Help. Jess help me,' he shouted. 'I'm in danger ... and Spider-Man is about to save me.' His raised voice disturbed the sleeping Buddy and Jack now found himself pinned to the floor, with the spaniel bouncing and barking around him. 'Oy, oy, oy ... Enough ...' he said, in an attempt to calm the dog. 'You'll go outside,' he threatened.

'Yeah, go on, Buddy, get him,' Poppy yelled and giggled as she too joined in with Buddy and jumped on top of Jack, while waving her arms around in the air.

Jess sat down at the table and watched the pair play. Jack really was everything she'd ever wished for in a man. He was kind, fun and she just knew he'd make the best father in the world.

'Oh, I'm not saving you, Jack,' Jess said with a laugh. 'You deserve all you get for teasing her.' She picked up the teapot and shook it. 'I think I'll take a pot up to Emily. I'm sure she'll be ready for one by now.' Jess had left Emily sleeping a couple of hours before and always checked on her before supper.

'Serves me right, does it? Well ...' Jack moved onto his hands and knees. '... this nice guy just turned into the Incredible Hulk, and he's gonna get ya,' he shouted, scurrying across the floor to chase Poppy, who had now run to Jess and jumped up and into her arms.

'Aunty Jess! Ahhh, save me!' She buried her face into Jess's neck, while giggling and squirming as Jack came closer.

'Taken refuge with Aunty Jess, have we?' Jack growled, still in Incredible Hulk mode. 'Well, if I catch you, I'm going to tickle you till you scream and then ... then I'm gonna blow raspberries on your tummy.' He advanced on Poppy who squirmed and clung to her aunt like an overgrown baby orangutan. 'And, you, protector of the little one, you ...' He paused and leaned forward, giving Jess just a moment to catch the sparkle in his eye. '... you, my dear, get a kiss for your trouble.' He planted a firm kiss on Jess's lips, and then turned to the back door, opened it and threw the ball across the lawn for Buddy to chase. 'Go on, boy, off you go, have a run.' He watched as the spaniel ran out and across the grass, before happily heading for the woods.

'What's all this talk about kissing?' Bandit asked as he entered the kitchen and automatically threw his arms around Madeleine. 'If there's any kissing going on, then I'm sure that we should be involved.' He planted a kiss on Madeleine's lips, leaned back, looked into her eyes and kissed her again. 'In fact, I definitely think we should be involved,' he said, making them both laugh.

'Now then you soppy lot, put each other down while you're in my kitchen.' Nomsa laughed. 'I won't have kissing going on in here, no, sir.' She swiped at Bandit with her tea towel. 'And you, young man,' she said, pointing to the utility room, 'go and wash your hands and then you can try my cake.' She turned to Jess. 'I'll make up a tea tray for you to take up to Emily ... you can take her some cake too.'

Chapter Three

Emily sat up against the array of pillows and looked out of the window over the vast gardens that surrounded the Hall. The flowers had long since gone with the autumn, but the shrubs and trees still remained, although most of the trees had now lost their leaves. No matter what the season, she never tired of this view; after all, this same room had been hers since she was a very small child. And now, at ninety-three years old, she'd had a good life and, for most of it, all the beauty Wrea Head Hall had to offer had surrounded her. She'd known love, companionship and, even though she had never expected it, she'd had her final moments back here at the Hall.

She looked down at her hands; the paper-thin skin that covered them and the dark veins that stood out from beneath. How had she got so old, she wondered? And when had life taken over her body and turned her from being a vibrant young woman into an old one? She took in a deep breath and held onto her chest. The pain was there every time she breathed in and she took short shallow gasps until it subsided.

Emily leaned out of bed. She needed her pen and writing paper and so pulled open the top drawer of her dressing table, where the letters she'd already written looked back at her. There was one for Jack and one for Madeleine. There was also one for her son, Arthur. But there was one more letter she needed to write. She needed to write to Jess before it was too late and before every ounce of energy finally left her body. It was a time she knew wasn't too far away, and yet, a time she'd come to terms with. But how to start her letter? All the letters had been important in their own way, but the one to Jess just had to be right, and what to say to her was a decision in itself, which was why she'd left it until last.

Emily thought of Jess and smiled. She'd become more like a daughter to her than a friend. But how would she say goodbye, for that's what the letters would be, a final goodbye to the people she loved. She closed her eyes and thought for a moment before starting:

My dearest Jess

My dear girl, how I wish I'd had a daughter and how I wish she'd been just like you. There would have been nothing I would have changed, for you are beautiful both inside and out.

Over the past year I've tried to tell you my story, tried to teach you from all that I got wrong and, through my stories, you know that I have kept far too many secrets. My stories and secrets are my legacy to you. For secrets, as you know, cause trouble. They are never a good thing and the secrets that are held within this house, and within the people in it, really need to stop, for all of your sakes. After all, why do we keep a secret in the first place? Is it to protect ourselves or others around us? And if it is to protect others, why oh why do we feel they need our protection? Isn't that for them to decide?

We should always remember that every secret is preceded by an action. And it's normally an action that should never have happened in the first place. So, think twice, my darling girl, think twice about everything you do, especially if you think it's something that you shouldn't, because secrets are crippling, they never bring joy, or should I say they never brought me any joy. And me, I made the biggest mistake of all. I was keeping everyone's secrets for them and making sure that everyone around me was happy. Even though, most of the time, other people's happiness was at the cost of my own.

Now, don't mistake my words. I have been content for most of the time and I've had a good life. I loved my Eddie with all my heart and with that love I bore my son Arthur. If my Eddie hadn't been injured in the war, if his mind hadn't been taken from him, I'm sure we'd have married and lived happily – but a happiness such as that was not for me. I was frowned upon and brought shame to my family for living with a man that was not my husband, but I loved him so much, even though with his mental state he had no idea who I was. But I wouldn't have had it any other way. My life was exactly how it should have been. So please, don't be sad at my passing. Just smile in the knowledge that you made my last days the best that they could have been.

Emily broke off from writing, leaned back and sighed. She breathed in and out, taking short shallow breaths. She was afraid of the pain and wanted to finish her letter before it got too bad. She spent a few moments concentrating on her breathing before pushing the quilt back and getting out of bed. She pushed her feet into her slippers and then, with hesitant steps, she made her way over to the wardrobe, all the while using the furniture to steady her balance. Opening the wardrobe doors, Emily stood back and studied the few clothes that remained, the few possessions she'd brought with her and the memory box that sat in one corner of the shelf. Carefully, she opened the box and peered inside at the photographs, small pieces of jewellery and the letters that Eddie had sent to her during the war. With shaking hands, she moved the items from side to side, until she put her hand on a small, thin jewellery box. She stared at it for a moment before opening it to reveal a necklace. It was a small silver love heart that had been a gift for her eighteenth birthday. She smiled as she remembered the tears that had filled her mother's eyes as she'd presented her with the chain and the words she'd said: 'This, my darling, can be worn at your wedding, once your father approves of a suitable man, that is.' Emily knew that her parents had hoped that she would marry a doctor, a solicitor or an accountant, but she'd rebelled and had only ever loved her Eddie, a simple gardener who had loved her back, much to her parents' disgust.

'Just perfect,' she whispered as she replaced the lid to her most treasured memories and carefully made her way back to the bed, where she covered herself with the quilt and collapsed against the pillows. She took a moment to regain her strength before once again picking up the pen and completing the letter.

I'm thinking of secrets, Jess, and I'm pleased you chose to share yours with me. I know it's early days, but it's time you spoke to Jack. You have to tell him what you know. He's a good man, the right man for you, and he'll look after you and support you. He'll make the best husband you could ever wish for, I promise. Oh, I see the sparkle in your eyes when you look at him, the way you blush and smile and, what's more, I see the way that he looks at you too. It's more than obvious how much your love for each other has grown over the past year. So, please, take control of your life while you have the chance. Be happy together, and have the kind of good, real, loving relationship that I could never have with my Eddie, not after the war.

But living life through a loving relationship comes with a responsibility of its own and, as you'll have found within this envelope, I've given you my necklace. It was a necklace

that my mother gave to me. A necklace I never ever wore,
because with it had been the condition that I should only
wear it on my wedding day, but only if I married the man
that my father chose. But that was never going to happen.
I would never have chosen another, not over my Eddie,
so it's lain in my memory box for far too many years. But
you, my dear Jess, I hope you will wear it on the day you
marry Jack. I'm sorry, my darling, I don't think I am going
to live long enough to see you two married, but hold me
in your heart and I'll walk with you every step of the way,
for always. You go together so perfectly and I just hope
that the happiness you share now will last you both for the
whole of your lifetime.

Sending you love as always
Emily x

Chapter Four

Jack took the stairs two at a time, his hand barely touching the carved oak balustrade as he leapt from one step to the other. He reached the top, turned onto the landing, and burst in through Emily's bedroom door.

For a moment he felt as though he were either in the wrong room, or on a film set and definitely intruding on something he shouldn't. The sight that met him stopped him in his tracks while he gasped for breath. The normally peaceful room was a hive of activity, with Emily central to the attention. She lay flat on the bed; her pillows had been tossed to the floor and two paramedics worked feverishly on her. Meanwhile, his Jess was crouched down in a corner, humming, rocking and sobbing with her eyes tightly closed and her fingers pressed into her ears. It suddenly occurred to him that he'd never seen her look quite so small, or as fragile and defenceless, like a very young child who was upset or hiding.

'Jess, I'm here, come on, I'm here, I've got you.' He went to her, reached out towards her, almost afraid to touch her, and in a gentle loving gesture he used just one finger to stroke her cheek, knowing that in her current state he'd have frightened her even more if he'd taken hold of her. He waited for a moment until she opened one eye and acknowledged him, and then carefully but firmly he pulled her towards him, turning her away from the bed, so as to block her view. He didn't want her to see what the paramedics were doing, even though he knew she'd already witnessed too much.

He shook his head, annoyed with himself that he hadn't been here when Jess needed him. A walk in the woods with Buddy had taken him out of range of any mobile signal and only when he'd heard the ambulance had he realised that something was very wrong. He had run back across the fields and into the Hall, where an inconsolable, sobbing Nomsa had pointed to the stairs, while all the time shepherding guests into the conservatory and away from the commotion.

For a moment he just stared at where Emily lay, watching carefully as paramedics rushed around with oxygen, defibrillators and more swabs and syringes than he'd ever seen. Then the men gave each other a look, a look that told Jack that Emily had gone, that there was nothing more they could do, and he began mentally preparing himself for how Jess would be, how he'd tell her and how he'd look after her during the days to come. Nothing seemed real, the room felt as though it were full of fog, like a mist enveloping them all.

The pandemonium had stopped. The fog lifted and one paramedic checked his watch; a time was muttered, a phone call was made and paperwork completed. Then Jack watched as they began packing equipment away, placing syringes and swabs into tubs and bags, before respectfully covering Emily's body with a sheet and leaving the room, carrying all the equipment down the stairs with them.

Jack felt hot and nauseous. His head began to spin and he could feel himself trembling. It was a trembling that started in his toes and travelled up and into both of his arms that were wrapped around Jess. And then, suddenly, he gasped and took a breath, realising that the whole time he'd been watching the paramedics, he'd been holding it; wishing, praying and hoping that they'd perform a miracle, but all the time knowing that there wouldn't be one, not today. For a moment or two he concentrated on breathing, in and out, an action that should have been automatic. Automatic, that was, until, like Emily, your body chose not to.

Both Madeleine and Bandit burst into the room and Jack immediately caught Bandit's eye, and shook his head. 'I'm so sorry,' he mouthed as he moved Jess past them in an attempt to take her out of the room and onto the landing, where a group of guests hovered, all watching with tear-filled eyes.

'I'm sorry, but please, give the family some privacy. I believe Nomsa is serving tea in the conservatory.' He ushered the guests towards the stairs, all the while holding onto Jess. He looked back into the room and prayed that Emily's passing had been fast, and that she hadn't felt any pain. After all, wasn't that what everyone wished for? Didn't we all want to pass without trauma, pain or suffering?

'I ... I ... can't leave her,' Jess suddenly whispered, lifting a hand and wiping her face, while her eyes pleaded with Jack. 'Please, please, Jack, I ... I can't leave her, she's ... she's all alone.' She began to move back towards the room, but Madeleine stepped forward and wrapped her arms around both Jack and Jess.

'Jess, it's okay. Bandit's with her.' She paused. 'She's gone, Jess.' A deep sob left Madeleine's throat as she spoke. 'There's nothing more you can do. There's nothing any of us can do. Not any more.'

Jack loosened his grip and turned back to see where Bandit stood quietly and respectfully beside his grandmother's bed. He gently held her hand, stroked it and then leaned forward to kiss her on the forehead. 'Rest now, Grandma. Rest in peace.' The words were simple but final and, on hearing them, Jess fell to her knees as a long piercing scream that seemed to go on forever left her lips, a scream that was quickly followed by heart wrenching, uncontrollable sobs.

'No, no, no,' she shrieked. 'She can't be gone ... she was talking to me. She ... she was sitting there, in bed, drinking tea and talking ... like normal. She ... she even insisted I open the window, just as she liked it.' She looked up and pointed to the bed. 'She'd wanted the fresh air, but was cold and I got her an extra blanket to keep her warm. So, so ... she can't be gone, can she?'

Chapter Five

Bastion Collymore used his body to shield his eight-year-old daughter. It was the only way to protect her from the driving rain that pounded against his back and onto the pavement beyond the shop doorway, in which they'd made their home for the next few hours. He sighed, satisfied that, at least for now, Lily was dry, albeit he knew that she was cold and almost certainly hungry.

There were so many noises that surrounded them, every one amplified beyond normality. They were noises that during the day would hardly register, would pale into insignificance, but on a cold, dark night were emphasised and felt louder and more dangerous. There was the sound of traffic, the screeching of brakes, the tireless bleeps of a pelican crossing, and the joviality, shrieks and laughter of clubbers and partygoers, all on Christmas party nights out. They were all having fun, all intoxicated and all spending more money in one night than he'd most probably have earned in the past month.

The whole area was lit up with coloured, flashing Christmas lights. They were hung across the street between flashing Santas, stars and Christmas fairies. The flashing was annoying him and he glanced over his shoulder in the hope that they'd magically stop, only to see a man and woman in their late twenties, only ten years or so younger than he was himself, both tightly entwined and pressed into the corner of a see-through polycarbonate bus shelter. He could tell by the way their urgency was growing that their actions would soon turn into a sight that he wouldn't want Lily to witness and he manoeuvred his body to hide the view from his daughter's eyes, before nervously resting his own from the flashing onslaught. His eyes hurt with an overwhelming tiredness that he knew wouldn't go away, not until he could sleep properly, not until he knew they were safe.

It had been a long, cold and relentless afternoon of travel that had begun in London. Their day had involved sitting on platforms, waiting for the cheapest trains or buses. He'd even slipped them both into a toilet cubicle on the last train, where they'd hid, silently, until reaching the next stop. The stolen journey had saved them money, yet still they'd arrived in York just a little too late to catch the last bus to Scarborough.

Once again he closed his eyes. He was desperate to sleep, but didn't dare. Not tonight. He'd lived in London for far too long, had seen far too much and knew exactly what could happen on its streets. Deep down he knew that York would be no different. So tonight he had to stay vigilant, he had to know who was creeping around them and, at all times, be prepared for the unexpected. Above all else, he had to protect his child, and keep her safe. He felt in his pocket for his old army knife, a gift that his father had given to him. It was a weapon that he didn't want to use, but knew that he would, should he have to protect Lily.

He sighed. He wished he'd had time to plan for this journey, to save up and maybe then he could have afforded a hotel, or at least a bed and breakfast or even a hostel. Anything would have been better than having to sleep on the street, but even after the stolen journey, he only just had enough money left to catch tomorrow's early bus, meaning the luxury of any kind of safe environment wasn't an option.

He took in a deep breath and immediately wished he hadn't. He winced with pain. His arm immediately shot up and clutched at his ribs as a strange crackling sound came from within, quickly followed by the persistent coughing that had plagued him for the past few weeks.

'Daddy?' Lily's young voice whispered in the darkness. Her body inched closer to him, her arms encircled his waist and he felt her lips kiss his cheek. 'You okay, Daddy?'

She felt cold to his touch and he pulled his overcoat further around her body in an effort to keep her warm. He knew she was scared and hated himself for having to put her through this night. It was a night when most children would be counting down the days as they sped excitedly towards Christmas. With only ten days to go, most little girls would have thoughts of presents under a tree, of family gatherings and of food galore – all while waiting for Santa to arrive with an abundance of gifts for all.

'I'm fine, I'm fine. Don't you worry yourself, my beautiful girl.' Bastion's deep, Caribbean twang bellowed out louder than he'd intended and he tried to smile as he looked down at the child. He'd chosen the doorway for its depth and location. He'd guessed it to be one of the less populated areas of town, close to the bus station, yet far enough away that he'd hoped he'd get just a little privacy. The constantly flashing Christmas lights lit up Lily's beautiful big brown eyes, which stared back up at him like saucers. At just eight years old, she was already a picture of beauty, with the most perfect white teeth and dark, wild Afro hair that had formed a halo around her soft chestnut face. It was a hairstyle that never looked brushed, yet had always looked perfect and Bastion found himself carefully brushing the hair away from her face with his fingers and tucking it behind her ear.

'I'm so sorry, my girl. You shouldn't be here; this is no place for you to sleep. Not on a night like this.' His voice cracked with emotion. 'I'll make it up to you.' He leaned forward, kissing her gently on the forehead. 'Tomorrow will be a good day. I promise.' Again, he took in a breath. The breaths were becoming more and more shallow. Every part of his chest hurt, every inch of him felt the cold and a violent trembling began at his toes and worked its way up and through his body, which burned with the heat of a furnace but cooled quickly as the persistent rain soaked through his coat and reached his skin.

He pulled at the old army duffel bag that lay by their feet and dragged an old jumper from within. 'Here you go, princess. Put this on.'

Lily pulled her thin cotton school dress down over her knees, pulled at the coat that was far too small and forced a smile. She looked down at the jumper in his hands, and he watched the tears fill her eyes. 'I'm okay, Daddy. You wear it.' She pushed the jumper towards him. 'You're poorly, Daddy, you need to get better.' Her chattering teeth gave her away and a tear dropped down Bastion's face as he realised that even at such a young age, his daughter was willing to stay cold, just so that he could be warm.

He shook his head. He felt selfish, cruel and had gone beyond self-hatred. Lily was young, innocent and precious. So much wrong had already happened in her life that she hadn't deserved, which had begun with her mother leaving so many years before.

He thought of Lily's mother, of Annie. She was a typical working girl, just one of the many that London had to offer. But, of course, she hadn't been a working girl when they'd met – or so he'd thought. They'd met in a club, he'd asked her to dance and he'd been the perfect gentleman – taking her out for dinners, buying her flowers and courting her just as he'd thought she deserved. The attraction had been mutual, they'd spent every minute they could together and the hours had turned into days. To Bastion she'd been the perfect woman; he'd loved everything about her, from her shoulder length auburn hair, and her petite frame, to the freckles that scattered themselves across her nose. She'd been younger than him by a good ten years but it hadn't mattered. They'd fallen into a routine; both had had to work, him on the docks and her in the clubs. She'd worked every weekend, but Monday to Thursday of every week they'd be inseparable. Every single thing they did had been in unison, they'd shop together, sleep together and they'd party together. But they'd partied too hard and had gone to one party too many where far too much heroin had been available, and after night after night of abuse, it had been more than obvious that the drugs had finally won – Annie had become addicted. He'd always stayed clear, kept himself clean, and had tried to look after her, tried to help her, and did everything he could to keep her away from the drugs. But the call had been too strong and it was only then that he learned the truth about who Annie really was. She was a prostitute; a high-class escort that only needed to work a few days a week to earn a fortune from rich clients. He'd always thought she'd worked in a bar, that's what she'd told him, and the revelation of what she really did had been a huge shock. But her need for a heroin fix changed her – she began to lie, began to steal and had quickly lost her job. No one wanted an escort with a drug problem and she'd had no choice but to work the streets, where she was ruled by pimps and soon found herself owing them money. Slowly but surely she'd come to rely on one pimp in particular, Griff, and after losing her own flat through debt, he'd convinced her that she was safer living and working in his brothel, under his protection.

At first Bastion had been furious. He hated what she did and had tried to walk away, but he'd loved her and had hated the thought that other men were near her. After all, in his opinion she'd been far too beautiful to be on the game. He became obsessed and spent every penny he earned paying for her in an attempt to keep her away from the others, not realising that he was helping to keep both her pimp in pocket and her in drugs.

But then, like a miracle, Annie had become pregnant. From an early stage her petite frame had made the pregnancy more than obvious and, much to Bastion's relief, her pimp had lost interest. He'd stopped making demands and had thrown her out of the brothel, giving Bastion the perfect opportunity to offer her a home, and to clean her up. It had all been a risk, he'd known from the beginning that the baby might not be his, in fact there was a strong chance that it wasn't. But he didn't care. This was his only opportunity to get Annie back, this was his chance to be a father and this time he intended to get it right.

At first they'd been happy. They'd decorated the flat, bought a crib, a pram and baby clothes. And, for a while, Annie had tried, especially during her pregnancy and when Lily was first born. But for her, drugs and alcohol had been as much a part of her life as the air that she breathed, and it wasn't long before once again the heroin became a daily addiction. Every day, after work, Bastion returned home expecting her to be either dead or gone. The longer she stayed, the more he hoped that one day she'd clean herself up and they'd finally have a normal family life. It was a future he wanted and wished for, a future that had both Annie and Lily in it.

But he should have known better, he should have never wished for his very own 'happy-ever-after', not with Annie. The track lines on her arms became more and more apparent. She'd stopped caring about her appearance, stopped bathing, washing her hair and spent hour after hour crying, shaking, rocking or throwing up. She'd leave Lily to cry and on most days Bastion would come home from work to find that Lily hadn't been changed, cleaned or fed, and all because Annie had either been as high as a kite or in need of a fix. One way or the other she hadn't been capable of being a mother.

Bastion's love eventually diminished. He began to hate her for neglecting Lily. He couldn't believe how little a mother could care about her own baby and in the end even looking at Annie was so painful that he began to wish her gone. It was something he'd never previously wished for. All he'd ever wanted was to be happy, to be a normal couple with a family, with holidays, Christmas and birthdays. He'd wished so often for a good and happy home, but now, all he wanted was a home without Annie in it.

It had been a cold, dark, winter night, almost eight years before, when he'd returned home from work to find a completely empty flat. He'd opened the door, and been totally shocked by what he'd seen. He'd quickly closed his eyes, slammed the door closed, and had stood on the landing, looking around, double checking that he'd opened the right door, on the right landing, to the right flat. He'd shaken his head violently, and pinched himself repeatedly, before once again slowly opening the door and peering inside. Annie had gone and taken every single one of their possessions with her. The only thing she'd left behind had been Lily, cold, sobbing and alone in her cot in the empty room. In a split second his whole life and dreams fell apart and he was suddenly alone, with a tiny baby who needed him in order to survive.

Bastion shook his head and brought himself back to the present. He'd long since stopped loving Annie and on most days he wondered what he'd seen in her in the first place. She wasn't the woman he'd originally loved, she'd changed so much and he'd spent years doing everything he could to keep her as far away from Lily as possible. On many an occasion he'd found himself wishing she'd disappear without a trace or that she'd overdose on the drugs and be gone forever.

Annie hadn't wanted Lily when she'd had the chance, but now, for some reason, she insisted on coming back each Christmas and birthday. She'd turn up, sit for hours, pretend she cared, and even bring a gift for Lily, normally something small, something she'd obviously stolen, whilst all the time rocking, scratching and shaking.

Was he so wrong not to want Annie around? Did he owe it to Lily to allow her mother to visit? Did his daughter have the right to know who her mother was, even if that mother was a dirty, drug-addicted prostitute, who'd abandoned her soon after birth?

He knew he'd wished her gone. But deep down, the good in him had hoped that one day she'd surprise him. Hoped that one day she'd turn up, clean from the drugs, and suddenly become the mother that Lily deserved. Had he hoped for too much?

Bastion gave Lily a stern look, followed by a smile, before pushing the jumper over her head. 'No arguments, young lady. Don't I always tell you that you need to do what your daddy says?' He coughed again, before he pulled the jumper down and over the top of her dress and coat and then laughed as it hung loosely around her legs, covering her feet like a long woollen duvet. He then dug for a second jumper and repeated the exercise. 'It's just for one night,' he said. 'Tomorrow will be a new day, you'll see.' He positioned the large duffel bag as close to the shop door as he could, and placed a third jumper over the top of it to make a small mattress, just big enough for the child. 'Lie down, princess. Lie down. Try and get comfy.' He indicated the corner.

Bastion rubbed his tired eyes and watched as Lily curled up and pretended to sleep. He stroked her cheek and prayed that he could stay awake long enough to keep her safe. He saw her eyes flicker and a half smile cross her lips.

'Hey, do you know what, princess? There are people out there that pay a fortune to go on a camping trip.' His deep laugh echoed around their small space. 'Yet here we are, my girl, doing it for free.' He tried to make a joke, to lighten the mood, but again the coughing began to tear through his tormented body.

'But … Daddy.' She opened her eyes and a sob left her throat. 'We're not camping, Daddy, are we?' The trembling in her voice told him what he already knew. She was terrified. 'Please, Daddy. I want to go home.'

'I know you do, honey. I want to go home too.' Nothing was further from the truth, for earlier that day Annie had broken in and had once again emptied the flat. He'd arrived home from work and from bringing Lily home from school, and for the second time all their possessions had been gone, even Lily's toys. He'd stood, shaking with temper and with sadness, knowing that he couldn't do it again, he couldn't replace everything, not a second time. He hadn't got enough money left and knew that the little he did have wouldn't last to the end of the month. Their home had become an empty shell and in truth he knew he had no choice but to leave. While they stayed there, Annie would keep coming back, keep taking what she could and he'd never know what they were going home to.

Bastion looked over his shoulder. The flashing lights dazzled his eyes and he caught sight of a man urinating in a doorway across the street, making him gag. The doorway they slept in would most probably have been used as a public toilet too and he swallowed hard in the knowledge that not only was he putting Lily through this awful night, he was exposing her to germs, and disease. His coughing began again; he clutched at his chest. He'd never felt so ill in his life and knew he needed medical help. Help that he hadn't wanted to ask for, not until Lily was safe and could be properly cared for.

He pulled a piece of newspaper from his pocket. It was old, creased and wrapped in cling film to protect it from the weather. It was an article he'd cut out over a year before. One he'd read over and over. The article showed photographs of a hotel, Wrea Head Hall in Scarborough, which had been almost burnt to the ground. It showed its owner, who'd survived the most horrific of attacks, along with pictures of other people, some who'd survived the atrocity, but then there had been the ones who hadn't. One of the pictures was of a 'deceased' woman, Margaret Croft, and beside her was a picture of her grown-up daughter, Jess. But of course, he'd seen Jess many years before. She'd been so young back then, but he'd never forgotten those big, jet black eyes, that wild wayward hair, or that smile that would have lit up a sky. He coughed again, took in another painful breath and then he held the clipping up to the light so that Lily could see.

'Lily, do you see this … this young woman?' He pointed. 'The one there, she's called Jess. She's your sister,' he said proudly, before pausing, gasping for breath and coughing again. 'She lives in this big house, do you see it?' He saw Lily's eyes grow wide and sparkle as she studied the picture of Wrea Head Hall. 'Tomorrow, my girl, tomorrow we're going to go to that house.' He nodded. 'That's right, we're going to go there. We're going to go and find your sister.' He sat up with a determined effort. 'Her house, it's by the seaside, not too far from here, and tomorrow we'll catch the early bus and go find it.' He nodded. 'You have to trust me, baby. I have a plan. All we need to do is get a little more money. Enough for some breakfast, and for us to clean ourselves up.' He patted the bag. 'I have my good suit in here, you know.' He nodded and smiled. 'Hopefully I'll get us enough money to catch a bus from Scarborough to the hotel. Otherwise we might have to walk, but it might be a long way. Is that okay, princess?' He watched his daughter nod and then he turned to face the street, held out his hand to a passer-by and lowered his eyes.

'Please, sir, please, could you spare a coin. We missed the last bus. I need to get my daughter home.'

Chapter Six

The rain poured relentlessly as Bastion smoothed down his
suit jacket. It had become just a little creased from being in
the duffel bag, and the rain was soaking it through. He was
disappointed because the last thing he wanted to do was to
give a bad first impression. He looked down at Lily, whose
eyes were as big as saucers. She stood beside him staring at
the Hall as it loomed up before them.

'Daddy, it's a castle. A really, really big castle.' She
gripped his hand tightly and skipped through the puddles.
They were both soaked, and he noticed that Lily shivered
continuously. Yet for some reason, they were both in good
spirits, even though their walk from Scarborough had been
a long one.

'It's not a castle, princess. It said in the paper that it was
a country house hotel, but, yes, I can see why you'd think
it so grand as to be a castle.' He took in the grandeur of
the building, the tall mullion windows, the stained glass
that had pictures of swans and serpents and the big, arched
wooden door that stood at least ten feet high. Planters stood
by its side, and two large bay windows stood to each side of
the house.

He took a step backwards, suddenly unsure of what he
was about to do. He began to doubt whether Jess would
want to meet him, whether she'd even care who he was and
wondered why he'd actually thought this a good idea in the
first place. He had nothing to offer her, no money, no job,
no home. He'd walked away from all of it in London. He
stupidly didn't have enough money to get home again and
had no idea what he'd do if Jess turned them both away.

Kneeling down he looked into Lily's eyes. 'Honey, I'm so

very sorry, we shouldn't have come here.' He paused and looked back up at the house. 'Your daddy is a crazy, stupid old man. We've come a very long way, we're getting soaked to the skin and I should have never brought us here. Not on this day.' He looked up at the grey swirling clouds and then heard the rumblings of thunder that echoed overhead. 'We need to take cover.' He ushered Lily under a tree.

'But, what about Jess? You said I had a sister.' Tears filled Lily's eyes. 'Won't I get to meet her now? Won't we get to go inside the castle?' Her shoulders slumped. 'And, Daddy, you're not so very old or so very stupid, but my feet do hurt.' She lifted her foot to show a hole in the sole of her shoe.

Bastion shook his head and looked down at his beautiful girl. 'Oh, Lily.' He shook his head, he knew he didn't have enough money for shoes. He leaned on the tree for support. 'Your sister, Jess, she doesn't know who we are, princess. She's never met me.'

Lily looked confused. 'But how come, Daddy? How come she never met you? Aren't you her daddy too?'

It was obvious to Bastion that Lily didn't understand why Jess wouldn't know him. To her a daddy was someone who was always there, someone who looked out for you, bathed you, dressed you and fed you. He was also someone who should buy your shoes and he pursed his lips, furious that he'd failed her. He tried to think of a way to explain, to tell her what had happened and why Jess had never met him, just as the front door opened and a beautiful dark skinned, voluptuous woman stepped out. She was dressed in black, but was wearing a brightly coloured apron with a green, yellow and black Jamaican flag on the front. Bastion not only approved, but he stood spellbound watching as with broom in hand she swept the damp leaves away from the entrance to the Hall and then turned to the hanging baskets and pulled one or two dead heads from the winter pansies. She stood in the rain, not seeming to care that she was getting wet, and stared out over the fields. But then she turned, caught his eye and her face lit up with the most beautiful smile he'd ever seen.

'Good day to you, sir. Can I help you?' she sang out as she walked towards them. 'And you, little one, aren't you the most beautiful little thing.'

The words made Lily beam and Bastion held out a hand to the woman. 'I'm Bastion Collymore,' he said, hoping that the name might mean something, but the woman just shook his hand and continued to smile.

'And I'm Nomsa, I'm very pleased to meet you.' Her eyes sparkled and Bastion loved the way her whole face lit up. 'I work here. But I'm so sorry, if you're looking for a room for the night, we can't accommodate you.' She sighed. 'We've had a death in the family and all the family and most of the staff are at the funeral today, including the receptionist.' Nomsa wiped away a tear.

'Daddy.' Lily pulled at his coat. 'Did … did our Jess die?' The tiny voice came from a worried Lily and Bastion turned quickly, wishing she hadn't spoken. He glanced back up at Nomsa, knowing he'd have to explain. But then he began to cough, and leaned against the tree, looking up apologetically.

'Oh no, darling, Jess didn't die,' Nomsa said. 'No, Jess is fine. You should have said you were friends of hers.' She looked at Bastion with concern. 'And if you don't mind me saying so, you don't sound so very well. You're soaked and look like you need a sit down.' She put a hand out to steady him. 'Come on, let's get you in the house, you need to get dry and I'll put the kettle on.'

Bastion was unnerved. He didn't know what to say, didn't know how to explain why he was here. He picked up the bag that he'd dropped while coughing. 'No, no. I really don't want to intrude, not on such a day. We'll be on our way. Come on, Lily.'

Lily let go of his hand. 'But, Daddy,' she shouted. 'We came such a long way to see Jess and I want to see her, you promised.'

'Lily, today is not the day. Now, come on, be a good girl, follow your daddy.'

'Oh no you don't,' Nomsa said as she patted Lily's shoulder. 'You are not well, you're soaked and, by the sound of it, you've come a long way. The least I can do for a friend of Jess's is give them a cup of tea. Besides, the family won't be back for a good hour. By then, we could have you both dry.' Nomsa took the bag from his hand and marched back towards the Hall. 'Come on, I've made my best fruit scones for when the family get home from the funeral. I'm sure you'd like one,' she said, looking at Lily, 'wouldn't you?'

Chapter Seven

Thunder began to echo through the sky as the rain fell in torrents onto the already saturated ground. Puddles turned themselves into miniature ponds and a small group of mourners protected by umbrellas stood by the open grave trying to avoid them, whilst the priest carried on with his sermon, regardless of the weather.

Jess shuddered. She was both heartbroken and terrified. She held tightly onto Jack's arm and cowered each time the thunder boomed above their heads, making her repeatedly look up at the swirling black clouds that hovered above her and filled almost every inch of the blackened sky. It was a sight that made her close her eyes, and she felt thankful that for some reason there was no lightning, either before or after the thunder. Ironically, it seemed quite fitting that Emily Ennis would leave this earth during a loud and fearful storm. She'd been the calmest and most peaceful person who had ever lived, spending most of her life doing her best to keep others happy and avoiding any kind of angst.

Jess took a step backwards. Her shoes sank into the mud, her feet were wet and she stumbled, dropped her umbrella and looked around in a daze as she felt someone push it back into her hand. She felt numb, her mind was swimming in what felt like a thick and indescribable mud and nothing felt real. Nothing, except that Jack was there, right by her side, just as he had been for the past two weeks, holding her up, protecting her and saving her from falling or feeling alone.

She felt Jack's body heave with grief and she immediately pulled herself into his frame, wanting to feel close and warm. Her hand went protectively to her stomach. She'd been keeping a secret of her own and she closed her eyes, knowing deep down that she'd never be alone again, not once the baby was born. But Jack still didn't know he was about to become a father.

Jess had told Emily about the pregnancy a few days before she'd died. Jess knew how much Emily had loved her own child and had hoped that the announcement of new life would make her happy. And it had. Emily's health had picked up, she'd eaten, she'd even walked down to the kitchen and had drank coffee at the kitchen table, just like she had the year before. The very morning she'd died she'd been sitting in the garden. It had been one of the warmer days and she'd commented on how she looked forward to the summer when they'd sit out there with the pram, sipping lemonade.

Jess still hadn't told anyone else and now with all that had happened, it seemed wrong to celebrate a new life, while grieving for the loss of another. To announce the news at this time would be indelicate and Jess decided to wait a few days before she told the others, deciding she might even wait until Christmas. It would only be ten days until they would stand in the gardens, with the Christmas tree all lit up. The villagers would arrive, along with local school children of all ages, and they'd sing carols, say prayers, and afterwards they'd eat together, as a family. Just as they had the year before.

She felt Jack's arms surround her. He kissed her forehead and Jess closed her eyes, wishing that she were anywhere else in the world other than here. Only to open them moments later to realise that she was still standing by the graveside, Emily had still lost her battle for life, and they were still there to say a final goodbye.

Nothing had changed. And after all, why would it?

She looked to the head of the grave where her sister Madeleine stood, holding onto Bandit, her fiancé, a man normally strong and brave, but who today unashamedly allowed the tears to roll down his face as he mourned his grandmother. She was the grandmother he'd only just got to know, a woman who he'd come to love through the diary that he and Maddie had found, only to realise that she'd been so much closer than he'd ever imagined, living alongside his father in a nursing home. And, just a year before, he'd brought them both back to live at Wrea Head Hall, and back to the home where they belonged.

Jess tried to suck at the air, she felt the need to fill her lungs but couldn't, and she found herself taking short sharp gasps as she tried to concentrate on the priest who stood beside Bandit. His words became lost and distant, as her foot once again slipped in the mud, making her squeal and grab at Jack to steady herself. She then stood with her eyes tightly squeezed together, praying, as terror began to fill her mind; it occurred to her how easy it would be for either her or one of the other mourners to lose their footing completely and drop down into the depths of the grave, like Alice falling down the endless rabbit hole and into a world where she had no control.

Jess felt herself begin to shake uncontrollably. She pulled her coat tightly around her body, turned away, and pulled Jack with her. A sob left her throat and the tears that she'd held onto for so many days began to fall. She once again turned to Jack. His arms encircled her and again, he pulled her into the warmth of his body like he'd done on so many occasions before. It was a feeling of safety and security. A feeling she didn't think she could live without and she had no idea what she'd have done over the past year without him.

'Jack, please, I really need to go,' Jess whispered as she noticed people begin to move slowly around the grave. She presumed that the priest must have said his final words as she watched both Maddie and Bandit walk gingerly over the AstroTurf to the head of the grave, where they both picked up a handful of soil. It was soil that had now turned into mud and as they threw it down onto the coffin, it landed with an eerie thud, making Jess recoil and take yet another step away from the grave.

She swallowed hard and watched as Bandit returned to where his father's wheelchair stood. He wiped his hands on a cloth before gripping the wheelchair's handles and forcibly pushing it through the sodden ground and to the head of the grave, so that his father, Arthur, could pay his own respects. Bandit picked up another handful of dirt, took control of his father's hand and helped him to throw the soil. But the look on Arthur's face told Jess that he had no idea of what he'd just done, or why, and it occurred to her that he too battled daily just to live and that in the not too distant future Bandit could find himself back here, at this same grave, burying his father alongside Emily, just as she'd planned.

'Why, Jack? Why do we discard people this way?' She thought about death, of how close she'd been just a year before and of how we loved a person in life, cherished them, protected them, but then once the life had gone, we put them in a box, nailed down the lid and tossed them in the ground, alone, to rot. It seemed wrong, and cruel.

She thought of her niece, Poppy, who was just four years old and wondered how on earth her sister Madeleine had managed to explain the death of Emily to her. Of course, Poppy had known death before, they'd been surrounded by it, but she'd been far too young the year before to fully understand what it had meant. Now she asked far too many questions and persisted until she got the answers to questions that most of the adults around her didn't comprehend themselves.

Jess continued to take in the short, sharp breaths. She passed Jack the long stemmed rose she'd carefully held in one of her hands. 'Throw it for me,' she insisted as once again she took a step back. 'I ... I can't do it,' she said and she momentarily let go of his hand, watched as he stepped forward and threw the rose down onto the coffin and then returned to her side, where she grabbed onto his hand again and pulled him past the many gravestones. She'd seen enough, grieved too much. She walked back to the path and to the car, where she waited until Madeleine came towards her. She and Maddie caught each other's eye, a silent, knowing stare that said nothing, but meant everything. They both climbed into the back seat of the limousine, along with Jack, and waited while Bandit attended to his father, ensuring he was seated in the front seat of the car, before folding the wheelchair and passing it to the funeral director, who took it from him to store in the boot.

The funeral car stood for what seemed like an age with its engine purring. The windows steamed up and the air in the car became more and more humid. Jess held her head in her hands. She felt dizzy, and nauseous. It was a feeling that hadn't left her for the past few weeks, but today it was worse. Her head spun, her stomach cramped and she continued to take in short, sharp gulps of air. She needed to escape, to get out of the car and she looked around to see if anyone would notice if she ran. But her eyes fell upon the two men who now worked at the graveside, dressed in black. Both held spades and, due to the weather, they wasted no time before they began shovelling mud into the grave, where a loud thudding could be heard as it landed heavily on top of the coffin. The sudden realisation of death hit her. Emily was in that box. The same Emily who used to have her chair placed right in the middle of the lawn because she loved being in the open air. The same Emily who'd sat out there right through the year, even when it was cold and had slept all year round with the bedroom window wide open because she hadn't wanted to be cooped up in the house. She'd insisted on walking to the woods and back every single day just to touch the trees, even though her legs were not as capable as they'd once been. A deep sob left Jess's throat as she realised that Emily was in the box and about to be buried in the ground, forever, and that she would never be seen again.

Suddenly the air left her lungs. For her, Emily's death was one death too many. It was as though everyone she knew, everyone she loved had been taken away far too soon. She could no longer breathe and inhaled without success. The more she tried to breathe, the harder it got and a feeling of claustrophobia surrounded her like a thick, grey fog. Her hands went to her throat before she waved them around wildly, grabbing at the door. She scrambled to wind the window down, her finger punching at the button and she felt Jack take her hand in his.

'It's okay. Jess, Jess, please … Listen to me. You're fine.' Jack helped her open the window and she leaned out, allowing the wind to blow through her hair. She gasped for breath as the car set off through the village and climbed the hill towards the Hall. 'That's it, take deep breaths. We're nearly home.' Jack's voice was calm and Jess did as she was told as she squeezed the air into her lungs. 'There you go. Come on, sit back. You're safe. I've got you.'

Jess felt Jack pull her back into a sitting position, just as they turned into the driveway, past the gatehouse where Madeleine and Bandit lived with Bandit's father, and followed the lane until the Hall came into view.

'Deep, deep breaths, that's the way.'

Jess turned to her sister. 'Maddie, I … I … I can't breathe! Please. Stop … stop the car. Tell them … tell them I need to get out.' Jess continued to gasp for breath, and counted the seconds until the car came to a halt, before throwing open the door and jumping out. Her head was in her hands; her knees felt weak and she stumbled to the Hall's entrance, where she leaned against the stone arched doorway, her face hidden against her arm, while dragging air into her lungs. And then, as always, Jack was beside her, pulling her into his arms, supporting her and stopping her from falling to the ground. A ground that suddenly felt so very, very far away.

There was a noise. There was the sound of footsteps that made her turn. Then there was a man, a man who came from within the Hall. He stood before her, his hand reaching out and landing on her shoulder, making her look up into his deep, pitch black eyes and for a moment they stared at one another without speaking. A brief moment of recollection crossed her mind, making Jess wonder where she'd seen him before. But then she watched in horror as the man's eyes flickered, and he collapsed in a heap on the stone steps before her, making her scream.

'Arrrgghhh … Daddy …' The second scream came from a child. A small girl, who now knelt on the floor beside the man. 'Daddy. Please … help him.' She pulled at the bottom of Jess's skirt, as Jess looked between the man, Jack and the funeral car, where both Maddie and Bandit were hurrying towards her.

'What the hell?' Bandit moved quickly, checked the man's pulse and moved him swiftly into the recovery position. 'Did he hit his head? Get an ambulance. Now.' He turned to Jack, who'd already set off in the direction of the reception.

'What shall I say?' Jack shouted as he ran.

'You know the drill. Tell them one of the guests has collapsed. His breathing is weak. It isn't good. Tell them to be quick and then go find Ann or Len, they should be following in one of the funeral cars, ask if they'll come and identify him.'

The young girl once again tugged at the bottom of Jess's skirt. 'You're Jess, aren't you?' she asked, sobbing and looking hopefully at Jess, who was still holding onto the stone archway. 'Jess … he … he's not a guest. He's our daddy. We came to find you.'

Chapter Eight

Jess stood with her arms crossed, as Jack paced up and down the darkened landing before her.

'What do you mean, you went to the hospital?' Jess whispered in a growl. 'Why the hell did you do that?' She moved across the landing and towards the staircase. 'He'd just collapsed on our doorstep. The last thing he needed was a full on interrogation, especially by you.'

Jack sighed. 'All right, all right, I'm sorry. But someone had to find out who he is and what he is up to and right now, you don't look entirely capable.' He looked down. 'I might be being just a little sceptical here, and I know that he said he was your father, but guess what, Jess?' He pursed his lips. 'He might not be.' He lifted his hand, rubbed his eyes and then ran it through his dark overgrown hair. 'He could be just about anyone.'

'I know.' Jess's simple response was quietly spoken. 'I know he could be anyone, but do you know what, Jack? I really, really want him to be my father.' She stepped nervously from foot to foot, and looked at the bedroom door behind which Lily now slept. She was fully aware that if Lily woke up, she'd be able to hear every single word. The child had been through enough and the last thing she needed to overhear was raised voices or to think she wasn't welcome.

'Jess, his story. It's not great. He's penniless, he's homeless and he left London after Lily's mum cleared out their flat and sold it all to buy heroin. He had only just enough money to get here, which seems a little odd, don't you think?' He paused. 'He had absolutely no one else but you that he could turn to, and, what's more, he seems to have an eight-year-old daughter who needs looking after.' He took in a deep breath and stared at Jess. 'You were his only option, Jess, his last resort. He had nowhere else to go, so he thought he'd come and find you, his daughter, twenty years too late. Twenty years after he should have first introduced himself to you as your father.'

Jess fixed her stare on Jack's face. His jawline looked more chiselled than she'd ever noticed before and it occurred to her that he was maturing more and more by the day. 'Do you think I hadn't worked all of that out, Jack? Do you think I hadn't wondered if he was just some random, black, homeless guy that had turned up looking for somewhere nice to live?' Anger and sarcasm ran through her voice. She'd been so happy that Bastion had turned up and right now the last thing she needed was to fall out with Jack.

'So, what are you going to do?' he asked as Jess walked towards the balustrade that provided a gallery to the grand hall, in which the twenty-foot Christmas tree sparkled with brightly coloured lights and the sound of Bing Crosby's 'White Christmas' echoed. The whole room had taken on an amber hue; the fire crackled within the huge, stone, inglenook fireplace, its flames reflecting in the numerous pictures and the smell of burning logs and pine needles filled the air. Jess sighed. The atmosphere in the Hall was normally happy, warm and comforting, yet at that moment she felt none of those emotions.

Jess needed to think. She took a moment to lean against the railing and watched the way that Jack walked back and forth along the landing, with his hands on his hips. He was restless, he obviously had more to say and she took in a deep breath as he moved forward to lean against the balustrade beside her. It had been a long and tough day for them all and Jess was surprised at both Jack's attitude and his tone. He was normally the most supportive person she'd ever met, but tonight he seemed sad and anxious. She realised that he was talking to her, though she hadn't really been listening.

'... and what do we do in the meantime, Jess? Babysit? Look after a child we've never met before? I mean is that even legal? And for how long? Do you have any idea how long the hospital will keep him or do we call social services?' Jack had continued. 'Well?'

'I don't know, Jack. Why didn't you ask Bastion while you were interrogating him?' she snapped. She felt betrayed. Jack had gone to the hospital without telling her and the more she thought about it, the angrier she got. It was as though he didn't want her to have a father, didn't want her to have that joy, or even the knowledge of who he was. She shook her head, trying to dispel the fog that had taken over her thoughts, and it crossed her mind that Jack might be jealous that Bastion was here, disrupting the status quo and giving her the father figure that he'd never had.

'So ...' Jack's voice burnt through her thoughts.

'What do you expect me to do, Jack?' Jess walked towards the bedroom door. She looked inside at the sleeping Lily before pulling the door to a close and then pointed to the window. 'Did you take a look out there tonight, Jack? Did you ... did you see the weather?' She walked down to the turning point on the grand staircase and stood before the huge stone mullion window. She tapped on the glass. 'It's winter, it's been raining for days and she's just a child. A cold, homeless child, who has nowhere to go and, what's more, my father brought her to me.' Jess pulled her cardigan tightly around her body. 'As far as I know, Jack, she's my sister, my own flesh and blood, so I can hardly throw her out on the streets to look after herself, now can I?' She lifted her hands and shoulders in a shrug. 'And, Jack. It's Christmas. It's just nine days till Christmas. She's just a tiny little girl, not the bloody enemy.'

Jack looked up. 'Oh, Jess. I'm sorry.' He walked to her and pulled her into a hug. 'Look, I know it's Christmas. But ...' His voice was now barely a whisper and he sat down on the steps, pulling her to sit down with him. 'I love you so much, Jess. I really do. But all this, it's too much and I'm totally out of my depth. I have no idea what to do, what would be for the best. I mean, what if he doesn't survive? What happens then? Does she have any other relatives? Or do we take on the responsibility, Jess? Is it up to us to bring her up, you know if ...?'

Jess looked up. 'Wow. Is that what this is all about, Jack?' She turned and stared at the bedroom door. She had no idea how to answer him. She hadn't thought that far ahead, in fact she hadn't really thought beyond that night and for a moment her thoughts went to Lily. What would happen to her if Bastion died? Would they really send her to live with the woman who'd apparently emptied their flat to pay for heroin? Is that where she'd have to go? 'I really don't think he's about to die, Jack. The paramedics said it was a mild case of pneumonia, nothing more. He collapsed due to exhaustion and they said he needed some intravenous antibiotics and a lot of rest, that's all. They said he'd be okay.' She tried to convince herself with the words.

'I know, Jess. But what if he isn't? It's just a few weeks until our wedding and I need to know where we stand. I'm not ready to be a parent. Especially to an eight-year-old.'

Jack's words spun around in her mind. He wasn't ready to be a father. Her shoulders slumped as the realisation of his words hit her. She closed her eyes and thought of all the times she'd dreamed of having a baby, of what it would be like to be a mother, especially since Poppy had been born. Jess clearly remembered Poppy coming home with Madeleine and how Madeleine had lain her down in the Moses basket, and how she'd sat for hours staring at her, praying for her to wake so she could pick her up, cuddle her and help with feeding. The basket had been so beautiful, with a white broderie anglaise cotton lining and a pretty pink blanket, and Poppy lying in there, so tiny and perfect.

'I'm just worried about you, Jess,' Jack said into the silence that had engulfed them. 'I'm worried about what will happen … this man, he … he could be anyone and …' He paused and looked out of the window.

'Jack,' she pleaded, 'if you love me, you need to support me.'

'You know I will always support you.' Jack looked back at her with saddened eyes. 'Haven't I been there for you, through everything? Wasn't I the one to hold you together after what that nutter did to you?' He paused. 'I waited, Jess. I waited for all of that to be over. I waited in the hope that one day I'd get you to myself, just for a little while. But then, out of nowhere, Bastion Collymore turns up, claiming to be your father.' His voice was filled with an emotion that Jess had never heard before.

'I want it to be true, Jack. I really want him to be my father, I really want to have some family left that I can hold onto.'

Jack shook his head. 'But what if he isn't? I love you, Jess. I love you so much, and I can't bear to watch you fall apart again.' He held his head in his hands. 'You know I'll support you, Jess, no matter what. But, please, for me, ask for a DNA test and I promise you, if Bastion is your father I'll welcome him with open arms.' He placed a hand on his heart. 'I promise.'

Jess concentrated on her breathing. She realised she'd been intermittently holding her breath and once again felt glad that she was sitting down, fearing that if she hadn't been, she'd have most probably fainted. She needed something to do, something to concentrate on and began to stroke the oak balustrade affectionately. It was solid, beautifully carved, and had all been replaced after the fire, yet had been made to look original, as if it belonged.

'This house, our lives here, it is about us. We rebuilt this whole place, together, and it's what we have here that means so much to me, especially after what we all went through.' Jess closed her eyes. 'I hoped we'd have a future here, Jack. I thought this house would be a place where we'd become parents and raise a family and maybe that family will end up including Lily.' She inhaled, and placed a hand on her chest. Her heart seemed to be fluttering rather than beating and she made an attempt to calm herself, in the hope that the fluttering would stop. She wasn't stupid. She was well aware that Bastion Collymore might not be her father, she didn't need Jack to remind her of that. However, she'd already become attached to Lily. She'd watched her as she'd tossed, turned and finally slept and all the while she'd watched, she'd stroked her hair and wondered how she'd feel when she could watch her own son or daughter sleep.

Jess had sat with Lily for hours. She'd been nervous, uncomfortable and for a while had sobbed for her father. Jess's heart had broken. The child's love for her father was more than obvious and Jess would have done anything to take away the pain, but Lily's words still haunted her. 'She took everything, even my toys. We had no money left, Jess. Daddy was sick, he couldn't work and we couldn't pay the rent or buy food and we had to leave, before the bad men came.' She'd lain beside Jess on the bed and had curled her body up in a self-protecting ball. 'Daddy said they'd probably come soon, especially if we couldn't pay the rent, so we counted every penny, you see, it was important to us that we got to you. We even slept in a shop doorway. It was cold and scary and Daddy, he made me wear most of his clothes to keep me warm and then … then we walked all the way from Scarborough, just to get here.' Her hands had gone up to indicate the Hall and Jess had gasped, knowing that the child had gone through hell and had walked at least three or four miles in the freezing cold rain.

Jess had given Lily a bath, washed her hair, put plasters on her blistered feet and had provided her with an oversized nightdress. Then she'd held her and rocked her until she'd fallen to sleep. But Lily hadn't slept calmly, she'd tossed and turned, going from one nightmare to another, making Jess wonder how much a child of eight could have already been through to make her dream so badly.

'... lost you once, Jess. I can't risk anything happening to you again.'

Jess drifted out of her thoughts to once again hear Jack speak and realised that she hadn't heard most of the sentence. 'Sorry, what?'

Jack tutted. 'I was saying that after the fire, after you were kidnapped, I thought I'd lost you. At first we all thought you'd been trapped in the flames, that you were dead, but then to realise you'd got out of the Hall, only to find out that he had you, Jess, we were all beside ourselves. I can't bear for you to be hurt again. I just can't.' He pulled her towards him and Jess took in the homely, musky smell of his aftershave. It was a smell she loved, it was a smell that meant she was close to him and she had an overwhelming desire to feel his body next to hers. But then, Jack pulled away, stood up and walked to the window seat where he perched and looked outside.

Jess thought back to the year before. To the way Liam, Madeleine's ex-fiancé, had hunted them all down, almost killed them in an arson attack that had all but destroyed the Hall and then, when they'd all thought it safe, he'd struck again, taking both Jess and Madeleine hostage in different ways, with a view to killing them both. Jess felt her stomach turn as she remembered the fear she'd felt, the pain of being confined in a cage and when she'd finally escaped, when the police found her, the despair she'd felt when she found out that Liam had also been responsible for the deaths of so many people, including their mother, and Madeleine's first husband, literary agent and father. He'd tried to kill or destroy everyone that Madeleine had loved. The police had called it obsession, but Jess knew that it had been much more than that and for months after, she and Madeleine had clung together in a silent unity that only sisters could have shared.

Was this a similar sister-like unity she could share with Lily? She and Madeleine had always been close, yet so very different. Not only in personality, but also in looks. She had dark chestnut skin and wild Afro hair. She had a fiery personality and normally wouldn't think twice before fighting her own corner. Whereas Madeleine had fair skin, a clear complexion, shoulder length blonde hair and was so very beautiful, brave and caring. Jess closed her eyes for a moment and took in a deep breath. For the first time in her life she had a relation that looked like her. Lily was her younger duplicate. A younger version of herself and, with that in mind, she really wanted her to be a sister too.

But, if that was the case, why hadn't Bastion Collymore come forward before? Why had he waited twenty years to come to her, to introduce himself? And how, when their mother had called it a one-night stand, when it obviously hadn't been, had he known who she was, or where to find her?

'But what if he is, Jack? What if Bastion is my father and for the first time in my life, I could have a family member who actually looks like me?' She looked hopeful and put her hand on her heart. 'Think about it, I've never had that. Both Mum and Maddie, they were both fair and blonde, whereas me, I was a cuckoo in the nest. The little black kid, the odd one out. I'd have done anything to look the same or even similar to them. And now I have it, I have someone who's like me. Did you see Lily? She's my double. Everything about her is similar to the way I looked at her age.' Her thoughts went to her baby, to how it would look when it was born and she wondered whether it too would take on her colouring, or whether the baby would be more like Jack, with his pale skin and dark hair.

'Jess, my God, look at you, you're so beautiful. I've always thought so.' Jack moved back to sit on the step beside her. 'You're no cuckoo. You're stunning and I feel so proud to be with you. I just think you've seen enough hurt.' He pulled away and looked directly into Jess's eyes. His hand rested on her knee. 'I'm worried about you. As far as we all know, your mother and father ...' He paused and looked away. '... well, from what you'd been told, it had been a quick fling, a sailor who'd gone back to sea. Your mother told you that she'd never seen him again. Yet now, over twenty years later, up pops Bastion Collymore all the way from London, homeless and needing somewhere to live; as far as I'm aware, he never went to sea, he was never a sailor and from what he said, your mother was not a one-night stand. Their stories don't match and I just want you to be careful, Jess, that's all. And it's not like your mum is here to confirm what he's saying now, is it?'

'Well, I guess it would all have been easier all round if my mother hadn't been murdered and that he'd turned up a millionaire, wouldn't it, Jack?'

Jack sat quietly and shook his head. Jess saw him momentarily close his eyes, and knew that he was tired. It had been a long day and they were both exhausted.

'Jack, if you had a child, if you were to be a father, you'd stand by it, wouldn't you?' It was a question she hadn't wanted to ask, but felt she had to.

'Jess, seriously, come on.' He put his arm around her shoulder. 'You have nothing to worry about on that score. You know I wouldn't leave you. But … but it's not going to happen, not for a good few years. We're both young and far too sensible for that. Besides we have the wedding coming up.' He kissed her on the cheek. 'Once we're married, I want to find us a house of our own, with a garden full of swings and climbing frames, and security, Jess. I need us to have security. Especially after all that happened here, after all the nightmares we went through. I know you love this place, but for me it's the last place I'd want to bring my children up. Don't you see that?'

Jess inhaled and a sob left her throat. 'But, Jack.' She paused, turned and stared into his eyes. 'I … I'm pregnant.'

Chapter Nine

Bright sparkling Christmas lights lit up the street, and shop windows danced with displays full of bright red bows, Santas, elves and sleighs full of sacks with toys spilling out, showing the promise of delights to come. All of this gave the whole world expectations they couldn't meet and put people into debt they couldn't afford.

Both men and women went from pub to pub, singing, dancing and laughing, dressed in their party clothes, and all seemed to have more money than sense. None of them looked as though they had a care in the world.

But Annie wasn't laughing, nor was she waiting for a Christmas promise. Punters in the brothel had been thin on the ground, so she'd headed out into the streets to find the party revellers. She'd worked all night, but after the last hit of drugs, she no longer had any money. But she didn't care. The drugs had overtaken her mind and she pulled herself, inch by inch, from shop to shop, holding onto the walls, doors and windows for support. She needed to sit down, close her eyes and more than anything else, she wanted to sleep. She needed to recover for just a while, and for her head to stop spinning, before she went back to work, before she looked for yet another punter, another good for nothing slob of a man to pleasure and endure for what would feel like the millionth time that year.

Her mind spun and she looked around for somewhere to sit. She knew that at thirty years old she ought to be wishing that her life too was one big party. That she'd be out there drinking, singing and dancing with the partygoers, that she'd be having fun and enjoying life. Or perhaps she should be wishing for an armchair, a fire to sit before, hot tea or cocoa and a place where she could curl up and be warm. She couldn't remember being warm for such a long time and the thought of a cosy room, with a fire, a Christmas tree and gifts brought a lump to her throat. All of this was what normal people would wish for at her age, but no, not her; all she wanted in her life was heroin. The drugs – the heroin – was like air itself to her and once she had it, she was happy. She knew she'd begin to feel calm, she'd escape the turmoil of life and sink into the darkness, a place where she'd finally find solace.

'Come on, love, you looking for a bit of work?' A man sneered as he grabbed at her arm. 'I could do with a bit.' He began to unzip his trousers. 'How much for a quickie? Will a fiver do it?' He pushed her against a wall, but Annie shrugged him off.

'Get off me, asshole, and no, a fiver would not bloody do it. What do you think this is?' She pointed up and down at herself. 'Bloody charity? Now, get off me.' Annie moved away from the man, looking up in an attempt to make out his face, but his features were blurred. The image of him swam around before her, and she steadied herself as a feeling of nausea overtook her.

'I think beggars can't be choosers, love, don't you?' Once again he grabbed at her arm, pulled at the tight, black top that barely covered her and exposed her breasts. 'There you go, that's what I want to see.' His mouth suddenly fell upon her, making her squirm and scream. She grabbed at his hair, pulling his head backwards, and lashed out with her nails.

'I said get off me, you asshole.' Her fingers clawed at his face. 'You don't touch me unless I say so. Do you get that?'

'Or what, you damned slapper?' Again his mouth was upon her, his teeth sinking into her flesh, and she squealed. Then he froze. His body suddenly left hers and was catapulted backwards and into the roadside, where a car swerved and narrowly missed him. Through the haze, Annie saw him grab at the kerb, before crawling at speed on his hands and knees in the opposite direction, and for a moment she just stood there without moving.

'What the hell do you think you're doing?' Griff's voice seemed to come from every direction. It echoed around her like a bass drum, but she couldn't focus and didn't know where he was. 'You're off your goddamned face again, Annie, aren't you?' he growled. 'Was he paying for that shag, you tart? Because from where I was standing he looked as though he was getting a damn freebie.'

Panic set in and she tried to move. She had to get away, she couldn't face her pimp, not right now. She needed to escape. 'He ... he was taking advantage of me, Griff, honest,' she yelled. 'Wanted it for a bloody fiver.' She felt Griff grab her by the shoulders and she could just about focus on his face, which she quickly realised was now within inches of hers and she didn't like it.

'What the hell did you take this time, Annie? Heroin ... again?' His voice bellowed and her whole body began to tremble. She felt him release her, giving her the opportunity to try and move away from his reach.

'You don't understand, Griff. I need it. I ... I just have to have it.' She stood up and set off in a haphazard zigzag motion, her legs seeming to travel in different directions, and she held onto everything she could grab, her long auburn hair bouncing around her face. She stumbled and fell against a wall. Pain shot through her shoulder, her whole body became disorientated, her arms and legs struggled to work in unison and she tried in vain to inch her way along the cold, wet pavement.

Every movement took effort, but Annie kept going. The road was long, the crowds were thick and groups of young men were congregating outside the pubs where they stood together chatting, smoking and drinking. The music seemed to get louder. Multi-coloured Christmas lights swam brightly before her eyes, and one road morphed into the other. Everywhere looked the same. Annie tried to make her way between the crowds, but found it difficult to negotiate her route as she crashed into men, spilling their drinks, causing them to shout after her as she went. She searched the side streets; she was close to the brothel and she was sure there was an alley, but this was London, the whole city was a maze, and in her confusion, she failed to find it. She looked up and down. She was sure there had been an entrance she'd used before. It had been between one of the shops and a car park, but was it on this street or another? She shook her head, there were hundreds of car parks in this area. But she seemed to remember a ramp, it was above the shops and it occurred to her that she'd once used that same escape route to outrun the police.

'Come on, where are you?' A fire escape, that's right, there'd been a fire escape, it had led to a rooftop that had then led her to the back corridor of a hotel. But which hotel? By rights she shouldn't be able to remember anything, especially after she'd taken enough drugs to floor an elephant. But constant use made her more tolerant and now the more she took, the more she wanted.

She looked over her shoulder. She had to escape Griff, but she couldn't run. Her stilettos hurt, her heels were raw, and she felt sure that they were bleeding. She pulled at her skirt; it was short and tight and she felt the seam tear as she stumbled. She was out of breath, her heart palpitating and her mind spinning when she found herself being pushed from behind and forced into an alley, where she was suddenly thrown to the ground. She landed heavily on her hands and knees, only to look up and straight into Griff's blurred, furious, contorted face.

It was then that she felt the pain. It seared through her head as Griff grabbed at her hair, pulling it from the roots. 'Where's my money, bitch?' he shouted, right before she felt the sharp slap strike her face and she was sure that Griff's hand would have left a mark. A second slap saw her whole body propelled across the rain-soaked tarmac. She landed heavily against the alley wall, screaming as her ribs crunched, her ankle twisted and the heel of her stiletto snapped. She closed her eyes and kicked the shoes from her feet and into the gutter, while she waited in fear, wondering where the next blow would come from.

'I haven't had any punters, Griff. Honest,' she cried, opening her eyes and hoping that he would believe her. 'It's Christmas and everyone just wants to get pissed.'

'For fuck's sake, Annie, don't lie to me! I've been watching you. Saw you had a couple of punters but guess you used your earnings to score. You need teaching a lesson. You can't get so frigging high, not when you're supposed to be working and not on my money. I've told you this so many damn times, Annie. Are you crazy?' Griff's voice had turned into a high pitched squeal and he stamped to the other side of the alley, kicked an empty beer can at the wall and then yelled with pain as he smashed his fist into a metal rubbish bin. 'See what you made me do, Annie?' He walked towards her showing her his injured bright red knuckles. 'Did you see, Annie, did you see that?' His knuckles were millimetres away from her face. 'And look at you. How the hell are you supposed to attract a bloke if you look like that? Hey? You look a fucking mess. You're old, you're dirty and you stink, do you know that? You need a goddamned bath, preferably in bleach,' he yelled. 'And that geezer, he'd have paid for it. But you, you were too friggin' high to negotiate with him.' He turned away and kicked at the kerb. 'You do know how much you owe me, don't you? And I need my money, Annie.

If you're high, you can't work, and if you can't bloody work, you can't pay me and if you can't pay me, I can't pay the rent on the house. Don't you get any of that?'

Annie fumbled with her unwashed hair and pushed it away from her face. She was sure she looked okay, sure she didn't need a bath, not for a few more days, and she fumbled around in the dark, looking for her bag. 'I ... I'm sorry, I'll sort my make-up out, honest. I'll try harder, Griff, I promise. I'll do better.' She spotted the bag and made a sudden dash across the tarmac on her hands and knees in an attempt to put some distance between herself and Griff. But the drugs made her weak and she stumbled over litter that filled the gutter and landed heavily on her face. 'Griff, please.' She began to laugh but didn't know why. 'I'll pay you ... another day. That's right ... yes ... I'll get some work ... I'll pay you another day ... tomorrow ... I'll pay you tomorrow.' Her mind spun round like a spinning top; she could barely speak, darkness threatened. She got back up and onto her knees in another attempt to crawl across the alley. But then a sudden pain hit her as broken glass cracked under her knees, making her scream as she felt the flesh tear.

Annie turned and sat down while she inspected her knees. Then she looked up to where a blurred image of Griff hovered above her. He glared for what seemed like forever and then suddenly, without warning, she felt his hand grab her throat. He squeezed hard and she couldn't breathe. Her whole body left the floor, her legs dangled in the air and once again she felt him strike her, a sharp heavy slap that hit her square across the face. Griff let go and she fell back to the floor. She spat the blood from her mouth and made a feeble attempt to creep to safety, as nausea once again overtook her. She began to vomit uncontrollably, before managing to find a space beneath a fire escape, where she curled up in a ball. It looked like a fortress of metal, a place that would surround her, like a protective cage. If only she'd realised that Griff could easily climb under it too.

'Annie, don't be stupid, you can't escape me. You do know that, don't you?' Griff's voice echoed. 'Besides, where the hell would you go? You owe me, you bitch. You owe me for looking after you, don't you? I give you somewhere to live, I protect you and for what? You pay me a tiny bit of what you earn, that's not too much to ask, Annie, is it?'

Raindrops continued to fall. They'd previously been gentle and sporadic, but now they fell heavily, splashing down and creating puddles. A black cat scarpered past. It headed to the fire escape, spotted the couple lurking below and leapt out of their way and up the steps without effort.

For a moment Annie sat staring into space, wishing that she too could escape in an upward direction. Nothing seemed to matter any more. She knew that Griff could and would easily kill her if he wanted to, yet still she smiled. She looked up at the sky and for a moment she wished she could die, wished she could disappear or fly upward to heaven. But then Griff kicked out and another more powerful blow struck her. She landed heavily and, with tears streaming down her face, she stared into a muddy, oil-filled puddle on the ground. The puddle was like a mirror, a black, glassy mirror into her life. She looked at her reflection. Griff was right; she was old for a prostitute, she was dirty, her hair was messy and her mascara was smeared across her face. For just a moment the puddle was like looking down a deep, dark, endless hole and straight into hell.

'Hell … That's where I'll be going, Griff. I'll be going to hell.' She continued to stare into the puddle, convinced that nothing could be more true. There would be no beautiful ending for her, no rocking chair by the fire, no Christmas tree or cocoa, and definitely no pearly gates. No. She wasn't a good person, she'd never really done anything worthwhile and had been evil to those around her her whole life. After all, how many mothers would empty their child's home and take their toys in order to pay for drugs? Especially just before Christmas. Everything she'd touched had turned bad, and it was no wonder that everyone she'd ever loved had turned against her. It had all been her own fault.

There had been a time when she'd wanted it all: a normal life with real people around her, and a real family. Just a few years before she'd tried to get out of the game. Her life had been okay, for a while. She'd met Bastion. He'd been a good, caring and loving man who'd given her time, respect and a home, and she had a daughter, Lily. She'd tried so hard to make him happy, but had failed miserably at making herself happy. But she'd been young, just over twenty years old, and the responsibility of caring for a baby had been far too much for her. No one had ever told her how hard it would be, and in the end her whole mind had shut down. She'd begun resenting Lily and had made a complete mess of being a mother to a beautiful, innocent child. Besides, she'd needed the drugs, the call from them had been strong, and finding her next fix of heroin became more important to her than anything else. There had been days when her mind had been totally consumed and she'd thought of nothing else. The shaking, scratching and nausea had taken over and she'd walked around in a zombie-like state; she had thought nothing of stealing Bastion's money or possessions to get her next fix.

'Get up, Annie, you're going back to the damned house,' Griff demanded, while his foot kicked at the tarmac. 'Get yourself cleaned up. I want my money, and I want it now or else.'

Annie began to shake. 'Griff, please, I've … I've said I'll pay you tomorrow.' She knew what Griff was capable of and she instantly began to look for a way to run, or for a person who might help her. But the sound of the road was distant and the cars sped past the end of the alley without caring.

'Get up.' His voice was more demanding and Annie found herself on her hands and knees staring up at him. She was more than willing to beg. Her eyes followed his stride as he stepped out from under the fire escape. She pressed herself against the wall and wiped her mouth; she needed to rid herself of the taste of blood which had accumulated on her tongue and the taste, along with the stress, once again made her gag. She spat at the floor, before she looked up and watched as Griff paced up and down in the rain.

'How are you going to pay me?' He laughed. 'Do you even know how much you owe, Annie? And, if you do, where the hell will you find that sort of money in a day? Eh?' He kicked out at her, catching her knee with his boot. 'Ten grand, Annie. That's what you owe, and every day you owe it, it goes up just a bit more.' His nose was almost touching hers. 'You've got just over a week. One week ... I want my money by Christmas Eve, Annie, and then you know what has to happen.' He stood back and once again he punched at the bin. 'You can't use the house for free, Annie. It's not right. The other girls ... they'll think I've gone soft and I haven't.' He paused and leaned forward. 'You know I don't want to hurt you, Annie.' His hand reached out and stroked her face. 'It'd be such a shame to have to cut you. But I will if you don't pay. Do you get that?'

Annie cowered, sobbed and leaned back against the wall. She may as well let him kill her now. There was no way she could pay him so quickly, not ten thousand, not in a week – not even in a year! She had to think of something to stall him.

'I need longer. You have to give me longer.' Her mind

spun around like a Catherine wheel on Bonfire Night. Sparks shot around behind her eyes and once again she looked down and into the puddle, in an attempt to make the image stop. She needed an excuse. 'I … I have a child to feed. It's Bastion, her father, he's cruel, he expects so much, and Lily, she's a demanding child, she always needs clothes, food and I have to pay for that flat too or she'd be homeless,' she lied. The truth was that Annie had never provided for her daughter, not in money or in love. 'Bastion, he's lazy, he doesn't work, hasn't worked for years, blames it all on looking after the girl and I have to give him money, she'd starve if I didn't. You do know that, don't you?'

Griff stopped abruptly. A leery smile crossed his face. 'Oh, Annie. How could I forget about sweet little Lily?' He rubbed his chin, stuck his tongue in his cheek and then pursed his lips. 'How old is she nowadays?' He leaned against the fire escape, hovering aggressively above her. 'She must be getting real grown up by now.'

Even through the fog that surrounded her mind, Annie had caught the tone in Griff's voice. 'No … No … No … She's just eight years old, Griff,' she slurred. 'She's just a baby and you wouldn't want a baby, would you?'

Griff nodded, his hand rubbing at his unshaven face. 'Annie, I think you should bring her to visit me.' He paused. 'Yeah, I'd like that, and I'm sure she'd like to come pay me a visit before Christmas, wouldn't she?' He smirked, cracked his knuckles and nodded. 'I bet she's grown up a lot, I mean, how long is it since I last saw her?'

'Oh, no, you don't, Griff. No way. I've told you, she's just a baby. You can't have her.' Annie sat up with her back against the wall. 'She's too young, you bastard. You can't do that.'

Once again he grabbed her throat, and she felt the pressure intensify as his hand began to squeeze. 'Annie,

Annie, Annie, do you think I'm some kind of ogre? Do you really think I'm the kind of man that would do that to a tiny little girl?' He let go of her. 'I wouldn't do that, not to a baby … No … I wouldn't, but do you know what, Annie? I have a list of men a mile long that would and what's more they'd pay me a lot of money for the damned privilege.' Again he stopped and paced up and down the alley. 'Truth is, Annie, I have to be paid and whether you like it or not, you owe me … You owe me a lot of money. So, you either pay up … or you bring me the girl. And if you don't do either, I'll kill you. And then, I'll find her … I'll hand her over to the men, I'll let them have her and then, once she's no use to me, I'll kill her too. Do you get that, or are you really that stupid that you think you can rob me of what's rightfully mine?' He began to laugh. It was a shrill piercing laugh that could have easily broken glass and Annie felt a violent shaking begin from within. Griff was evil. He'd killed before and she knew that he meant every word. She closed her eyes, realising that she had no choice but to do what he said.

Chapter Ten

Jess looked at the clock for what seemed like the tenth time in less than an hour. Its bright blue numbers illuminated the corner of the darkened room and Jess put her arm over her eyes to stop the glare. They hurt from lack of sleep. The conversation with Jack the night before hadn't gone well. They'd talked for far too many hours, gone round in far too many circles. Deep down she knew that Jack loved her, but he'd made it more than clear that being a father had been the last thing on his agenda, which made Jess more than aware of the tension that now hung between them. It was a tension she hated and one she wanted put an end to as soon as she possibly could.

She'd known that springing the pregnancy on Jack had been bad timing. Yesterday had been traumatic for everyone, but she'd hoped he would have been happy or just a little excited and that he would have embraced the news. But all that had happened over the course of the day had left him far too mixed up. She'd only found out she was pregnant a couple of days before Emily had died; she'd tried to tell him how confused she'd been, how frightened and full of doubt, but then how quickly she'd come to realise that whatever happened, she already loved their baby, and was already prepared to protect it with her life. She knew he'd come round, and felt sure that given time, he'd feel exactly the same. All he had to do was get used to the idea that becoming a father would be a good thing.

It had been midnight when they'd gone to bed. Jack had kissed her gently on the lips. A single kiss that had promised nothing, before standing up and going to their room, alone, while Jess had gone to stay with Lily, knowing that she couldn't risk the child waking up in a strange house, scared and alone.

Jess had eventually sobbed herself to sleep and now squinted in order to look back at the clock. It was just after six o'clock in the morning. It was still cold and dark outside and Jess quietly climbed out of bed. She inched herself into her slippers and walked over to the window to peep out over the national park. She smiled as she caught sight of the deer in the distance and noticed a doe and her fawn feeding on the dew-covered grass, a sight she often saw early in the mornings. The views that could be seen from the Hall were something she'd never tire of. Each month or season had its special moment, and its own miracle of nature. The view from every single window was stunning, picturesque, and she still found it hard to believe that Jack didn't see the Hall as somewhere they'd live forever. He'd spoken of getting a house, a home somewhere else, somewhere to bring up their baby away from the Hall, away from this beauty. Leaving Wrea Head was the last thing she ever wanted to do. She was happy here, and more than anything she wanted to stay and be close to Madeleine, especially after the baby was born.

Jess glanced back at the twin bed that stood behind her and squinted in an attempt to make out the tiny shape of Lily, who like her had tossed and turned for so many hours that at one point, Jess had climbed into her bed with her and had held her as she'd whimpered and sobbed in her sleep. Jess felt her own heart shatter into a million pieces, not only for herself, but for a child, who at just eight years old was so distressed that her sleep was disturbed in such a sad and dramatic way.

Jess inched closer to Lily's bed and carefully pulled the duvet down. Just a little at first, in an attempt to expose her face, but the bed was empty. The sudden realisation sent her into a blind panic and she dropped to her knees, looked under the bed, under the unit and then ran to the bathroom, throwing open the door. She switched the light on, but the room was empty.

'Lily, come out, honey, where are you?' She hoped that the little girl was hiding, but it soon became obvious that she wasn't and Jess wondered how a small, defenceless child had somehow managed to get herself up and out of the room without being heard. She had no idea how that had happened. Jess was sure she'd barely slept, or had she?

She threw on a pair of jogging bottoms and a T-shirt, before running out of the room. Her feet were cold and bare, but it didn't matter, she didn't care. Her eyes searched the hallway, looking over the balustrade and scanning all around her.

'Lily.' Her voice was just above a whisper. 'Lily, where are you?' She spun around on the spot, pulled open the door that led to a small corridor, where rooms one, two and the Ennis Suite stood, but the corridor was empty, making Jess turn around and head for the stairs. 'Lily, come on, honey, come out,' she whispered as she ran.

Where would you go? Where would you hide? Jess wondered as she reached the bottom of the stairs and stepped into the reception area.

'Ann, did ... did you see Lily?' she asked as the night manager looked up from her paperwork, put her pen down on the desk and smiled.

'Of course. I think you'll find she went that way.' She pointed towards the kitchen. 'She's with Nomsa. She came down around twenty minutes ago. Chatted to me for a bit.' She smiled. 'She's such a lovely girl,' Ann said, unaware of the panic Jess was in. 'You should have known where to find her. Kids today, they always head to where the food is. It's what Poppy always does, especially when Nomsa is making pancakes.'

Jess felt relieved, but then angry all at once. Was this what it would be like to be a mother? Would her life be consumed by the terror of keeping her child safe? Would she always panic, each and every time she lost sight of them? And how capable was she of being a mother, when she'd managed to lose Lily from an enclosed room, within twenty-four hours of taking responsibility for her?

Jess moved through the dining room and opened the door that led towards the warmth and security of the Hall's kitchen. The smell of fresh baked bread, bacon, and chocolate brownies seeped out of the room and Jess breathed in, just as her stomach let out a humongous growl. It was certainly loud enough to give away the fact that after not eating the night before, she'd become beyond hungry.

It was then that she heard the sound of little girls giggling and stopped in her tracks to take in the noise. It was beautiful, and without a doubt the most innocent sound she'd ever heard. She listened for just a few moments more before stepping forward and into the kitchen.

She stared at the sight before her and couldn't help but laugh at Nomsa who was dancing on the spot, wiggling her broad hips while holding a pan in each hand, from which she flipped pancakes simultaneously, much to the delight of both Lily and Poppy, who sat eating them as fast as Nomsa could make them.

'Eat them up, my lovelies, there's more in Nomsa's pan when you've eaten those,' she sang as she turned to Jess. 'Ahhh, there you are, my gorgeous girl. How are you doing this morning?' Nomsa's eyes searched hers. 'You look a little peaky. Now, you sit yourself down and let Nomsa get you some breakfast. We have pancakes with blueberries, banana and chocolate sauce, or you could wait just another six minutes and there will be chocolate brownies hot out of the oven. Do you fancy some?' She sang out the words, then turned to put the frying pans down and leaned across and picked up the kettle. 'Tea or coffee?' she asked as she placed a mug down on the long oak table in front of where Jess had now sat. 'Ah, let me guess. Coffee in the morning, tea at night. Isn't that what you normally say, my girl?'

Jess smiled. No matter what was happening or what had happened around the Hall, Nomsa was almost always jolly, kind and generous. Jess took in a deep breath, smelt the air and came to the conclusion that even at that early hour, she could have murdered the chocolate brownies, but didn't trust herself enough to eat the sugary content and not throw them straight back up.

'Just coffee, thanks. I'm going to the hospital later. Thought I'd take Lily into Scarborough first, get her some new shoes and a coat and then take her to see her father.' Jess saw Lily's face light up, but Poppy's frown. 'Don't worry, Poppy. Aunty Jess will buy you something too,' she said as Poppy began to giggle.

'Aunty Jess, we had chocolate sauce … for our breakfast,' Poppy announced, pushing a huge piece of pancake into her mouth, making her cheeks bulge out like a hamster.

Jess smiled and shook her head as Nomsa filled her mug full of fresh aromatic coffee. 'That father of yours, he seems like a really nice man,' she said, and blushed as she put two slices of bread in the toaster. She then passed Jess her coffee, picked up her own mug and stirred the contents, before taking a sip.

The smell of the coffee immediately made Jess's stomach turn and she pushed the mug away. 'Actually, wow … err, can … can I have tea instead? Yes, tea. Tea would be good,' she rambled as she stood up from the table and walked to the back door, opened it and allowed the fresh winter air to blow over her face.

Nomsa looked over at Bernie the chef, who turned away,

pursed his lips and continued stirring his hollandaise sauce. 'Two eggs Benedict, ready to go,' he shouted as he poured the sauce over the poached eggs and passed the plates to head waiter Len, who was ready to take them to the guests.

Jess had seen the knowing expression on their faces and she'd had no choice but to look away, out of the door and across the yard towards where the greenhouse stood and where Bandit was working. He waved and Jess thought of the day he'd saved Poppy from the falling glass. Since then the greenhouse had been restored; the wooden structure was now all new and the original glass had been replaced. So much had happened here in the past year that everyone had got to know each other just a little too well. Which meant that she couldn't lie to Nomsa. She couldn't trust herself to look her in the face without telling her about the baby and knew that if she did, one too many questions would be asked and, for now, she wanted to wait until both she and Jack had come to terms with the idea before telling everyone else. Suddenly she realised just how difficult keeping her secret might be.

'Here you go, these are for table seven,' Bernie said as he finished loading a tray of toast, tea, cups, saucers and miniature jam pots. He passed them to Len, who'd returned to the kitchen. He smiled and took the tray.

'Thank you,' Len said. 'Now, table two would like eggs Benedict, one with ham, the other with bacon. And table four is a full English breakfast, with poached eggs and no black pudding.' Len had worked at the hotel for years; he, like Nomsa, had been one of the original staff and Jess smiled as he turned and walked out of the room. She then watched as Nomsa began to fill a miniature wicker box with a couple of brownies, a piece of carrot cake and a buttered scone, before she sat down and patted the bench, insisting that Jess sat with her.

Jess did as she was told and received a quick hug from Nomsa.

'But, Nomsa, when did you meet my father ... I mean ... I didn't realise you'd spent that much time with Bastion.' Jess popped a cube of sugar into her mug and began to stir the tea.

'Awww, of course I met him. He was here waiting for you yesterday. You both sat right there ... didn't you, chicken?' Nomsa directed the question at Lily, smiled and watched as the child nodded with enthusiasm. 'It took him a while to admit who he was, but once he did, he was just a little more than excited that he was going to finally meet you in person. Told me how happy he was, how he'd seen the article in the newspaper last year and how he'd hoped that one day he'd pluck up the courage to come here and find you.'

Nomsa's hands automatically went to Poppy's knife and fork; she picked them up and cut what remained of the pancake into pieces. 'Did you know you were named after his grandmother?' She looked Jess directly in the eyes and raised her eyebrows. 'Yes, you were, he told us all about it.' She laughed. 'Your daddy, he liked my baking, didn't he, Lily?' She nodded while filling two glasses with milk from the jug, and pushed them in the children's direction. 'He was starving, ate two of my scones, said they were the best he'd ever tasted and then he drank a whole bucketful of my tea while he waited for you to come back from the funeral.'

Jess laughed. 'Ahhh, that's what it was ... it was your scones. They're what probably put him in the hospital.' She tried to lighten the mood, but still felt puzzled. Lily had told her about going home to an empty flat, that they thought her mummy had taken their things. But it still wasn't clear why he'd set off to travel across half the country in the middle of winter to find her.

Nomsa stood up and swiped at Jess with a tea towel. 'Hey, cheeky, people drive for miles to eat my scones. The Women's Institute come every Monday and Friday, they all love them,' she said, filling the kettle and placing it back on the Aga. The smell of fresh toast filled the room as it popped up in the toaster. Nomsa grabbed it and placed the slices on a plate, where she buttered them and then pushed the plate across the table to where Jess sat. 'I think you should eat something. Might help you feel a little better, you know, a little less on the peaky side. And help yourself to the jams. They're a good pick me up.' She pointed to the selection that stood in the centre of the table. 'The sugar, it might help,' she said, with a knowing smile.

'But ...' Jess's eyes pleaded with Nomsa's. 'How did he find me?'

'He recognised your mother, of course. What happened here was big news, it hit all the national papers and he spotted your mum, along with a picture of you and the others.' Nomsa sat back down and lovingly held her hand.

'There were a lot of newspaper articles, but none of them were really about me. More about Liam, about what he'd done and how he'd almost killed Maddie. He was her fiancé, not mine, and the fact that he almost killed me too was pretty much brushed over by the press. So, I don't get it.' Jess looked down at their entwined hands. Nomsa had become a huge part of her life, and for a moment Jess wondered what she'd ever do without her. The thought brought tears to her eyes. She had no doubt that Nomsa had taken to her father, but had no idea why he'd told her so much, and in such a short time. 'He told you I'd been named after his grandmother?' she questioned. 'Why would he do that? I wasn't even aware that my mother knew his grandma, she'd always been quite certain that I'd been the result of a one-night stand. And apparently he'd travelled all the way from London? What the hell was he doing right down there?'

Nomsa nodded. 'Maybe your mother had a good reason to let you think that, honey. Maybe she needed to keep him a secret. Only he can explain now and as for London, that's where your mother used to live, when they first met. Bastion said that it was where she lived with Morris, Madeleine's father. You were just a toddler at nursery when you moved to Yorkshire.'

Jess shook her head. 'But I don't remember moving.' She pondered for a moment, and sighed. 'Why all the secrets and lies? Why did Mum let me think that he'd been a sailor who'd gone back to sea, without ever knowing that I existed?' She paused and looked at Bernie who'd stopped cooking and was listening. 'Do you think he was more than a one-night stand to her? I mean, it sounds as though he was.'

'Honey, I don't know. All I do know is that he's here now. He came to find you and you have a chance to get to know him, to be with him and to learn all about him. Don't throw that chance away. As I said, he seems really nice,' Nomsa said as Poppy climbed onto her knee. Her arms immediately went around Nomsa's neck and the four-year-old snuggled in. 'Hey you, don't get comfy.' Nomsa laughed as she began to tickle the child. 'I've got some work to do and you … you have to go and play with Lily.' She kissed Poppy on the forehead before picking her up and placing her back on the floor. 'Now then, Jess, will either Maddie or Jack be going to the hospital with you?'

Jess shook her head and sighed. 'No, Nomsa. I think that this is one trip that Lily and I should do alone. I guess that this is one conversation that's waited for far too long and, to be honest, I guess there might be a few tricky questions that I need to ask. Besides, Maddie has things to do here.

Christmas is nearly upon us and Jack ... well, Jack's kind of busy too.'

Nomsa smiled, nodded, turned and pulled Jess into a hug. Jess held onto her as tightly as she could, knowing that here, in this kitchen, with this wonderful woman, everything was good and she always felt safe and loved.

'Oh, Nomsa, what would I do without you?' Jess wanted to tell Nomsa everything, wanted her advice, and a small sob left her throat as she tried to decide what to do. Did she tell Nomsa all, or did she wait to tell everyone until after Christmas or even after the wedding?

'There, there, my girl. I'm not going anywhere.' She patted Jess on the back and then held her at arm's length to look into her face. 'I'm always here for you, honey, you know that.'

'I know you're not going anywhere, Nomsa. But I'm not so sure about Jack.' She swallowed hard as she spoke, knowing she'd already said more than she should have. 'Things have gone all wrong,' she whispered, careful not to speak too loud. 'Last night he was so very different. He doesn't like the fact that ...' She looked around, checking to make sure no one else was listening, and whispered, 'Bastion. Jack isn't happy. He's talking DNA tests and everything.' A second sob left her throat and she buried her face in Nomsa's shoulder.

'Oh, Jess. Don't you ever doubt his love for you, my lovely girl. Whatever's been said, he loves you. I just know it. And do you know what? He's right. You should get a test, it's the right thing to do.' Her voice sang out as she rocked Jess back and forth in her arms. 'And if he is your daddy, then you can get on with your lives without any doubt in your mind. Think of the positives.' She leaned back and smiled. 'Anyone from twenty miles away would be able to see how much you and Jack love each other.' Once again she pulled away and looked directly into Jess's tear-filled eyes. 'Trust me. He's probably just a little confused, some things take a little getting used to. A lot has happened over the past year. He's been patient, he's stood back and waited and, if I'm right, he won't want to be sharing you, not with anyone. Not for a long time.'

Deep down Jess knew that Nomsa was right, as always. Jack had as much as admitted that he didn't want to share her. He'd never wanted to share her. Not with Emily, not with Maddie, and now not even with her father or his own child. But she wanted this baby so much and she couldn't imagine it not being there, not now. Already she felt protective towards it and she knew with certainty that she'd never do anything to hurt her unborn child. In fact she'd do everything she could to protect it.

She felt torn in two and sighed. She loved Jack so much, the whole wedding had been planned and every little detail discussed. She had the most beautiful dress, and she had the shoes. But now she wondered if there would be a wedding at all – Emily's death, Bastion turning up and Jack's reaction to the baby had shaken her badly and she just wasn't so sure about the direction her life was taking her in any more.

She took a deep breath and pulled herself out of Nomsa's arms. 'Nomsa, maybe this last year has been too much for him. I mean, not many fiancés have had to go through what he has.' She tried to smile. 'He might have had enough, and this … Bastion turning up … this could all be just one thing too many for him.'

Chapter Eleven

The sound of bleeping, mumbling and chairs being dragged across floors reverberated through the air as Jess walked along the hospital corridor. The feeling of nerves, sickness and trepidation all passed through her body at once, and she turned to look back at the hospital entrance, wondering if she should make a run for it and leave now, rather than face Bastion Collymore, the man who claimed to be her father.

She'd spent the whole night wondering what she'd say to him, how she'd act and, most of all, how she'd feel when she actually got to look him in the eye. Was she supposed to have an immediate love for this man, a natural affinity, purely because he was her father? Should she hug him, kiss him, shake hands with him, or just sit back and ask him where the hell he'd been hiding for the last twenty years? There were so many emotions running through her body, with her pregnancy making them worse, and she had no idea how she was supposed to feel or think. Nothing had prepared her for this day. Especially now, just after losing Emily.

She took a deep breath and looked down at Lily who happily trotted beside her in her new, more comfortable fur-lined boots. A huge smile covered her face, and her small hand continually stroked the red material of the new coat that Jess had just bought her. 'It's the prettiest coat, Jess. I look like Little Red Riding Hood, don't I?' She suddenly stopped skipping and looked up. 'But ... but ... she was pretty, with curly blonde hair, wasn't she?'

Jess's heart went out to the child. She knew exactly what thoughts were going through her mind, because they were ones Jess had had herself as a child of a similar age. 'Oh, Lily. You're not just pretty, you're beautiful. Just look at you.' She stopped in her tracks, knelt down in the middle of the corridor and took the child by the hands. 'Do you know how many people want to look like us?' She paused and stroked Lily's cheek. 'People pay a fortune to be like us. They go on exotic holidays, lie in sunbeds, or pay for tanning creams, just so they can have lovely tanned mocha skin, like we do.' Jess wiped a tear from the little girl's eye. 'It's true, Lily. I know you think that the only girls that are pretty are the ones with the curly blonde hair, but all of those girls, do you know what they want?' She paused and smiled. 'They all want to look like you, honestly. And they wouldn't want that if you weren't really pretty, now would they?'

'But all the fairy princesses have white skin,' Lily replied.

'Oh, my darling, that's not true. What about Jasmine from *Aladdin*? And Moana? Always remember that you're surrounded by people who love you and skin colour doesn't matter, in fact it's the last thing that matters. We're all the same in here.' She placed a hand on her heart and smiled. 'And your daddy, you know for a fact that he loves you and … what … what about your mummy? I bet she loves you too?' Jess beamed as she remembered the unconditional love that her own mother had given her. But Lily looked thoughtful.

'I don't see Mummy very often. She isn't very nice.' Lily drew circles on the floor with her foot. 'She smells, and acts funny and she always wants to talk to Daddy and tells me to go to my room and play. Which is really hard 'cause my room was the living room. I had a settee that turned into a bed.' She continued to stare at the floor and shook her head. 'So, no, I don't think she likes me very much, and I'm really sure she doesn't love me.'

Jess was shocked at the child's words. She was still kneeling before Lily and she looked up and down the hospital corridor, wishing they were somewhere more private. 'Oh, Lily, I'm sure you must be wrong, how can anyone not love you?' she questioned. 'You're such a great kid, and I'm so lucky to get you as my very own sister.' Jess stroked her cheek and smiled when she saw the immediate delight in Lily's eyes. But deep inside Jess felt the guilt sear through her. To tell the child that she had a sister felt like a betrayal, when in reality it was still possible that Bastion was not her father and she might not be related to Lily at all. For the hundredth time in as many hours, Jess wished that her own mother was still alive. It was now that she needed her the most and maybe if she were still here, she'd be able to ask the questions and get the answers that she so desperately needed.

Jess opened her handbag and searched inside. She spotted an old envelope and pulled it from the bag along with a pen. 'Okay, I'll tell you what I'm going to do. On this envelope I'm going to write down my phone number and inside it ...' She reached for her purse. '... inside it I'm going to put two pound coins. This means that if ever you feel scared, afraid or if you just need me, you can call me. Okay?' She placed the envelope in the top zip pocket of Lily's coat, fastened the zipper and patted Lily on the shoulder.

'Can we go and see Daddy now?' Lily asked. 'I'm going to tell him all about Nomsa and the pancakes. I'm going to tell him about how I slept in a real bed, and I'm going to show him my new shoes and coat,' Lily said as she pulled on Jess's hand. 'He'll be so excited to see you, Jess. Are you really excited too?'

Bastion Collymore was in a four-bedded bay. A monitor continually bleeped by his side. It was loud, persistent and annoying and he tried his best to ignore it while using his arms to hold his chest as he coughed. His mind was doing somersaults with the anxiety of not knowing how Lily was. He needed to know who was looking after her and if she was all right. Oh, he knew he'd left her at the Hall, and hoped that Nomsa would have taken care of her, or maybe she'd met with Jess and she'd taken care of Lily. It was either that or already his princess would have been taken into care and would already be with foster parents, the place where he least wanted her to be.

He mentally kicked himself for travelling up country in the first place. It had been a long way, not only for Lily, but also for himself. It had been a cold, harsh journey and deep down he'd known that if he'd stayed in London one of their neighbours would have taken them in. One of them would have fed them and looked after them for a week or two. But no. He'd wanted better for Lily. He'd wanted her as far away from Annie as he could get her and had set off from London knowing he was sick, knowing he should have stayed and knowing that he should have got some medical help.

So why hadn't he? Why hadn't he spent the money on a cheap second-hand mattress? It wouldn't have cost that much, they could have shared and he guessed that they'd have managed for a few weeks, at least until he'd got himself well and back to work. After all, they'd become quite adept at making a corned beef stew feed them for three days at a time. So why had he wanted to come here? Why had he wanted to escape from London? Had it all been about Annie? Had he hated her so much that he'd taken her daughter so very far away, just to stop her messing with her life?

He'd brought Lily up here in search of strangers, people who'd never met either of them, and now all he could hope for was that his Lily was safe, and those strangers in that house were looking after her. He'd left her with people she didn't know and she was probably scared, terrified even, and it was his fault. He only had himself to blame and guilt tore through him.

He needed to get well again. He needed to leave the hospital, contact the authorities and find somewhere to live. Somewhere where he could look after his daughter and keep her safe. He closed his eyes and leaned back against the pillows. He knew that he was running out of options. Without money he knew that finding a new place would be close to impossible, but hoped that with having Lily he'd go to the top of a housing list, especially if he told them what Annie had done and that he'd felt the need to leave the flat in London for Lily's own safety.

Yes, that's what he'd do. He couldn't imagine living without Lily, therefore he had to man up and do something to keep them both together. When her mother had left, he'd promised to look after her, promised she'd never wish for anything, promised her that she'd always be happy, yet here they were with nothing, not even a roof to put over their heads. He'd failed her.

Bastion closed his eyes and once again tried to ignore the bleeping. He wanted Lily to have what all other children had at this time of year. They had homes, they had wishes and dreams, with Christmas trees, gifts below it and an anticipation of what was to come, all while they waited for the big man, for Santa, to visit. But his Lily, she had none of that, not this year and the thought of it all broke his heart.

'Daddy, we're here. Did you miss me? And look, I have new shoes and a coat. Me and Jess, we went shopping. She bought them for me, aren't they beautiful?' The sound of Lily's voice rang out as she ran into the ward, jumped up and onto the bed and quite literally threw her arms around him, making him hug her as tightly as he could while he sighed with relief. 'And look, they don't have holes or rub me like the old ones.' She pointed to the shoes. 'The old ones gave me blisters, Daddy. Look, do you see? Jess had to put plasters on my heels. They were bleeding.'

'You … you didn't have to buy her clothes.' He looked across as Jess entered the room. 'I can buy her clothes.' He glanced down at the coat. It was snug, well made and Lily looked warm. He knew he should be grateful, and knew she desperately needed the coat, but felt more than embarrassed that someone else had not only seen that need, but had acted upon it so swiftly.

'Well, we needed some sisterly bonding time, so we hit the shops. Didn't we, Lily?' Jess said as she stood before him, shuffling. Bastion looked up to where she stood and smiled. He knew that she too must be nervous. After all, him landing on her doorstep, quite literally, had all been quite a surprise to her. She'd had no idea of his pending arrival and from what her boyfriend had said the night before, his appearance had been the last thing she'd needed following the funeral. For that he felt sorry, as well as knowing that not many girls got to be twenty year olds before they got to meet their father.

'Look, I'm sorry. It's just …' He leaned back against the pillows and coughed. 'The shoes and the coat, they're beautiful, I appreciate what you did, thank you.' He then ruffled Lily's hair. 'Did you say thank you, Lily?' Once again he hugged the child as close as he could. She smelled of soap, and of posh shampoo and for the first time in days he saw a sparkle in her eyes.

'She did say thank you, honestly,' Jess cut in, once again shuffling on the spot. 'We got new socks and underwear too. I hope that's okay? The ones Lily had were a little past their best.'

Bastion nodded. 'It's more than okay, it's very generous and as soon as I'm on my feet, I'd like to pay you back.'

Jess shook her head. 'Seriously, there's no need.' She didn't know what to do and moved to sit in the chair. 'Did the doctors say when you'd be released?'

Bastion looked down to where Lily snuggled in and nodded. 'They said that I could leave tomorrow. So long as I rest.' He sighed, knowing that he had nowhere to go and would need to contact the authorities before he'd be allowed to leave.

'That's great. Isn't that great, Lily?' Her question was directed at the child, who was still cuddling into her father. 'I'll ask Nomsa to make sure the bed is changed in room five, as soon as we know. It's one of the only twin rooms in the hotel, and where Lily slept last night. I stayed with her, I hope that's okay? You see it's a big house and I thought she might be frightened if I left her alone.' She paused. 'But once you're back, I'm sure you'd rather be the one to share the room with her.' Jess's enthusiasm shone through and Bastion swallowed hard with emotion as he realised that she was offering him somewhere to stay.

'I ... I can't ...' he stuttered. 'I mean, it's very kind of you but I didn't come here to impose.' His voice broke; by turning the offer down he'd be rendering himself homeless, rendering Lily homeless and possibly losing the only opportunity he'd ever have to get to know Jess. When he'd decided to come here, he hadn't had a plan, he hadn't known what would happen, all he'd known was that he couldn't stay where he was. The last thing he'd ever intended was to take advantage.

Jess's face lit up with kindness. 'Don't be crazy, where else would you go? Lily told me what happened and that you slept in a doorway just to get here. Besides, it's the week before Christmas and if you're planning on staying in the area, you'll need to contact the council, but they'll be closed until the New Year. So, if you want to, you can stay for a week or two until you are well enough to sort something out.' She smiled at him. 'What's more, Nomsa would be so annoyed with me if I didn't bring you back to the Hall. You certainly left an impression upon her. She was singing your praises only this morning and as far as I'm aware she's already baking and getting ready to feed you back up.'

'Did someone mention my name?' Nomsa laughed as she entered the ward, carrying a small wicker basket. 'I thought you'd like some of my chocolate brownies, I made them special this morning, I did.' She looked directly at Bastion, their eyes connected and he smiled in appreciation of the basket. She was a fine woman, and he wondered which heaven he'd fallen into. 'Besides,' she continued, 'I thought that Lily and I could pop along to the hospital shop, give you two a little while alone.' She glanced back at Bastion and then at where Jess sat by the side of the bed. 'Come on, sugar.' The words were directed at Lily. 'Let's go find you some proper food, 'cause all I remember you eating today was my pancakes.'

Lily jumped up, took Nomsa's hand and happily followed her out of the ward, leaving Bastion and Jess alone.

Jess stood up and moved to lean against the wall. Now she had the opportunity to ask Bastion anything she wanted, she had no idea what to say.

'So ...' she began. 'Now we are expected to talk.' She laughed and looked at the men in the other three beds. Two of them were asleep, but the other seemed quite interested in what she had to say and so she moved to the side of the bed, pulled the curtain closed and once again sat down on the chair.

'Jess, I don't know what to say, but ... I'm so sorry.' He

looked down as he spoke, genuinely sad and Jess believed that he really was sorry. She just didn't know what for. Was he sorry for leaving, or was he sorry for not having been in touch for the first twenty years of her life?

'You're sorry for what?'

'For everything.' He began to cough. 'First, I'm sorry about your mother. She was a good and fine woman.' His hand lifted to his square jawline. He rubbed his chin and then looked over at the bathroom. 'I ... I'd have had a shave if I'd realised you were coming, so I'm sorry for that too.'

Jess let out a deep sigh. 'I want a DNA test. It's for the best and everyone says that I should get one done,' she suddenly blurted out. 'I looked into it this morning. We can get a result within just a few days. Only problem is it's just under two hundred pounds.' She closed her eyes and looked down at the floor, but Bastion reached over and took her hand.

'My dear girl. I'd have the test tomorrow, today even, anytime you ask, if that's what you want, but I'm sorry, I just don't have that sort of money.' Once again he looked embarrassed. 'Maybe in a few weeks, once I've seen the authorities, once I've got Lily and I somewhere safe to be.' He stopped and swallowed. 'Then, my beautiful girl, then I'll make it a priority.'

Jess nodded. She'd known he wouldn't be able to pay and kicked herself for mentioning the price. 'It's okay. I'll pay for it,' she whispered, still looking down at their hands. 'But if it's negative, you'll be owing me the money. Is that a deal?'

Bastion lifted her hand to his lips. He kissed the back of it and then looked up and into her eyes, while his other hand patted hers. 'Positive or negative. It's a deal. I'll pay for it either way.' Jess could see the tears in his eyes as he spoke. 'But I can tell you now. I have absolutely no doubt in my heart that you're my daughter, Jess. No doubt at all.'

Jess was silent. She didn't know what to say to him. She felt as though her demands could have offended him and tried to think of a way to explain. 'I'm sorry if you think I should just believe you and I don't mean to doubt you, but you see … we've had a hell of a year.'

Bastion once again patted the back of her hand. 'You don't have to explain … I don't mind taking the test.'

Jess liked him. He seemed genuine and she left her hand held within his. 'I kind of do have to explain, Bastion. My sister—'

'Madeleine, ah yes, how is she?'

Jess nodded. 'She's fine. But last year she was with a man we all trusted, a man she went to live with. It … it was him that killed Mum. He also killed Madeleine's husband, her father and her literary agent. Sounds like a novel, doesn't it?' She took a deep breath. 'Then … then he tried to kill both Maddie and me. He burned down the hotel from which both Nomsa and Poppy only just managed to escape and that's what you'll have seen in the papers. So now, and unfortunately for you, we're all a bit on the cautious side.' She pursed her lips. 'Sorry.'

Bastion sat forward on the bed. 'First, I'm so sorry I wasn't allowed to get to know you before now and second, I owe you such an explanation.'

Jess nodded. 'An explanation would be nice. I mean where the hell were you for so many years?' She looked down at her feet, wishing she'd been just a little more tactful.

Once again, Bastion took hold of her hand. 'If I could have been, I'd have watched you grow, I'd have tucked you up in bed every single night and I'd have read you every book that the library would lend us. But, my dear girl, it wasn't my choice.' He stopped and rubbed her hand in his. 'Your mother and I, we loved each other, we did. But she was a mother first and foremost. She thought that by staying with Morris, by pushing me away, she was doing right by her children. After all, until the moment you were born, she had no idea which one of us was the father.' He looked up and directly into her eyes. 'I should have fought harder for you, but she made it clear that her choice had been made and I loved her enough to let her go. I thought she'd be happier without me.' He closed his eyes, released her hand and gripped his ribs while coughing.

'But, after I was born … When you knew that you were my father, you could have come back, couldn't you?' Jess was clutching at straws. 'But you stayed away.'

'My dear Jess, I once saw your mother pushing you in your pram and you were so beautiful that the moment I saw you my heart burst with pride. There would have been nothing I'd have loved more than to go home with you, but your mother forbade it. She wouldn't allow me to see you, so I became your number one stalker and used to watch you as often as I could. I resorted to hiding behind bushes, bus shelters and parked vehicles just so I could watch you walk down the street. I'd sit in the park reading newspapers in order that I could watch you play on the swings, but then your mother moved away. I had no idea where you were, except that you were somewhere in Yorkshire and, as you know, Yorkshire is a big old place and I had no idea where to start looking.'

Jess sighed and stared down at the floor. She knew that finding someone twenty years ago had been so much more difficult than it was now. There hadn't been the internet, there'd been no such thing as Twile, Find my Family, Facebook or search engines. Finally she looked up to see Bastion's eyes which searched her own.

'Jess, I want to be your father, I always wanted to be your father and I prayed that one day … one day …' He began to cough, picked up the glass of water and took a small sip, all the while looking Jess in the eye.

'Daddy, look what I got.' Lily ran in, a soft rag doll in her hands. 'Nomsa bought me a dolly. It's just like my favourite one, like the one that Mummy took.' Once again she jumped up and onto the bed, clung to her father with an obvious need to be close to him and Jess felt a pang of jealousy shoot through her. It was a surge that took over her whole body as she realised how many years she'd missed out on, how many hugs she could have had and how much love they could have shared. For years she'd had so many questions she might ask if ever they met, but now she was here, wishing she'd made a list. Jess took a deep breath and made a mental note to ask him next time about her mother and how they'd met. She smiled, hoping it was a good old romantic tale.

Chapter Twelve

Jack ran through the woods. He needed to run, needed to feel the burn in his lungs, but most of all he needed to clear his head. Now that his shift for the day was finally over, he needed to get out of the hotel and away from the constant questions that Nomsa had been firing at him like bullets for the past two days.

He knew she meant well, knew she loved both Jess and himself like a part of her own family, but he had no idea how to react, not at the moment. Jess was pregnant, and as far as he was aware no one else knew. What he really wanted was to get some time alone with Jess to talk about the baby, about how they both felt and, of course, he needed to know if Jess was as confused and scared about it all as he was. The problem was, every time he and Jess got the chance to speak, there seemed to be three or four other people in the vicinity who wanted to join in, which quite often included an eight-year-old little girl who seemed to cling to Jess like a limpet.

He'd never thought about becoming a father. Right now it had been the last thing on his mind, but now it was here, he wondered what the reality would be like. Would he know what to do? Who would teach him? He thought of how Nomsa and Madeleine would both help Jess, but for him there was no role model to look up to, no father figure to ask advice of and definitely no friends who'd already become parents. All he could think of was how he interacted with Poppy; was it the same with your own child, or different? He felt numb at the thought of it all and wasn't sure what he should be feeling. Was the numbness normal?

He inhaled as he ran, stumbled over a fallen log covered in a pile of old, wet, fallen leaves, steadied his pace and then came to the conclusion that he felt as though a pressure had been placed on his shoulders, like a set of dumb-bells weighing him down with no chance of the weight relenting anytime soon. And that weight, he decided, was called responsibility. He was going to be a father, so much sooner than he'd ever thought, but now he had to 'man up', and take responsibility for a child he hadn't planned. The thought spun around in his mind. The pregnancy was as much his doing as hers. It had taken two of them to have sex, and both of them had been more than aware of the consequences. He shook his head knowing how irresponsible they'd been. He hadn't wanted a child. He hadn't wanted this pregnancy. But he did want Jess. He loved her more than anything in the world. He couldn't imagine life without her, but the reality was they were about to be married, about to become parents and they had nowhere to live. It hadn't seemed important before; they lived in the hotel. But now he needed to find them somewhere to live as a family, a home to call their own.

Jack jumped over a small water inlet and almost tripped over a rock. He grabbed at a tree branch, caught his breath and then continued to run. He pushed on harder than normal, the need to feel the burn on his lungs overwhelming, and ran as fast as he could.

Everything in his life was going to change. Damn it, it had already changed.

After the trauma and upset of the year before he'd only just begun to settle. He'd finally allowed himself to relax and enjoy the little time he managed to spend with Jess outside of work. She'd decided that she'd train as a nurse, and had even enrolled on the course, initially spending a lot of hours studying. But Emily had been so dependant, and Jess found that she felt more useful at the Hall, helping Emily. So she'd quit and had taken on responsibilities here. She worked on reception each weekend and when they needed the cover during the week. The rest of the time she'd shared her day between Emily and Jack. But working alongside Jack was different to them spending time together. Quite often their shifts were different, or overlapped and it was on the days that Jack worked that Jess spent most of her time with Emily. She'd walk her around the garden, some days on foot, other days pushing her in the wheelchair, with Poppy and Buddy happily trotting behind. And on the days when Emily didn't feel well enough to be outside, they'd sit together drinking tea, whilst all the time laughing and giggling, and talking about anything and everything they could think of.

When they'd least expected it, just two weeks before Christmas, Emily had taken to her bed mid-morning and died before tea. Then Jess's father, a man she'd never met, had arrived right after the funeral, promptly collapsed on the doorstep, and to complete the whole explosion of events, Jess not only had an eight-year-old sister who she now had to look after, but she was pregnant with his baby. There was no wonder he felt confused.

He slowed his pace, came to a halt under a tree and tried to catch his breath while he thought things through. He had a list of all the things he wanted them to do together, all the places they should go, the holidays they should take and all the experiences they should have, all before having children. He'd wanted to do things properly, with the wedding coming first, but then he'd had ambitions of buying a house. Just a small one to start with, but somewhere away from the Hall. Their home would have been and should have been their new start. It should have been a place where they could spend a year or two of married life. Just the two of them. And in time he'd have most probably decorated a nursery, all ready for when they decided, together, to have a baby. He'd wanted to do that. He'd wanted to do all of that. But most of all he just wanted to be with Jess.

But now instead of the dreams of what they could or should have done, everything was decided. Their whole lives were now set in stone, and it was now up to him to take responsibility. Was everyone this nervous? Was every new father this scared of what was to come, of how they'd cope and how they'd provide everything that was needed?

It had been raining overnight, so the ground was sodden, and the puddles were larger than normal. He leaned against a tree and immediately droplets of water fell from the branches above, like a thousand raindrops falling at once. He sighed, shook the water from his hair and looked up and into the branches. He'd spent most of his childhood climbing trees, rummaging for apples and running through the woods. He thought back to his mother, how happy she'd been when he'd brought the apples home. She'd hug him and make a pie for tea. Jack smiled. His mother had been a single parent, one who could seemingly turn any foraged food into a banquet. Even so, he'd watched her struggle for years. The terraced house they'd lived in had been old, with single glazing, and they'd burnt anything they could in the open fire grate each evening just to keep warm. He'd watched her going without, making do, and not just with material things, but food too. He'd not seen it as a child, but as an adult it had become more than apparent that she'd spent years making excuses to him of not being hungry, or pretending to have eaten earlier, when in actual fact she'd have barely eaten at all. And all because she had a responsibility to him, to ensure that he was always fed and well looked after. And he applauded her; he'd never gone without. He'd been almost an adult before he'd asked her what it had been like for her, a question he should have asked so many years before. But as only a mother could, she'd simply replied, 'My darling boy, I would have given my last breath for you and to bring you up alone was not a hardship. Not to me.' Jack had never known who his father had been. Had never known how life would have been with a father in the house, or what a father's role was.

Jack's mind was engulfed with questions. If he was about to become a father, then he wanted to do it right, be the best he could be, but how could he do that when he'd never experienced how a father was with their children?

He felt the anger grow within him, his whole body beginning to shake. He wondered where his father was now, what had become of him and whether he too would turn up on the doorstep of the hotel one day, hoping for a big reunion. And what if he did turn up? How would he feel? Would he be like Jess and welcome him with open arms? He shook his head. No, he wouldn't, he just knew he wouldn't. Was that why he was acting so out of character with Jess's father? Was he angry with him for being Jess's father and not his? And if that was the case, was that fair to Jess?

He kicked at the tree causing more drops of water to fall. He'd wanted more for his own children. He'd wanted them to have so much more than he'd ever had and had always promised himself that by the time he had a son or a daughter, he'd have a home with a garden and savings. He'd wanted them to have somewhere they could play, somewhere he could run around and play with them, and somewhere he could keep them safe.

Was that too much to ask? Was he being unreasonable? Did he have a right to feel angry that his plans had been thrown up in the air?

He sighed. He knew that Jess was still annoyed with him, that he'd been wrong to go to the hospital to challenge Bastion with an onslaught of questions. But he'd only been trying to find out who Bastion really was and why he was there. He'd only been thinking of Jess. He'd been trying to protect her because he knew how hurt she'd be if Bastion Collymore was a fraud, and wasn't her father at all.

'Were you annoyed? Annoyed that it wasn't your father that turned up?' Jack questioned himself. But then he kicked himself; he'd seen how excited and happy Jess had been. She'd been to the hospital with Lily and spent time with Bastion. She'd spoken of how, through the newspaper clipping, he'd found her. How he and her mother had been more than a one-night stand. He'd used the word love, said that he'd loved her enough to let her go. What did that mean? What's more, he'd told Jess that he was more than willing to take a DNA test, that he had no doubt what the result would be. Jack remembered how silently he'd sat at the kitchen table while Jess had rambled on to him and Nomsa. How on the one hand he'd wanted to be excited for her, but on the other he'd wished for none of it to be true and how he wanted to turn the clock back by at least two weeks, to a time when life had seemed so much simpler and he'd felt more in control.

Jack began to run back towards the house, through the trees, down the lane and into the clearing. He stopped in his tracks to take in the Hall's beauty with its bell tower, gargoyles and the new windows that had been recently placed in the tower room, giving the room a whole new existence after having been hidden away for so many years. He loved to see the house at this time of night, as darkness began to fall and the Christmas lights shone out from the lower windows, and big white puffs of smoke bellowed out from the chimneys.

He took in a deep and determined breath. He needed to speak to Jess. He needed to tell her that it would all be okay and that he'd find a way to look after her, even though right now he had no idea how. He looked up to the sky. 'I don't normally pray, God, but if ever you wanted to throw me a miracle, now would be a great time to do it,' he said with a smile, and ran back to the Hall.

Chapter Thirteen

Annie rolled onto her back and pulled her dressing gown up and over her partially naked body. The material was practically see through and didn't make much of a difference, but to Annie it was a way of ending the session, a way of showing a punter they'd had their money's worth, that her body was now out of bounds. She lay back against the pillow for a moment and sighed, before allowing her eyes to close. She was tired, but she couldn't sleep, not yet.

She had a lot more work to do before the night was over. It was a continuous cycle of punters and with one job finished, she needed to move onto the next. Opening her eyes, she glanced across at the overweight man lying beside her. His hair was greasy, his shirt un-ironed, his teeth were either black or missing and his saggy old skin was covered in liver spots, freckles and hair. Annie guessed him to be around seventy-five years old. He was a man who at his age ought to be at home with his feet up by the fire, drinking hot chocolate, rather than being in a brothel, with her. She wiped her nose on the back of her sleeve, and turned away, wondering if he was married or had kids. But in reality, she didn't really give a toss who he was, or where he should or shouldn't be. A man like him was the easiest money she ever earned; she never had to do much before it was all over, not with men like Charlie. His vigour had left him years before, along with the use of his legs and his eyesight. And fast results meant fast money. He was the fifth 'easy money punter' she'd had that night; in fact, most of the punters these days were like him, as the young and good looking ones took themselves into the town and got their sex for free from girls willing to drop their pants for a meaningless promise and a quick fumble behind the nightclub.

She looked at Charlie and hoped she could get rid of him quickly. She needed to move onto the next. She had debts to pay, and needed to fit a sixth or maybe even a seventh punter in before she went for some food, a fix or even a quick drink in the bar. Tonight she was thankful; at least there were enough punters in the brothel to keep her from having to work the streets.

'Come on, Charlie. You've had what you came for, now get your fat arse out of bed and hand over the cash.' She pulled at the dressing gown, climbed out of the bed and allowed her eyes to scour the littered carpet, searching for his discarded clothes that lay amongst hers. She picked up his trousers. They were dirty, and covered in unidentified stains, but she didn't care. The trousers normally held the money and that's all she was interested in. She threw them at the bed. 'Here you go, Charlie. Get 'em on, and pay up.'

She walked over to the window, moved the thick, cream, nicotine stained net curtain to one side and looked out. Griff was walking up the road towards the brothel. He had a young girl draped all over him and Annie wondered if she was a one-night stand, or whether she'd be coming to live in the house. Was it possible that he was already looking to replace her? The girl was tall, at least ten years younger than her, and to Griff she'd be someone new to rent the room to, just as soon as she no longer needed it.

'Give me a minute, I'll pay you when I'm goddamned ready,' Charlie's satisfied voice rang out. As he turned over on the bed, a putrid smell expelled itself from his body and Annie could tell that he was settling in for the night, as suspicious snores began to fill the room.

'Oh no you don't, Charlie. You need to get up. Come on, get your arse up, it's time for you to go home.' She watched him wriggle on the bed, his hand searching for a cover that wasn't there. 'Are you cold, Charlie?'

He grunted. 'Throw us a duvet, cocker, just for a minute or two. I'm … I'm just a bit on the tired side,' he whispered between the pretend snores.

'No way, Charlie. You're getting no duvet, now come on, throw me the money and get your stinking arse out of here. I've got another punter waiting, I need to get back to work.' Annie knew her words were harsh, knew that some men preferred her to be loving, pretentious and act as though they were the only man that night, but not Charlie. He was there for the sex, nothing more, nothing less. 'Charlie, come on, pay me the bloody money!'

'Get it yourself,' he grunted and turned on his side.

The words were music to Annie's ears. She knew he wasn't really asleep, but he'd given her permission to go in his wallet and she eagerly pulled it from his trouser pocket, opened it, and turned it upside down, ready to empty it of cash, but scoffed at its content.

'Come on, Charlie, where's the rest? You owe me another thirty quid.' She poked his leg with a stiletto and heard him grunt with annoyance. 'Charlie, twenty quid isn't enough.' Annie sighed and looked down at the money that had dropped onto the bed. 'Charlie, are you listening to me?' She sat on the edge of the bed and picked her camisole up from the floor. She began to put her underwear back on, before she brushed her hair and began repairing her lipstick in the dressing table mirror.

She glanced back at the bed and then at the room. It was a simple room. Just as she liked it. She had everything she needed. A bed, and a dressing table, along with a greyish carpet that had originally been cream. It desperately needed a good clean, but Annie didn't see the grime. Just like she didn't normally pay any attention to the navy blue bedding set that was now covered in bodily fluids and would have been better burnt, rather than washed. She moved the sheet to one side, then thought better of it and folded it in half, in order to hide the stains. She shrugged. The state of the room didn't bother her, but she knew it most probably bothered others. She'd long since lost all love of possessions, had sold most of her things over the years to get money for drugs and right now all she cared about was earning enough money for the next fix. She sighed, knowing that paying off Griff should be her priority, but her need for drugs took over all other rationality.

She walked back to the window. Griff had gone which probably meant he was somewhere in the house, and she wondered whether to disturb him and let him deal with Charlie. Dealing with the men that didn't pay was part of his job, especially if he wanted his cut. Men coming up short were normally dealt with swiftly, and everyone knew that Griff could be brutal, which meant that most punters paid up the moment his name was mentioned. Annie looked back at the sleeping Charlie. At least by letting Griff sort him out, he'd see how hard she was trying to earn the money and what she was up against. But then again, she wondered if he actually cared or whether he preferred the option of killing her and getting hold of Lily?

'What's wrong, honey?' Bella asked as Annie stomped down the stairs and walked into the communal lounge. Bella sat with three other girls, all scantily dressed, in full make-up and lounging on the numerous mismatched settees that surrounded the room. All the settees had seen better days; they were threadbare and covered with throws to hide their condition and the one in the far corner, which no one ever sat on, was propped up with a brick under the back corner. 'It's a makeshift leg, till I sort it out,' Griff had said some months before, but he still hadn't done anything about repairing or replacing it and Annie guessed that he probably never would.

'Thirty quid short.' She stamped across to the cabinet, picked up a bottle of whisky and poured herself a large drink. 'What the hell do I do? I have to pay Griff, he's already pissed that I owe him so much, and it's bad enough that I have to screw the old bugger in the first place, without him coming up short on the cash.' She began opening drawers, rummaging and searching inside and then slamming them to a close.

'Oh, bejesus, Annie. You haven't fallen for Charlie's sock trick, have you?' Bella laughed as she stood up, pressed her feet into the bright red stilettos, tossed her long bleach blonde hair over her shoulder, batted her long, false eyelashes in Annie's direction and pulled the see-through robe around her voluptuous body in a pointless attempt to shroud herself. Then she sashayed up the stairs, one at a time, and into Annie's room, where a bare-arsed Charlie still lay on the bed, pretending to sleep.

'Jesus, Charlie, what you been eating? It stinks in here.' She pulled back the net curtain, unlatched the window and opened it as wide as she could, allowing the fresh ice-cold air to flood into the room. 'Come on, old boy, let Bella take a look at those socks of yours.' She picked up one of his feet. 'There you go.'

Annie stood back and watched as Bella began carefully tugging at Charlie's moth eaten socks. They were practically glued to his feet, but she managed to somehow remove them with the tips of her long, false fingernails and one by one she tossed them at the bed.

'He used to do this at the last place I worked,' she said as she pulled a wad of money from the sock. 'He's got a lot more money than you think, he just knows how to hide it. Don't you, Charlie?'

Annie shook her head and began counting the notes out onto the bed. 'He's done it here before too, comes in short on the money, pretends to be asleep and then sods off when he doesn't think we're watching,' she growled. 'But what I don't get is if you have money, Charlie, why the hell don't you just pay up?' Annie screwed her face up and picked up a glass from the dressing table, sniffed at its contents, swished it around and drank it down.

'Yeah, Charlie, and buy some new socks,' Bella said as she kicked at a condom wrapper from the side of the bed and turned to where Annie stood. 'And you. It's time you gave the place a clean, Annie. It's bloody disgusting, isn't it?' She bent down, knelt on the carpet and began throwing the litter at a red plastic bin, which stood in the corner next to the dressing table. 'There's no wonder men try to pay you short, my girl, is there?'

'Thanks for the advice,' Annie said, 'but I don't think the men give a toss, so long as they get laid.' She kicked at the bed. She didn't care about the mess, and didn't pay any attention to the litter, the half empty mugs, the half eaten sandwich that still sat on a plate next to the bed, or the dirty syringe on the sideboard. All she cared about was getting the job done and grabbing the money. 'Charlie, next time you're paying up front, or I'll be calling for Griff. Do you get that?'

Charlie grunted and sat up on the bed. 'For God's sake, do you two ever stop bloody moaning? All I ever get from you lot is bloody abuse. Where's my damned trousers?' He began shuffling around, picking up his clothes, and pulled a cotton vest over his head.

'Here you go, Charlie, get them on.' Annie threw the trousers towards him, quickly followed by the socks, all while watching Bella who still continued to tidy the room, turning her nose up at the grot and grime that covered the floor.

Annie was at least ten years older than nineteen-year-old Bella, yet Bella seemed a lot wiser. She took more care over her appearance, her clothes and her personal hygiene. She showered between each and every client, whereas Annie did not and most days took a quick strip wash by the sink, if that. The last thing she wanted to do was get her hair wet and have to blow dry it on a daily basis. It all took time, time she didn't want to waste.

She knew she should shower more often. When the men came in off the street she'd watch them carefully as they sat in the communal lounge, and after the normal pleasantries they'd normally chose the girl they preferred. Annie had begun to realise that more than half the punters would choose Bella over the others and the other half would only choose her if all the other girls were busy.

Annie looked down at her own attire. The outfit she wore was probably older than Bella was. She knew she was dirty, she looked like a tramp and she thought for a moment or two, wondering if she were a punter and had the choice, would she choose Bella too? She made a mental note to think about taking a shower before the next man came through the door and she looked up at the clock, trying to work out how much time she had before the evening rush. An hour, two at the most, which meant she'd have time to get out of the house, find a dealer and get a much needed fix to feed her habit.

'Annie. Go get the bloody vacuum and clean this carpet, it wouldn't hurt you to sort this place out, would it?' Bella stood up and held a hand out to Charlie. 'And you, Charlie, you have been told to bugger off home.' She pulled him up to his feet, just as he lurched forward with his hands grabbing hold of every part of Bella's anatomy he could manage. 'Any more of that, Charlie, and I'll be charging you for a grope,' she shouted and moved out of his way.

Charlie turned and laughed, and as slowly as he could, pulled on his coat and then staggered towards the door, with his walking stick in hand. He waved it in the air. 'I'll be in next Friday, right before Christmas Eve.' He smirked. 'Let's see if one of you can make this twinkle.' His hand went to his crotch and the sound of his cackle filled the landing. Both Bella and Annie forced a smile, which quickly turned into a frown the moment Charlie had left the room.

Annie made her way to the cupboard on the landing, pulled out the vacuum cleaner and stamped back across the landing in her bare feet. 'Bella, I don't have time for this, I need to get out, find a fix and then I need to find some work.' She threw the vacuum into the room. 'Griff's on my back for money. I owe him thousands and I need to find a way to get some earned.'

'But you need to clean too.'

Annie shook her head. 'No, Bella. What I need is to keep him happy, or else.' Her voice began to tremble at the thought of what Griff had threatened.

'Hey … or else what?' Bella grabbed at both of Annie's hands and pulled her towards the bed. 'Come here, sit down for a minute. What's he planning on doing?'

'Bella, I can't. I …' She looked for a way out. 'I really don't have time, I've told you, I have to work …' She took a huge inward breath. 'Jesus, I need a fix.' Her eyes implored Bella. 'Do … do you have anything? Because I could really do with something right now and if you do …' She tried to think of an excuse. '… well … it'd save me going out, and then I'd have time to clean up a little, wouldn't I?'

Bella sighed as her hand went up to her hair and pushed it away from her face. 'Okay, okay, I have some heroin in my room. I'll get it for you.' She patted Annie on the knee, stood up and then disappeared momentarily. 'I hide it, so Griff doesn't know,' she said when she returned from her room. She raised an eyebrow. 'You know how he feels about us being high, I'd hate him to know I was using again.' She held out a small packet to Annie. 'Knock yourself out, but you owe me, darling. I want some back when you next go out.' Annie took the bag as Bella continued, 'There isn't much, but it might get you through tonight.'

Annie smiled. It was obvious that Bella had been using and if she didn't realise that Griff knew everything, she was sadly mistaken. But still, she hurriedly set to work warming the drug, picked up the dirty syringe and drew up the fluid. Once the heroin was injected, she leaned back against the wall with a satisfied sigh. 'Thanks,' she eventually said. 'Now, get out. I need to work. I can't risk Griff coming in. He's in the house somewhere, I saw him earlier, with a new girl. If I'm not careful, he'll be showing her my bloody room.'

'Come on, Annie, tell me what's up. Griff is always around the house, you know that. Why are you suddenly worried about him? What did he do to you?'

'He doesn't like me sitting idle.' She went to pick up an old screwed up newspaper, but her hands shook uncontrollably and she ended up sitting on the floor in a heap. 'He'd be annoyed with me, and I've seen him annoyed once too often with the others. He's a big man, Bella, he can do a lot of damage and it's not pretty when he starts.'

Bella took Annie's hand and held onto it. It was a gesture of kindness, of compassion, and for a moment Annie stared down at the hand as a warmth travelled through it. 'Why does he get annoyed with you, Annie? Did he do this to you?' Bella moved Annie's hair away from her face to reveal the bruise that covered her left cheek. 'Why do you stay, hun? You could leave, find a new patch, set up somewhere else, somewhere away from him.'

Annie began to tremble. It began in her shoulders and travelled down both of her arms. She closed her eyes, unsure as to whether the trembling was from the drugs or the fear. 'Are you crazy? He'd find me. Besides, I owe him and he wants his money and I have just a week left to pay, which gives me till Christmas Eve, or …'

'Or what, honey?' Bella held up her spare hand. 'What would he do?'

Annie crumbled; she'd never had anyone be kind to her, not since Bastion. Tears began to fall down her face and a continual shaking began to rattle her inside. 'If … if … if I don't pay … he wants my child … my little girl, but … how can I give her to him? I don't know where she is. And I'll end up having no choice, 'cause how the hell can I earn ten grand in a week?'

Bella stood up and dropped Annie's hand. 'Jesus, Annie. You owe him what?' Bella paced around the room. 'How the hell did it get to be so much?'

'Ten grand. I owe him ten grand and every day it increases with the interest. Bella, I've got no chance of earning it, not in a week. That'd be two hundred blokes at fifty quid each and that's if they all want the works. But most don't, you know that. Most want a twenty quid hand job or the other day, a guy just wanted to sit in the bath for an hour and get covered in custard. I mean, come on, it's weird. What the hell do you charge for that? Twenty, thirty quid?'

'Okay. Let me get this right. If you don't pay Griff, he wants the kid, but isn't she just a little 'un, a baby? What the hell does he want with her?' Bella shook her head. 'Actually, oh bejesus, don't tell me, he wouldn't, would he?'

Annie nodded between sobs. 'She's gone. Bastion is gone too. I went to the flat yesterday and the neighbours said he went a couple of days ago, right after—' She was going to add, right after she'd broken in and emptied the place of everything she could sell, but stopped herself at the last moment.

Bella paced up and down for what seemed like forever. 'So, you'd seriously give him your daughter, hand her over, just like that?'

Annie wiped her eyes on the sheet. 'What else can I do? He said he'll kill me if I don't and then he'll find her and he'll kill her too.'

Bella once again sat on the bed. Her hands were clasped together so tightly they had the appearance of wringing out a dishcloth. She looked ashen and for a moment Annie sat back and stared. 'Is that what ... what Griff does to those who owe him money?'

Annie looked through the haze, her mind now swamped with the drugs. She felt far too calm and distant to really care what Bella was saying. 'Oh, honey, without a doubt he'd either cut you or kill you.' She laughed. 'Please tell me you don't owe him money too? You're far too pretty for Griff to get hold of.'

Bella nodded, her eyes searching Annie's. 'It's just a couple of grand, nowhere near as much as you. But I do owe him.' Once again she stood up and began pacing up and down the room. 'I didn't cover my rent for a while. My dad, he was ill, and my mum couldn't cope any more, she needed a break, needed to put him in respite care. I had no bloody choice but to give her the money, Annie. She was at the end of her tether.'

The reality of what Bella had said brought Annie out of her daze. 'You have to pay him, honey. He can be cruel and you, you really don't want to see what he's capable of, do you?' She paused and turned away. 'But that means it's you or me. If one of us gets the punter, the other can't and, Bella, I'm telling you, for the sake of my baby girl, I need to stop the other girls taking them too, I need them all. Can you make a few calls, you know, drag a few of your old regulars in?'

Bella stared at the floor. 'Come on, Annie. It's Christmas. I've tried. Nobody's interested. They're all off buying their wives expensive gifts of jewellery, chocolates or clothes, which they'll hand over Christmas morning and pretend they're the perfect husband when in reality most of them come in here once or twice a month, even the posh ones.'

Annie leaned back against the bed. She watched Bella's torment, and then her mind went back to what Bella had said earlier about the drugs. They'd been hidden in Bella's room, somewhere Griff wouldn't find them, and Annie wondered where they were. There weren't too many places and she immediately thought of the drawers or the floor. She'd seen false bases in drawers before, but in Annie's opinion Bella would have used the old floorboard trick. She shook her head, even high on drugs working it out was just far too easy. After all where else would be a big enough space for her to hide both drugs and money? Was she saving the cash, waiting to give it to Griff in one go? After all, the punters chose her. They loved her voluptuous figure, which meant she must be earning it. She smiled. Bella took at least three showers a day and Annie made a mental note to watch her movements. Only then would Annie know how much time she'd have, and how long she could search for a hiding place without being caught. She nodded. It was her or Bella, and if Bella had money, then Annie was intent on stealing it.

Chapter Fourteen

'Oh, Mr Collymore, I'm so glad you're back,' Nomsa said as she moved to the bed and paid a lot more attention to plumping up the pillows than normal. 'Now, Jess says you'll be staying for a week or two, so let's get you all settled in.' She finally moved away from the bed and to the sideboard where she rearranged a vase of flowers and then turned to watch as Bastion gingerly walked across the room, quickly followed by an overexcited Lily, who held onto his hand as tightly as she could.

'Daddy, quickly, come and look.' She let go of his hand and ran ahead to jump onto the bed. 'This will be your bed,' she said as she bounced from one bed to the other. 'And here, in this bed near the window, this is where I sleep. Do you see it, Daddy? It's a real bed, not a settee and it's all mine, isn't it, Nomsa?'

'It sure is, sugar,' Nomsa said as Lily jumped down from the bed and skipped across the room to fling open the bathroom door.

'And in here we have our very own bathroom. Isn't it beautiful? And look, Daddy, a toilet of our own. Watch how it flushes.' Her eyes were wide open. 'Do you see? We don't have to go down the corridor, or use a bucket, or share with the neighbours.' She shone with excitement as she buzzed around the room. 'And the nice lady who comes in every morning, she brings lovely bubble bath and shampoo and really soft toilet rolls. Daddy, feel the toilet rolls.' She pulled a sheet off the roll and passed it to Bastion who stood, with mouth open, looking around the room.

'It sure is pretty in here.' He stood still, barely moving while he took in his immediate surroundings. 'I think we sure did fall into heaven, Lily, didn't we?'

'Now then, Mr Collymore, you're looking a bit wobbly on your feet. Come and sit yourself down before you fall down,' Nomsa continued, helping him to an armchair. 'I've changed the bed, and Jess went out and bought you some new pyjamas, slippers and a dressing gown.' She looked Bastion up and down. 'I'm sure they'll fit you just fine. So, when you're ready, you can get changed into them and jump into your bed. That's right, you just make yourself all comfy and I'll be back up in a few minutes with some of my nice French onion soup.'

Bastion watched, and nodded. His hand reached out and stroked the satin throw that covered the foot of the bed and tears sprang to his eyes. He was grateful for having somewhere warm and comfortable to sleep, for the new clothes and for the soup.

'Oh, Nomsa, you're a good, good woman. I don't know how to thank you,' he began. 'And please, my name, call me Bastion. No one calls me Mr Collymore any more.' He laughed, but as he did he began to cough repeatedly, and Lily looked up at Nomsa for reassurance.

Nomsa stayed calm, walked to the bathroom and filled a glass with water. She turned and pushed it into his hand, and he gratefully took a sip, before leaning back in the chair, where he closed his eyes and rested them for a few moments, until the urge to cough had subsided.

'It's been a long day for you, hasn't it? All those doctors poking at you, and then all that time you had to wait to be released, you'd think they'd do it all a lot faster, especially when they say they need the beds,' Nomsa said as she walked towards the window, opening it slightly. 'The fresh air will help, but if you get too cold, I can easily close it again. Now, can I get you anything else, other than the soup?' she questioned, and looked over to where he was sitting and caught his eye. A blush suddenly tinged her already rosy cheeks. 'A bath, maybe? Should I run you a nice hot bath? We should have some bubbles in here, ah yes, here they are.' She picked up a bottle and waved it in the air.

Bastion smiled. Nomsa was a fine woman and if he'd felt well enough he'd have probably had a very cheeky, quick witted response to her question about baths and bubbles, but instead he took in a deep breath and sighed. 'No, no thank you, I'll run one in a minute.' He seemed to think for a moment. 'I just want to get settled, hug my Lily for a moment or two, and then I'd really like to take that hot bath and get all clean before putting on these nice new pyjamas. And then, after the soup, I think I'd like to sleep for a week.' He patted the bed. 'And I must say, this bed sure does look cosy.'

'Well, all of that can easily be organised.' Nomsa picked up a towel, folded it and placed it on the end of the bed. 'I'll leave you two to your cuddle time. And when you want your bath, you send our little Lily down. And you can use the phone to let me know when you're all done,' she said, pointing to the phone that stood on the dressing table, 'and then I'll bring the soup up for you, just so long as you don't mind me seeing you in your pyjamas.' She winked and smiled, before walking awkwardly towards the door.

Again Bastion smiled and tried to think of a quick response. He liked Nomsa, he was sure she was flirting with him, and more than anything he loved the way she referred to Lily as, 'our little Lily'. He closed his eyes and thought of how different Lily's life would be here, if only it were possible to stay. 'Well, you saw me in my pyjamas at the hospital, now didn't you?' he responded. 'And I don't think I minded too much then, especially seeing as you brought that lovely basket of cakes.' He laughed. 'Those nurses were wondering why my sugar levels were through the roof, till I let them try one of your brownies.'

His laugh bellowed around the room. He got up, picked up the pyjamas and placed them on the sideboard, then patted the bed and sat down again, allowing Lily to jump up and onto his knee. 'Wow, this bed is so comfy, Nomsa. Almost as good as your brownies, which I must say were the best I'd ever tasted.'

'Ah, get away with you. The brownies were no trouble, and if that's your way of getting me to bake some more, then I will,' Nomsa said. 'I brought them to the hospital because I was worried about you. One minute you were sitting in my kitchen, eating my scones, and the next you'd collapsed on the doorstep and they were rushing you away in an ambulance, all lights ablaze.' She paused and shook her head. 'You gave me quite a fright, you did. And, your Jess, she said it was my scones that had put you in hospital, the cheeky madam.' She laughed, but then looked seriously at Bastion. 'Of course the bed is comfy and until you feel all better, you can have your meals up here. But, when you feel up to it, maybe you could get yourself dressed and come down to sit in my kitchen and chat to me while you eat. I'd be sure glad of the company.' She smiled as Lily jumped down from Bastion's knee, ran towards her and put her arms around her waist.

'Nomsa's the best, isn't she, Daddy?' Lily's voice sang out and she looked up at Nomsa with the biggest, most beautiful brown eyes that Bastion had ever seen. 'And Nomsa, Daddy really loves your scones, don't you, Daddy? You even told Jess how much you liked them, didn't you?'

Nomsa smiled as Lily let go of her waist.

'I did exactly that,' he said. 'I could have eaten those scones all day long.'

Once again Nomsa blushed. 'Okay, you've convinced me. I'll tell you what, after you've had your soup, I'll send you a fresh baked scone up for afters. I'll even put you a spoon of clotted cream on with a strawberry or two, just to make them a little nicer.' She winked at him and then looked at Lily's hopeful face. 'In fact, I'll tell you what I'll do, I might send up two scones, just in case our little Lily might want to have a bit of a picnic with you. How does that sound?' She glowed with happiness and Bastion smiled, appreciative of her actions.

'That, my dear lady, sounds amazing, and, for what it's worth, I think your scones were pretty perfect just as they were. They didn't need anything adding, did they Lily?' His arms were now around his daughter who'd pulled herself back up and onto his knee. He nestled his face into her neck and blew a raspberry on her skin, making her shriek with delight. 'Now, go on my girl, go with the lovely Nomsa while I get a bath. This good lady has made soup and the last thing we'd want to do is let soup spoil or go cold, isn't it?'

Bastion watched as Lily ran to Nomsa. Their hands automatically connected and were gripped together like magnets, in a way he'd always hoped he'd see Lily do with her own mother. It was a sight he'd wished and hoped for with Annie, but a sight he'd never thought he'd see with Lily and another woman. He nodded in acknowledgment. It was something he should have realised many years ago. Lily needed a mother in her life, she needed a woman in her life, someone who'd nurture her, love her and teach her womanly ways.

He smiled at Nomsa, who smiled back. 'Thank you,' he whispered, with genuine feeling, as both Nomsa and Lily left the room and the door closed behind them.

Chapter Fifteen

As Jess climbed the staircase and took a step across the landing, she could feel herself hyperventilating. It was the first time she'd been near Emily's room since she'd died – the day that Emily had been wheeled out of the house, never to return.

'Come on, you can do this,' she whispered to herself as her hand touched the silver doorknob of Emily's bedroom door. She took short, sharp breaths and placed the key in the lock. She paused and for a few moments she thought about the last time she'd been here, the last time she'd seen Emily alive and the moments preceding her death. The paramedics had been there. They'd been desperately trying to bring Emily back. The room had seemed full of people, medical equipment and the terrifying sound of the defibrillator as they'd shocked Emily's frail body, over and over again. She remembered crouching in a corner of the room, her hands in front of her face and tears flooding down her cheeks whilst she rocked and hummed in an attempt to try and block out all that was happening before her.

And now, here she stood, in the hallway outside Emily's room, with the thought of going back in filling her with dread. But it was something she needed to do; she'd promised Emily, and she knew that she had no choice. After all, what was a promise if you didn't keep it?

Jess turned the key and slowly pushed the door open, inch by inch, and then with the door ajar, she stared into the room. The medical equipment was now gone – the swabs, sterile gloves, and syringes had all been removed – and everything was as it had been before the ambulance men had arrived. Except now the curtains were closed and the room stood in darkness.

Jess walked tentatively through the bedroom on tiptoes. She felt as though she were intruding, as though Emily were asleep and any moment now she'd turn over and give one of her smiles. Jess opened the curtains that had been closed since Emily's death as a mark of respect, and the sudden light that flooded the room made her squint and stand back. She allowed her eyes to adjust and then turned to stare at the mahogany four-poster bed with tear-filled eyes. It had been in this bed she'd held Emily's hand and told her about the pregnancy, and where Emily had recounted the time when she herself had been young, pregnant and scared. How she'd hidden her pregnancy from her family and had given birth, frightened and alone, in the bell tower room, only to be found a few days later by her father. She'd been sick and at first her father had pretended to care, but then on a day when he'd insisted she went into the main part of the house to take a bath, he'd been caught red-handed with two women from the adoption society. They'd tried to take her Arthur away without her consent and Emily had had no choice but to run, with her baby in her arms, in order to save them both.

A sob left Jess's throat. 'Poor Emily,' she whispered as her fingers traced the ornate carvings of the bed. Nothing about Emily's life had been easy; she'd never felt total happiness, and had spent most of her life caring for everyone around her. Jess swallowed hard and sat down in the armchair that stood by the bed. Was this how her life would end up too? Would she spend her life looking after others? Would she have to fight for everything she wanted? She shook her head knowing that at least she had Jack, which was already so much more than Emily seemed to have had.

She took a deep breath in. The room still smelled of Emily, of the perfume that she always wore and Jess looked down at the bedding as her hand carefully stroked the material.

She knew that once it had been removed from the room, once the bed had been changed and the room emptied and cleaned, the scent would be gone and with it the last trace of Emily would be gone too. Jess pulled a pillow from the bed and hugged it to her chest.

'Oh, Emily, you have no idea how much I miss you already,' she sobbed. 'What will I do without you?' She turned the chair, inched it forward and placed it in front of the chest. Her hand brushed against the brass cup handles, knowing that the drawers had to be opened and emptied, and after quite a few minutes of sitting and staring she finally pulled open the first drawer and peered inside.

She emptied the drawers, one item at a time. Each item was carefully and respectfully checked, before being placed into one of two piles. The first pile was for things she wanted to keep, things too personal or valuable to give away, and the other pile close to the door was for the items that had to be thrown away, or given to charity.

Jess made her way to the chest nearest the bed, pulled open a drawer and once again studied the contents before lifting out a small pile of envelopes that were all tied together with a pink bow. It was more than obvious that Emily had hidden them there, and the letters had been waiting to be found. For a moment Jess allowed just her fingertips to touch the ribbon, the bow and then the writing in Emily's hand. After what seemed like an eternity, she pulled at the ribbon and allowed the envelopes to tumble onto the bed, where she noticed that each letter had been addressed individually. There was a letter for her, and a separate one for Jack. There was one for her son, Arthur, and then there was one for Madeleine. Four in total.

Jess picked up the letter with her name on it. Its bulge intrigued her, and she felt its shape knowing that there was more than just a note within the envelope. Her fingers traced the spidery writing. Emily must have written the letters knowing they'd be read after her death, knowing that Jess would be the one to find them. For a moment Jess hesitated with the envelope in hand, not knowing how she would feel to read the final words of a woman she'd loved so very much. She gave a half smile. She knew that even though the words would hurt her to read, she was certain that they'd also bring her the comfort of knowing that Emily had written them during her final days, and that she and the people that lived in this house had been the last thing she'd cared enough about to use her energy to write each one a final goodbye.

Putting the letters back together, she tied the ribbon around them again and placed them on top of the chest, now turning her attention to the wardrobe. She began taking clothes from hangers, one piece at a time, and one by one she folded them and placed each in the charity pile. All were quite new – most had been bought during the past year during one of their weekly shopping trips – and Jess knew that Emily would want someone less fortunate than herself to have them.

Finally, and with a huge sob, she turned her attention to the bed and began to strip the duvet and sheets from it. A soft knock at the door made Jess turn and, with sheets in hand, she opened it and looked into Jack's solemn, miserable face. He looked awkward, and distant. He was wearing shorts and a T-shirt and Jess could tell he'd been out running. It was something he did daily, a way of getting his thoughts together and blowing off steam. She stood back, waiting for him to speak.

'I ... I asked Nomsa where you were and she said you'd be in here. Do ... do you need any help?' he asked nervously. His body leaned against the door frame in a way that made Jess wonder if he'd struggle to stand unaided.

'Do you know that Bastion is home?' he asked, almost as an afterthought. 'Nomsa keeps feeding him. He's already had soup and a bite out of one of her scones, with jam and cream.' He looked her up and down. 'Don't ... don't you want to see him?'

Jess nodded. 'Of course I do, but ... I had to do this first. I promised Emily ...' She looked over her shoulder into the room. '... I promised I'd do this, you know, take her personal things out of the room, before the cleaners come in. I think Maddie will have it decorated, before ... before it's used again.'

Jack's hand reached forward. He slowly brushed a wayward hair away from her face, and Jess closed her eyes as his hand lingered against her skin. With all that had happened she'd missed being with him, and the smell of the deep musky cologne that he wore, but most of all she'd missed his touch.

'Kind of odd, her not being here, don't you think?' He stepped into the room and closed the door behind him. His hand ran across the surface of the chest. 'Will it be used as a guest room?' he continued, without waiting for an answer to his first question.

Jess turned. 'I think they'll have to.' She walked to the window. 'Do you mind if I open it?' she asked as she lifted the sash window, and the breeze filled the room. 'I need the air and besides, Emily didn't like it so very stuffy in here, did she?'

There was a mutual silence in the room and an awkwardness that Jess had never known between her and Jack. She knew that Jack had no idea what to say to her; after all, this was the first time they'd been totally alone since she'd told him of the pregnancy.

Jess picked up the letters. 'She left these. I ... I don't know what to do with them.' She passed them to Jack, who swallowed hard, and Jess knew he was holding back the tears as he too allowed his fingers to stroke the ribbon.

'They have names on them. Maybe you should give them out?' He looked up and stared at her, his eyes full of confusion and, without thinking, Jess leaned into him and closed her eyes. It felt so good to be so close, and she rested her head on his shoulder as his arms immediately went around her. For a few moments she felt safe, happy and content. The feeling was all she needed before a tidal wave of sobs flooded from somewhere within her. Every emotion left her body all at once. Her knees felt weak and she clutched onto Jack as though her whole life depended on it.

'Hey, come on. It's okay, I've got you.' His words were soft and comforting. 'Here, let's sit you down.' He led her to the bed and they sat together in silence until the sobs subsided. 'There you go, that's my girl.' He leaned back and looked into her face. 'Do you want me to get Maddie?' he asked, but Jess shook her head.

'No, I just want to be with you.' She sniffed. 'I'm so sorry, Jack. I didn't mean for all this to happen. I didn't mean to get pregnant, please believe me.'

'Oh, Jess. I don't blame you for this. I think that …' He tipped his head to one side. '… I think there were two of us there that night, and two of us made this happen, not just you.' His hand lifted to cup her chin. 'So, I'm sorry too. I'm sorry I made you so sad, and what's more I'm sorry I've handled all of this so very badly.' He paused and placed a kiss lightly on her lips. 'I should have reacted differently, but … but I was so confused.' He nodded. 'I'm still confused. In fact, I'm terrified. And I'm not going to pretend that this is what I really wanted for us right now, Jess. You know it isn't.' He pursed his lips as though thinking what to say next. 'You know I wanted us to be settled before we had a family, didn't you? I wanted us to find a house, soon after the wedding, a home for us both. But things have changed now, and now I need to find a home for the three of us.' Again his lips grazed hers. 'I'm going to look after you, I'm going to look after both of you.' He allowed himself to laugh. 'I have no idea how right now, but if you want me, I'm here.'

Jess pulled herself into his warmth. 'Oh, Jack, of course I want you.'

'There's only one thing I ask, Jess.' His hands touched both her shoulders making her sit up and look him in the eye. 'All of this …' His hand went down to touch her stomach. '… It was all a bit of a shock.' He paused. 'Can we just keep the news to ourselves for a while, allow it to be our secret, just till I get used to the idea myself, maybe even till after the wedding?' His eyes pleaded with hers and Jess nodded in agreement.

Chapter Sixteen

Annie watched Bella as she stood on the brothel doorstep, waving her latest punter off and shouting goodnight. She looked down at the money in her hand, counted it and then tucked it into her padded bra, before closing the door and turning into the room.

'Oh bejesus, it's freezing. He was a good tipper, so I had to wave him off, didn't I?' she said as she turned to the drinks cabinet and poured a large glass of whisky. 'But then again, I did give him a few of the optional extras.' She gave out a dirty laugh, placed a tongue in her cheek and held the glass in the air. 'This and a hot bath will be my treat tonight,' she announced as she sipped at the drink. 'What about you, Annie? Are you finished for the night, or what?'

Annie seethed inside. Bella had asked the question in the knowledge that she hadn't had any work all night. All the punters had chosen either Bella or one of the other girls, meaning that Annie would have to hit the streets as the clubs came out and would most probably still be working way after they'd all gone to their beds. What's more all tonight's men had arrived, done the business and gone quickly. They'd all paid up without an issue and, by the sounds of it, Bella had ended up with a few quid extra for her multiple services.

'Think I'll take a walk down the road, see if anyone's looking to score a trick or two in their car,' Annie answered as she slumped towards the stairs. Her legs ached and her heels were raw with wearing charity shop stilettos that were far too tight. Kicking them off for a moment, she began to climb the stairs. It was winter and she needed to change; the skimpy underwear that she currently wore would be no good out in the cold and the rain, but her distinct lack of clothes meant that her choices were limited.

'Well, I'm going to lay in a bubble bath for at least an hour,' Bella said as she smugly turned on her heel to follow Annie up the stairs. 'Think I've got enough to pay Griff off now, so tomorrow, my darling, the punters are all yours. I might even have the day off and go do some Christmas shopping.' She smirked. 'Buy my mammy and daddy something nice for the big day.'

'All right for some,' Annie threw back. 'So how do you do it, Bella? Two grand is a lot of money for you to have come up with that quickly.' Annie tried to calculate the amount of work Bella must have had over the past two days. She pondered for a moment; at around fifty quid a go that would have been forty blokes, and surely there hadn't been that many that had come through the doors? In fact, she knew there'd only been twenty at the most, and with that in mind, Annie tried to think back over Bella's movements. Had she been in the house all the time, or had she been out working on the side? She shook her head. None of them could earn that in a day or two, no matter how many extras they offered, not unless those extras were drugs.

Annie tossed the stilettos through her bedroom door but hovered on the landing, while she watched where Bella went. Whatever Bella was up to, whatever she was doing, it wasn't a few quickies with the punters, and Annie's mind went to the small bag of heroin she'd produced to help her out. Was she dealing? Was she selling it along with the sex? If she was capable of earning two grand that quickly, and apparently that easily, then she could earn it again.

'Looking forward to seeing my mammy Christmas day,' Bella said, ignoring Annie's question. 'They've invited me for Christmas dinner. First time in three years and I reckon it's all cause I helped my mum. She must have really appreciated it.' She looked pleased with herself, but Annie was annoyed. She could feel the steam coming out of her ears as she stamped around at the top of the stairs. Bella was gloating just a little too much and Annie could feel herself getting more and more angry. But her anger would be short-lived. Annie had a plan and in the end Bella could gloat as much as she liked, but it'd be Annie that won the war and her that would have the money. After all, why shouldn't she? Bella had known what she'd been up against, she'd known what Griff had demanded, what he'd threatened and she'd known what he was capable of, yet even with all that at stake, she didn't seem to care. All she cared about was saving her own neck and paying her own debts.

Pushing the door to her room wide open, Annie went inside, kicking rubbish to one side as she went. She sat on the bed and began picking up her outdoor clothes from the floor, but then tossed them back where they'd come from. She didn't want to go out there tonight. It was too cold, it was raining and whoever wanted to score would be half paralytic by now. She sighed. 'There has to be an easier way,' she whispered to herself. Then she thought of the money. Could she really take Bella's money, or was it better to admit defeat, and to just give Griff the child? Annie knew what those animals would do to Lily, but did she care enough? Was it better to sacrifice her daughter than to take the wrath herself? It was the first time Annie had really wondered whether Griff would actually take her. Was it worth it to clear her debt? And if not, could she deprive herself of the drugs while trying to pay Griff off?

She thought of the heroin. Could she go without it? She shook her head. 'Not a chance,' she said to herself as she scratched at her arm. The track marks were more than apparent, her arm was filled with sores, and she made a study of where she'd next find a space in which to inject.

Along the corridor a door opened, and then slammed shut, right before she heard the water run in the bathroom.

'You said you were going to lay in the bath for at least an hour,' Annie repeated the words that Bella had used and walked to the door. 'Well, good for you,' she whispered as she stood with the door half open, listening to the sound of the water swooshing around and Bella singing. Her mind went back to the day before. Bella had drugs hidden in her room. Annie smiled. There were only one or two places big enough to hide anything and Annie thought about the floorboards, how loose they always seemed and how she'd often hidden things under there herself. And with a good-sized hiding place, she was sure that Bella would have hidden the money there too. Again, Annie listened to the noise of the water swishing around behind the closed door. With Bella saying she was going to take such a long and luxurious bath, she'd be gone long enough for Annie to go in, find the hiding place and take it all for herself.

Chapter Seventeen

It was still early in the day, but with only six days to go until Christmas, preparations at the hotel were well underway. All the staff ran around frantically, doing multiple tasks, and all the main rooms were being prepared, cleaned and decorated. Jess seemed to have the longest list of all and she began ticking each job off, one at a time. The Christmas tree was to be removed from the grand hall – being real it had soon lost its perfection and a new and pristine one was to be put in its place. Jack and Len were already getting on with it. The old tree was too big to remove in one piece and therefore had to be cut up and taken out, all with as little disruption to the guests as possible. However, the new tree was much easier to erect and could easily be brought in through the patio doors. It was still wrapped up tightly in netting and while that was still in place, it could be positioned before the netting was removed. The tree could then be dressed, with everyone getting involved, before the first guests came down for dinner.

Once that was done, the dance floor needed to be constructed, the disco confirmed, and the food, balloons, streamers and crackers were all to be collected from the supplier, along with the miniature wicker baskets. Every guest staying on Christmas Eve would receive a small wicker hamper, each filled with goodies, and placed in the bedrooms as a surprise to welcome them on their arrival. All the baskets still needed putting together and Jess had wondered if she might enrol Bastion to help with the task. Everything had to be ready, everything had to be perfect and it all had to happen on time. The guests were paying a lot of money to be there and they were all entitled to total perfection.

Her thoughts turned to Christmas Day. Dinner would be served promptly at one o'clock, preceded by champagne, an array of cocktails and the most sumptuous aperitifs. It was up to the whole team to ensure that everyone enjoyed every minute of their Christmas, but ultimately it was up to Head Chef Bernie, Nomsa and the kitchen staff to provide the best food possible.

'Jess, did you phone the disco man to check the booking and make sure he gets here early on Christmas Eve to set up? Christmas Day will be far too busy and we really don't need the disruption of him having the doors open, letting all the warm air out.' Madeleine flicked through the diary. 'I want him in the corner of the library, and a string of balloons hung from the ceiling and the same on New Year's Eve, just like last year.'

Jess smiled. Maddie was the most organised person she knew and never ceased to amaze her. She'd been a bestselling author before coming to the hotel. She'd written to earn money while Poppy was a baby, but the writing had had to stop as soon as she'd inherited the Hall. Running Wrea Head Hall took all of her time and she'd had to learn a whole new profession within weeks of her arrival. Her whole life had changed yet, without hesitation, and with the help of Jack and the management team, she'd blossomed in the role of running the hotel. She did everything as her father had, ensured that the guests came first and, above all else, she did it all with an air of professionalism that Jess truly admired. But today Madeleine looked tired and flustered. It was as though there were too many things on her tick list and she picked up one piece of paper from the desk after the other.

'Maddie, when you say the disco man, do you mean the DJ?' Jess walked towards her, smiling, and watched as Madeleine juggled three jobs at once.

'That's Mr and Mrs Kent booked into Room Nineteen on the twenty-ninth, tick. I've ordered room service for Room Two, tick, and the lady, Mrs Bramfoot, in the Ellis Suite would like an iron and an ironing board, which Nomsa is about to take up. Tick tickety tick.' Madeleine paused and looked up from the desk, caught her sister's eye and burst out laughing. 'Yes, of course. He's called a DJ. Now can you be a love and call him, check he's still turning up and at what time? And let Len know that I've put him in charge of making sure the dance floor is constructed properly. I can't risk people tripping on it, especially during the conga.' She turned back to the computer and tapped on the keyboard. 'Oh, and check the DJ man's fee, make sure he isn't going to charge too much. I think last year, let me see, yes, last year he charged three hundred for Christmas Day, and the same for New Year's Eve. If he wants much more than that, haggle.'

Jess put her clipboard down and glanced into the main hall where she watched both Jack and Len now moving settees, tables and chairs into more suitable positions, all in readiness for removing the old tree.

Jack stood upright, his hand going to wipe his brow, and their eyes connected. He raised a hand and gave her a smile. He then awkwardly put his hand in his pocket, took in a deep breath and looked unsure of what to do next. He wasn't good at keeping secrets and normally blurted things out the first moment he could. But for just a few days, knowledge of the baby would stay between them and she held a finger to her lips and smiled, making Jack do the same.

She looked back at where Maddie sat. She normally told Maddie everything and it was killing her not to tell her about the pregnancy, but she'd promised Jack and in her book a promise was a promise. Besides, there were other things going on at the Hall. She'd only just come to terms with the fact that she might have a father, who was slowly regaining his strength after his mild bout of pneumonia. Over the past few days Jess had spent as much time with him as she could, but Christmas was the busiest time at the Hall and there was much work to do, so they'd only had the chance to have brief snatches of conversation that lasted just minutes at a time. Most of the conversations had taken place in the kitchen, where he seemed to spend most of his time with Nomsa, and it seemed to Jess the two were fast becoming inseparable. She'd bought a DNA test online and had sat for over an hour that morning just looking at the box, wondering how and when she'd approach Bastion with it. Half of her wanted to run to him immediately, to get to the truth and find out if he really was her father, but deep down the other half of her was terrified, just in case he wasn't.

'It's all going to be all right, I promise,' she whispered as she rested a hand on her stomach. She looked up and noticed that Jack had been watching and once again she lifted a finger to her lips, before turning her attention to the room keys, which she systematically hung in order. She then picked up one of Maddie's to do lists and began ticking off things that had already been done. 'Right, looks like Jack and Len have got the Christmas tree organised. So, I'm now going to go and ring the disco man.'

Madeleine took the list out of Jess's hands and passed a different list to her. 'Here, sorry, I made a new list.'

'Why am I not surprised?' Jess said with a laugh, looking down the new list.

'You okay?' Madeleine asked. 'You seem distracted.'

She had to look busy, had to keep working, had to think of a reason that would stop Madeleine asking questions. 'Oh, I don't know, Maddie ... okay, yes I do know. It's the DNA kit. It came and I don't know what to do.'

'Hey, I thought we'd spoken about this, Jess. You don't have a choice. You have to do the test, and you have to do it sooner rather than later. Before you get too attached to them both … you know, just in case.'

Jess looked down at the floor. 'Just in case he isn't my father?' she questioned as she raised an eyebrow. 'I know you're right, Maddie. You always are. But … I really, really want him to be. And what do I say to him? Here's the kit, now take this swab and if you don't mind could you go and rub it around your mouth because I need you to prove you really are my father and not some random black guy who's taken up residence in a nice hotel for the Christmas festivities?' She tried to laugh, tried to pretend that everything was okay, but it wasn't and she knew that Madeleine would keep pushing until the test was done.

'I'd say yes, that's kind of what you do. Besides it's not like he isn't expecting it, is it? You did have this conversation with him at the hospital, didn't you?'

Jess nodded, but tried to avoid eye contact. Her normal bubbly personality had disappeared and she could feel herself begin to shake. 'But, what … what if he isn't, Maddie? What if he isn't my father? What do we do, throw them both out? They've got nowhere to go.'

Madeleine looked her up and down. 'Jess, you have to get a grip on this. If he isn't your father, then he isn't your problem and he certainly isn't mine. Now, yes, I agree it's Christmas, the hotels are full and not even I would throw them out, not if they have nowhere to go.' Again she tapped on the keyboard. 'But there is a limit to what we can do. He's a grown up, he has to take responsibility for himself. I mean, the council, surely they'd do something for them, especially as he has Lily, they'd be sure to push him to the top of the "needy" list.'

Jess nodded again while staring at Jack in the grand hall.

If only she could tell Maddie about the pregnancy. She knew exactly how Maddie would react. She'd bounce around, kiss her a lot and she'd want to celebrate the new life of her first niece or nephew. She'd want to arrange a family dinner to tell everyone else and she'd want to go shopping for baby clothes. Jess sighed, knowing that all of that had to wait. She'd promised Jack and so she would have to hold on to her secret for a little while longer.

'Jess?' Madeleine looked up at her. 'Is there something you're not telling me?'

'No, no, I'm fine,' she lied. 'I'm just feeling a bit lost today. I … I was cleaning out Emily's room yesterday. It took its toll on me, all the memories of that day, they all came back.' She hadn't known what else to say.

Madeleine's hand reached out and landed gently on her shoulder. 'Oh, Jess, that must have been hard on you. Why didn't you tell me what you were doing? I'd have helped you. We could have done it together.'

Jess shook her head. 'I promised Emily that I'd do it. It was the last promise I made to her and, anyhow, Jack helped me.' She paused. 'Emily had written some letters, you know, before …' Jess announced, making Madeleine jump up from her seat and pull Jess into a hug.

'Letters … really? Oh, Jess … I mean … what do they say?' Madeleine stood back and looked directly into Jess's eyes.

'There were four. One addressed to you, one for Jack, one for Arthur, which you'll have to read to him, and one for me.' She took the letters out of her pocket and passed Maddie the envelope. 'This is the letter she left for you.'

Madeleine's hand went to her chest and rested on her heart. 'Oh, Jess.' She turned away and sat back down at the desk. 'This makes me really sad.' She looked down at the keyboard. 'Do you think that she knew … you know …

that she was dying, and that she wouldn't be here … for Christmas?'

'I don't know. But she obviously wanted us to open them after she'd gone, and not before. She must have had a reason.' Jess looked back into the grand hall, where Jack and Len were wrestling with what was left of the tree in a comical Laurel and Hardy style, making her laugh out loud.

Her whole insides ached with longing; all she wanted was to walk up to Jack, hold him and kiss him. But that wouldn't be allowed, not down here. There was a protocol to be followed in front of the guests and Jess let out a deep breath.

'Well, are you going to open it?' Jess sat down and watched as Madeleine hesitated before she tore open the envelope.

'Maddie, my beautiful girl,' Madeleine read out loud. 'Oh, bless her.' She looked up at Jess before continuing.

'I am writing this letter to you because I know you'll share all the details with my grandson, Christopher, or Bandit as you all now call him. I also know that men are not much for the written word, so I'm hoping that you will kiss him goodbye for me and tell him how much I loved him.

I'm also grateful to you. You have no idea how much coming back to the Hall meant to me and you opened your home to me without a second thought. I feel at peace in the knowledge that I spent my last days here and that my Arthur will be well looked after during his final years, although according to the doctors, it's doubtful that he has long to go on this earth either. I hope that you see fit that one day we will be buried together. Just as we should be.

Now that I'm gone, I'd like to bequeath to you my diaries. The ones that you know of and the ones that you don't. There are still diaries hidden, just look where the dust motes hover. They are yours and all that is within them is yours too. I'm hoping that you might start to write again. I'd be delighted to think that you might finally tell the world the story of my life, tell of how my father ruled us, how he and my mother lived very separate lives and, most of all, I want you to bring this house back to life. For far too many years it's been the house of secrets. One too many secrets if you ask me and I want them to end, they bring no joy to anyone. There are some secrets that I've held onto for most of my life and there are one or two I wish I hadn't kept, but I did so to protect others, to stop them from being hurt, when, in actual fact, I should never have had to do so.

The only thing that kept me going throughout all the years was the love I had for both my Eddie and for my son, Arthur.' Maddie paused, and wiped her eyes. *'There is a final secret still to be told, again one that I've held for far too long. All will become apparent, my dear girl. All is told within the diaries and all will make sense once you find and read them.*

Yours, Emily x'

Excitement flooded Madeleine's face as she looked up from the letter. 'Oh, Jess. Where do you think they'll be? I mean, you must know where she hid them?' She put the letter down and watched as Jess picked it up and shrugged.

'Don't ask me, I have no idea. But isn't it typical of Emily to leave us with a little intrigue?' She passed the letter back to Madeleine. 'So, are you going to do it? Are you going to look for the diaries and write the book?'

Madeleine stared at the letter. 'I don't know. I mean, where would I start?'

'First you have to find the diaries. She can't have hidden them anywhere obvious or we'd have already found them during the refurb and she must be pretty sure they hadn't been damaged in the fire. What does she say? "Look where the dust motes hover." So I guess somewhere we don't go very often, somewhere within this house or in the cottage. Somewhere that no one goes on a daily or weekly basis.'

'Do you think they've always been there?' Madeleine looked puzzled.

'I don't know, but I don't think she's hidden them anywhere too difficult to find. She must have been confident you'd work it out.'

Jess stood up and kissed Madeleine on the cheek. 'I'll help you look later, but right now, do you mind if I take a break, Maddie? I think you have a lot to think about and me, I need to catch up with Bastion. I'm going to pop to the kitchen, see if he's there, and make a drink. Do you want something bringing back with me? Tea, coffee, carrot cake?'

Madeleine was still staring at the letter and shook her head, leaving Jess to take one look back into the grand hall before leaving reception. She walked through the back connecting passage that led to the kitchen, where both Nomsa and Bastion were perched at either side of the kitchen table. Their heads were close together, their eyes were locked, and Jess was sure their hands had been momentarily linked, making her literally stop in her tracks in order to watch them more closely. There was an exchange of whispers, smiles and giggles, which made Jess unsure what to do. Should she carry on regardless and enter the kitchen or was she about to disturb something she shouldn't? She was wondering whether the moment that Nomsa and Bastion were sharing was as obvious as it had looked, but then Bastion leaned in closer and, taking his hand to cup Nomsa's chin, he gently grazed her lips with his. Jess held her breath and glanced back towards reception. Should she reverse, disappear back where she'd come from and give both Nomsa and her father time to finish whatever it was they'd started? But one step on a creaking floorboard meant that the spell was broken. Nomsa looked up and, although she'd hesitated, Jess continued to walk forward.

'Ahhhh, there you both are,' Jess said as Nomsa jumped up like a naughty child, picked up a tea towel, turned her back on where Bastion sat and began drying the mugs that stood on the draining board. Jess continued to look between them both, and even though Nomsa had turned away, she could tell that both were smiling from ear to ear, and both seemed to be blushing. 'Okay, what's going on?' she blurted out, before sitting herself at the table. She picked a banana from the bowl, peeled the skin back and began to eat.

'You want coffee, or tea?' Nomsa asked. It was obvious she was ignoring Jess's question as she picked up the kettle, gave it a shake and then filled it with water from the tap, before placing it on the Aga to boil. 'And a banana, my girl, is not a substantial breakfast. Not unless you eat it with some nice yoghurt or something.'

Bastion chuckled. 'I'm glad it's not just me that she nags.' He picked his mug up and took a sip.

'Away with you,' Nomsa said as she flicked the tea towel at him. 'You know it's for your own good. I want you fighting fit and back on your feet by the time Christmas gets here. Now finish drinking your tea and I'll make you a fresh mug along with a nice bacon sandwich for your breakfast.' Nomsa gave Bastion a smile and Jess noted that it wasn't the same sort of smile that she'd give to everyone else, but a smile that lit up her whole face, making her eyes sparkle with happiness. 'And then,' she continued, 'if you put a warm coat on, you could go and sit out on the patio. Get you some fresh air.' Nomsa gently patted Bastion on the shoulder. It was a loving gesture and Jess smiled in the knowledge that there was the same look in both their eyes.

'I might even join you out there for a moment or two now I've finished with the guests' breakfasts.'

Jess waved what was left of the banana in the air. She wanted to speak to Bastion about the DNA test, but her mind was now full of wondering what was happening between Nomsa and her father. 'Hey ... what were ...' She hadn't got an answer to her earlier question and was going to ask them if they'd like to fill her in, but she stopped mid-sentence. They were both adults and if they were happy, then who were they hurting? 'Okay, Nomsa, in answer to your question, I'd like some tea, please.' She sighed. What she really wanted was coffee, strong coffee, but early in the morning the smell made her want to heave and she couldn't risk that happening, not in front of Nomsa or her father. Instead, she sat watching how the dynamics in the kitchen had changed. Nomsa, who normally ruled the roost and force-fed everyone who came near, had suddenly turned into a coy figure of a woman and she was hanging on every word that Bastion said.

Jess really wanted to ask more questions, but didn't feel she knew Bastion well enough to dig any further and decided to wait until Nomsa was alone. 'It's quiet in here, where are the girls?' she asked as she stretched up to look out of the window.

'Oh, they were both up bright and early, and seeing as it's a nice day, they've taken themselves outside in the garden. They've been playing hide and seek for the past hour. It's Poppy's favourite game at the moment, she can't play it enough. She even makes Buddy join in, but him being a dog means that he barks and gives her away more often than helping her hide. Look, they're over by the trees.' Nomsa pointed into the grounds to the edge of the treeline. Poppy knew not to enter the woods, not to go out of sight, which made Jess smile as she wondered how on earth the four-year-old managed to play hide and seek without actually hiding.

Nomsa picked up the teapot and poured the tea. 'Now then, I was just going to make Bastion a nice hot, fried bacon sandwich to eat before he goes out in the garden. Would you like one too?'

Jess began to think about the bacon, about the grease, the sauce and the stodgy bread. 'Excuse me, I … I have to go,' she said as she stood up from the table, held a napkin to her mouth and practically ran from the room, while carefully clutching her mug of tea as though her life depended on her not spilling it.

Chapter Eighteen

Bastion zipped his freshly washed coat up and pushed his hands into the gloves that Nomsa had borrowed for him from Bandit. He rubbed his hands together, appreciative that they were warm and stepped out onto the veranda that led to the garden. He walked along the path towards the lawn, where he'd spotted some wooden bench seating from his bedroom window. The thought of sitting outside had seemed like a good idea, but now he felt the cold begin to penetrate, making his lungs tighten, and he wondered if he ought to take himself back inside to the warmth of the kitchen, where he could sit at the table, drink tea and watch Nomsa dance around the room while making something amazing for lunch.

He shuffled around on the wooden bench in search of a comfortable position. The bench was to one side of the lawn, at the back of the Hall and was overlooked by the vast conservatory, which was now full of guests, some taking morning coffee, others sitting with newspapers outstretched, and one man pacing up and down looking out at the view. But all seemed sensible enough on such a cold winter's morning to stay inside, where it was warm.

He took in a deep breath. It was a relief not to cough every time he breathed in and he smiled in the knowledge that the antibiotics must have finally begun to work. He hoped that soon he'd be well enough to sort out his life, once and for all. He needed to take control, search for work and earn enough money to give Lily a proper home. She needed a place to live where she'd be safe, somewhere warm and cosy, with a real bed, a duvet and a bathroom of their own, just like they had here at the Hall. But he wasn't crazy, he knew that it would all take time. The council might offer them a place to begin with, but to get something of their own choice would mean earning money; even if he got a job right away and saved for a year, the best he'd manage would be a small deposit to rent an even smaller flat. But it didn't matter, he needed to get some self-respect. If he at least had that, he'd be in a better position to think about moving forward. And maybe then, he'd be able to ask Nomsa to go out with him for a drink, a meal, or even on a real date.

He took a moment to stare up at the Hall. To take in its beauty. He still couldn't believe that he'd got here, that he'd found Jess, his first-born child. That she'd not only accepted him, but had welcomed him with open arms, and that right now he was breathing in the clean country air, rather than the diesel fumes and smog of the city. It seemed like a different life and he nodded gratefully. It was a different life.

He listened carefully. Somewhere in the distance he could hear the giggles and squeals of both Lily and Poppy, interspersed by the odd bark from Buddy, who was no doubt bouncing around them both in true Springer Spaniel style. It was a pure and innocent sound that rippled through the bare trees like wind chimes. There were so many sounds, so pure that he'd barely ever heard them with the same clarity before. The city traffic normally overpowered any birdsong in London, except for the pigeons that just clucked and swooped at food. A smile crossed his face and he made a wish: he wished that the birdsong would be a sound he'd be able to listen to just a little more often.

Bastion looked through the dining room window and caught sight of Nomsa, who had stopped clearing a table, glanced up, smiled and waved. 'You're a fine woman,' he whispered to himself as he wondered what his chances were of staying in the north, and staying close to her. Not at Wrea Head Hall, of course, but here, in Scarborough. He liked it here; he wanted to stay in this place where he would be near all of these gentle, loving people, who for the first time in his life had made him feel part of a family, part of something worthy; where he'd always have the fresh air, the sea views; and, most importantly, where he could be near to both of his daughters.

He still couldn't believe he'd actually found Jess. But he was grateful for whatever madness had brought him here that day. Grateful that he had his little Lily, grateful that she was safe, that she'd got to meet her sister and, for however long they were allowed to stay, that she got to live in a house like this one.

His eyes drifted up to the roof, to the gargoyles that looked down upon him, and the multiple chimneys that pointed upwards.

'Bastion, do you have a minute?' Jack asked as he walked out of the conservatory with purpose, closed the door behind him and stepped onto the pebbled path with two mugs in his hands.

Bastion looked him up and down. 'Are you here to interrogate me further, Jack?' he replied, and pulled his coat tightly around himself like a protective cloak. 'Because if you are—'

'Hey, I come bearing gifts, it's a peace offering. Nomsa sent this.' Jack held a mug out towards him. 'It's beefy Bovril. I think she's worried you'll freeze out here. She keeps walking into the dining room, just to spy on you and make sure you're still alive.'

'Thank you.' Bastion took the mug and held it between his hands, allowing the warmth to seep through his gloves. 'I'm sure I won't freeze. Nomsa gave me a spare pair of Bandit's gloves to borrow, a scarf and an extra chunky jumper to wear. I think she'd have given me thermal knickers too, if only I'd have said I needed them.' He glanced back at the dining room window, to where Nomsa still hovered, duster in hand now. He smiled at her and raised the mug in thanks.

'See,' Jack said. 'She doesn't even trust me to pass on the Bovril to you without checking that I did it right.' They both laughed, as Jack sat down beside him. 'Nomsa sure likes to look after you, doesn't she?' Jack held onto his own mug and for a few minutes they both sat silently and stared at the view.

Bastion eventually nodded his head. 'If only I were worthy, Jack. She's a good woman, makes me wonder why she isn't married. She'd sure make someone a great wife.'

Jack sipped his drink. 'Are you digging for information?' He glanced across and smiled. 'Nomsa has never been married. We often tell her to go out more, to join an online dating site or something like that, but she's always here, looking after us, even on her days off. So I'd kind of say that the chances of her meeting someone would be a tad remote.' Jack once again sipped his drink. 'Only place she'd be likely to meet anyone would be here, at the Hall.' He raised an eyebrow as he spoke. 'But you normally find that most folk who come here are already part of a couple.'

Bastion took in the information. It was true, he did want to find out more about Nomsa, but he hadn't expected Jack to tell him so easily, or so freely. He sighed, and for a moment wished that Jack really had sat down to pass the time of day, to talk about Nomsa and give him the answers that gave him hope for the future, but he wasn't stupid enough to think that this was just a casual conversation. No, this was all about Jess, and about him turning up here.

'I know it's not my place to say this, but I'm guessing that Jess might be pregnant … right?' Bastion suddenly blurted out and watched as Jack went pale and almost jumped up from the bench.

'Yes, sir, she is.' Jack paused and nodded. 'Did she tell you?'

Bastion shook his head. 'No, Jack. She didn't say a word. But I'd be a fool not to work it out. She looks green first thing in the morning, has done each morning I've seen her. She's emotional, she can't stand the smell of coffee, and the mention of a bacon sandwich sent her running from the kitchen with a napkin held up to her mouth. Just one too many signs, I'd say and, to be honest, since I've been here, I've got to know Jess the least of everyone; if I've worked it out, I don't think the others will be too far behind me.'

'Ahhh …' Jack looked down at the floor. 'I see …'

'Do you?' The words were simple, but Jack looked as though he had the weight of the world pressing down on his shoulders. It was a weight that Bastion had known all too well, just over twenty years before, when Jess's mum, Margaret, had announced to him that she was pregnant.

'I guess I'm still in shock. Jess only told me a couple of nights ago.' He held the mug to his lips and sipped. 'So much has happened around here lately … it's all been a bit of a surprise, and … if I'm being totally honest, I really didn't want to be a father, not yet.'

Bastion stood up and stretched. 'It is a shock, I agree. Being told that I was going to be a father was something I never thought I'd hear, no, no, not in a million years, and, seeing as we're being honest with each other, I can tell you now that when Margaret, Jess's mum, told me she was pregnant, I didn't take it too well either.'

'So you knew about Jess, about the pregnancy?'

'Of course I knew. Margaret and I had been seeing each other for a few months. She'd been unhappy at home. Morris had changed towards her after Madeleine was born and Margaret felt as though the only reason he was still around was for the child. So she and I got close. Too close. And when she found out that she was pregnant, she was in quite a panic and told me right away. But she was married, you see, and even though things had been strained, she'd slept with the both of us and she had no idea which one of us the father would be.' He paused for a while and looked thoughtful. 'She was a good woman, Jack. She put her family first and, for Madeleine's sake, she decided to try and save her marriage.'

'I see.' Jack sighed. 'At least I don't have that problem, do I? You know, no other fathers in the running.' He kicked at the pebbles that covered the path. 'So what did you do?'

Bastion thought for a moment. 'Well, I wasn't really ready for responsibility, that's for sure, and when Margaret said that her marriage had to come first I acted like any twenty-year-old acts when the love of your life tells you that she'd rather be with someone else. I buried my head in the sand. I turned into a party animal. I went out on the town and decided that if I ignored the fact that I was about to become a father, it wouldn't be true.' He paused and sighed. 'It was self-preservation, Jack. I tried to distance myself, just in case the baby wasn't mine. Even though deep inside, I kind of knew that she would be.' Bastion's tear-filled eyes looked into Jack's, to see a young, confused man, who looked as though he was having a personal battle with the outside world.

'So you walked away, you abandoned them?'

Bastion sat back down, his hand patted Jack's knee. 'No, son. I didn't abandon them. I just did what Margaret asked. I stepped back. I didn't fight for them, when in reality I should have and, by the time I realised what was important to me, it was far too late.'

Jack cocked his head on one side. 'Meaning?'

'Meaning that by the time I saw Margaret again, she was pushing a pram down the street. Morris had realised that Jess wasn't his, and he'd left her. And then, because I hadn't fought to keep her, she didn't want me any more. I'd lost my chance.'

'But you loved her?'

'Oh, yes I did. I loved her very much, my boy, but you can't keep loving someone who doesn't love you back. She'd stopped loving me, you see.'

'But what about Jess?'

'Well, I can tell you now that I looked into that pram, and within a split second my heart filled with more love than you can ever imagine and then without warning my heart broke into a million pieces, all at once.' He stood up again and began to pace. 'I knew she was mine, but, from how Margaret reacted, I knew she'd never be a part of my life and that she'd never be allowed to look up to me and call me her daddy.'

Jack pondered the information. 'But when I saw you at the hospital you told me that Jess was named after your grandmother.'

Bastion looked sad. 'And she was. It was the one thing Margaret did for me.' He took a deep breath and began to cough violently, making Jack turn in concern.

'Hey, come on, sit back down. Are … are you okay? Shall I get you inside?' Jack stood up and held a hand out to where Bastion stood. 'Water, I'll bring water.' He turned to walk away, but Bastion grabbed his arm and shook his head.

'I'm fine,' Bastion said and caught his breath. 'It comes and goes.' His chest hurt like hell, but he knew that talking to Jack was important. 'Please, I need to finish the story, you need to know what really happened,' he continued.

Jack sat back down. 'Okay, go on.'

Bastion swallowed hard and stared wistfully into the distance. 'As I said, Jess was the most beautiful baby I'd ever seen, and my heart melted and I fell in love with her immediately.'

Jack looked puzzled. 'So why the hell did you disappear

for twenty years? She needed you so much, do you know that?'

'I didn't disappear, Jack. I was around, at least for the first few years, it's just that Jess didn't know.' Once again he began to cough, and took a final sip of the Bovril. 'You see Margaret didn't want me, she wanted Morris.' He stopped speaking and turned to Jack. 'She thought that Morris would come back, because of Maddie. She knew how much he loved her and was sure that he'd accept Jess as his own. So for her sake, for both Maddie and Jess's sake, I walked away with my dignity intact, and the only way I ever got to see them was from a distance.' Bastion once again cocked his head to one side. A shrill squeal was followed by a deep voice, another squeal, a giggle and then a bark or two as Buddy joined in the game. 'Do you hear that, Jack? Do you? That's the sound of children's happiness. Isn't it beautiful?'

Jack paused for a moment and Bastion saw a smile cross his face as the sound of little girl giggles filled the air. 'Bandit, he's been sent to play with them ... well, he was in charge of watching them, sounds like he's running around revving them both up.' They both sat for a moment and listened. 'So how do you manage to see someone, you know, from a distance?' Jack finally asked as he took the mug from Bastion's hand and placed it on the floor next to his.

Bastion laughed. 'Well, my boy, I pretty much turned into a stalker. I'd see them going out – Margaret, Madeleine and Jess – and I'd follow. I'd watch Margaret pushing the pram and deep inside, my heart was breaking and I wished I could push it too.' He paused and thought for a moment. 'As they got older, Margaret would take them both to the park and I'd sit on a distant bench and watch them play on the swings, the roundabout and the slide. I once saw Jess fall off and it took every ounce of strength I had not to run across the park, pick her up and cuddle her till she stopped crying. But I couldn't you see. Jess wouldn't have known who I was. I could have scared her and Margaret would have realised that I was there and what I was doing.' Once again he stood up and stretched before continuing. 'And on Jess's first day at nursery, I stood on the street corner, behind the conifers and watched her trot up the road with her mother and with her sister by her side, both of them all dressed up in their matching uniforms. They looked so very pretty in their red and white gingham dresses, I even took a photograph. Each night before I slept I said a prayer and hoped that Margaret would contact me. But then ... they moved. Margaret moved out of London. The next time I heard from her she was living in North Yorkshire. She wrote and told me she was happy, that Jess was doing okay and that moving away from London had been the best thing she could have done, for all of them.' He swallowed hard. 'It was hard for me to hear that the best thing for my daughter was being over two hundred miles away from me, but what could I do? It was much too far for me to travel, and besides I didn't have an address, just a location. All I knew was that she was in North Yorkshire.' He coughed, and sighed. 'Morris remarried soon after. Which meant that it had all been pointless. Margaret could have stayed in London and we ... we could have been a family. We could have had a good life and, if I'm honest, Jack, my heart tore itself in two.' He walked onto the grass and stared at the sheep. They were all standing by the wall looking up at the ha-ha and seemed to stare back at him with a look of hope that their food would come soon.

Jack simply studied the ground. 'It must have been hard. I can't imagine how I'd feel if Jess left, if she took the baby with her. It'd kill me if I never saw either of them again.'

Bastion nodded in agreement. 'It was hard, Jack. But I didn't fight to keep them. I should have and I only have myself to blame. And that's why, for all of your sakes, if you want this baby and if you want Jess to be a part of your life, you have to come to terms with what's happening … and real fast, my boy.' Again he coughed, paused and caught his breath. 'I really do wish I'd fought for them more. My whole life would have been different. I missed all those firsts with Jess, all the love, the cuddles, the bedtime stories, everything I should have been there for …' He paused and a sob left his throat.

'So why now? Why after all this time would you come and find her?' Jack looked up and stared out at the trees and Bastion followed his gaze, watching a squirrel who ran between the bushes, in and out, weaving a path through the longer grass, digging in the lawn for his food.

'You see that squirrel, Jack?' he asked and pointed. 'He's looking … no, he's searching for what he's lost. He knows he had food, knows he buried it somewhere, but he can't remember what he did with it. Yet he knows that if he tries hard enough, if he keeps sniffing around, searches and keeps going, eventually he'll find what he should have never let go of in the first place, and that's just like me.' He took a step towards the trees. 'When I lost Margaret and Jess, I made a decision that I'd never love again. It had hurt me far too much. So I spent my time working, and drinking and then I met Annie and for a while my life was good. But one hit of heroin too many turned her into an addict and only then did I find out who she really was.' He shook his head from side to side. 'I discovered she was a high-class hooker, an escort. She got paid for dressing up, for going out with rich clients and giving them the extras.' He looked back at Jack. 'That's right, my boy, my Lily came from a high-class hooker who turned into a dirty prostitute when the rich guys didn't want her any more.' He walked back to the seat and patted Jack on the shoulder. 'My beautiful Lily, she has a hooker for a mother, a mother who didn't want her, who abandoned her when she was just a few months old. A mother who chose drugs over her own child. Does that shock you, Jack?'

Jack spun and stared at Bastion with disbelief in his eyes. 'But, that's awful. Prostitute or not, why would she abandon her own baby, her own daughter?'

Bastion watched Jack's mannerisms and could see the moment the realisation of what he'd just said struck home.

Bastion stood for a moment, his breathing was laboured, and he patted Jack on the shoulder. 'Exactly, my boy. Why would she? And now I need to go and lie down. I think my work here is done and you, you know what you need to do.'

Chapter Nineteen

Jess pulled on her anorak, hat and gloves. She was determined not to be indoors for the whole day. She turned towards where Madeleine still sat in reception, still surrounded by her multiple lists.

'Come on, lazy bones. Bandit needs rescuing from the girls. He's been looking after them all morning, and I'm sure I just heard him screaming for help ... listen!' Jess threw Madeleine's coat towards her and pulled open the solid wooden door that stood between the grand hall's reception and the tree-lined driveway. The harsh wind rushed inside and Jess felt a shudder go down her spine as she stepped outside into the cold winter day.

She stamped up and down impatiently. 'Come on, Maddie, or poor Bandit will be tied to a tree with skipping ropes and both Poppy and Lily will be playing cowboys and Indians, running round him with duck feathers in their hair,' Jess called as she zipped up her coat. 'Unless, of course, it's Bandit that has the girls tied to a tree and then you could be in all sorts of trouble,' she joked. 'It could be him doing a tribal dance around them.'

Jess walked in front of the tall, mullion window and allowed her eyes to travel through it and into the grand hall where the newly decorated Christmas tree stood in the corner. Its lights were reflecting in the many pictures that hung on the walls and Jess concentrated on the amber hue that the room had taken on from the fire, which she couldn't see from where she stood, but she could imagine how the flames flicked and licked the back of the chimney breast, whilst busily crackling away as more and more logs were tossed on as the days grew colder.

She thought of the Christmas before, how she and Jack had curled up on one of those very settees that stood in front of the fire and watched the flames dance in the darkness. They'd sipped wine, made wishes and reflected on times gone by and, on just one occasion, when they'd thought that everyone had gone to sleep for the night, they'd gently and quietly made love, right there, in front of the fire, laughing and giggling. 'Shhh …' Jack had whispered to her. 'Is it just me, or do you feel like a teenager again?' he'd questioned as they'd hurriedly dressed, and picked up their wine glasses, just in time before Bandit had entered the room with his arms full of logs. Life had been so good. So settled. They'd found a daily routine, which had been so much less complicated than it all seemed right now.

She opened her eyes, walked back to the main doors and stepped through them, before staring through the dining room window beyond. She could see Jack sitting on the bench, chatting away to Bastion. They seemed deep in conversation and Jess found herself wondering what on earth they could be talking about. Or even why they were talking at all, especially after Jack had shown his initial distrust towards the man who claimed to be her father. She stepped forward as she saw Bastion stand, begin to cough and then sit down again. She had an overwhelming urge to run to him, but she couldn't, knowing that whatever her father and Jack were talking about, the words were probably better off said sooner rather than later. Besides, she needed to have a conversation with Bastion herself. Madeleine had been right; the test did need to be done. But now, time was against them. It was the nineteenth of December already and it would soon be Christmas. Even with first class post it would be doubtful they'd get the results before the big day, and now Jess wished she'd sent for it sooner.

Jess forcibly looked away from where Jack sat and

turned her attention back to Madeleine who was now standing beside her in the doorway. 'Hey, Maddie, come on,' Jess said, grabbing Madeleine's hand. She pulled her sister outside and then began to laugh as she saw the face that Madeleine was pulling. 'Hey, you used to love being outside, always running here and there. We couldn't keep you in at one time. What's wrong with you?'

Madeleine shrugged. 'I'm just tired, Jess. My get up and go has disappeared. I have zero energy and it's as though everything's gone wrong.' She spun around on the spot with her arms held out. 'I love this place so much but it keeps on taking from me and after all that happened last year, I'd just started to feel okay, we'd just started being a family again.' She wiped a tear from the corner of her eye. 'I mean, not just a family, but a real life, normal family. We hadn't had that for such a long time. Goddamn it, Jess, we hadn't ever had a normal family life. And then Emily died and Bandit's been a mess, after all she was his grandmother and he'd only just found her, and … well … it's all really shaken me, that's all.' She stopped and sat down on the stone step and sighed. 'Oh, and Bandit's dad, he isn't in the best of health either and, on top of that, it's Christmas and we have a hotel to run. We have to turn on the smiles, for the staff, and for the guests. Everyone expects us to be really happy, to glow with enthusiasm and Christmas cheer. And right now I haven't got an enthusiastic bone in my entire body, not one.'

Jess pulled her sister to her feet and into a hug. 'I know, Maddie. It's been hard on us all. I miss her too,' she whispered. 'It doesn't seem fair, does it? It's only a year since she came back home where she belonged.' Both sisters stared at one another with tear-filled eyes and shook their heads in unison, and then both jumped and screamed as a shower of leaves seemed to fall on them from above, making them spin around on the spot to see Poppy and Lily running off into the distance with Buddy, quickly followed by Bandit, who'd obviously instigated the whole game.

'Right, you three are really going to get it now,' Jess shouted as she threw her scarf around her neck and set off at pace, ducking and diving through the trees in fast pursuit. The leaves were wet making it slippery underfoot. 'Maddie, quick, you go that way,' she shouted, pointing to the left, as she ran to the right. 'We'll cut them off.'

Madeleine joined in and took up the chase, over the ha-ha wall, past the sheep, across the field and into the woods. She quickly grabbed hold of Bandit, who'd purposely slipped on the leaves, landed in a heap, rolled onto his back on the woodland floor, and allowed Maddie to catch him.

'Okay, okay, I submit,' he shouted as Madeleine's slim thighs straddled him. But the tables were quickly turned and the last thing Jess saw as she ran on was Bandit spinning Madeleine around, straddling her body instead, pinning her down to the floor, with his fingers waving in the air and coming down on her with full tickling intent.

'You're in trouble now,' he shouted as Madeleine's screams rang out. But Jess just laughed as she ran past. It wasn't her job to save her sister, not on this occasion. Anyway, she knew that if Maddie screamed any louder, she'd be attracting the attention of every guest in the Hall, who'd probably end up running to her aid instead.

Jess ran on. She'd been distracted by Madeleine and Bandit, but could see Buddy in the distance, and headed towards where he now played. She presumed he'd followed the girls, and ran in his direction. Jess laughed at him as he rolled on the grass, paws in the air.

'What are you doing there, boy? Where are the girls?' she shouted as she got close, but a thick, rancid smell drifted through the air and Jess turned her nose up. The smell had hit her way before she saw the remains of what may have been a squashed hedgehog and her whole body began to retch. 'Buddy, oh no, get off. Urgh. Stop that. Urgh.' She heaved repeatedly. The smell was unbelievable and she quickly grabbed at Buddy's collar. 'Stop that I said.' She dragged him away from the animal's corpse and back towards the Hall. But the fact that he'd being rolling in the decomposed animal meant that the smell was clinging. It was following him home.

'You, my friend, need a bath, and I think we may need the hosepipe first.' She looked down at Buddy's pitiful eyes, the look of a wounded soul. 'Don't you look at me like that, I didn't make you do it,' Jess growled. 'You stink, and, boy oh boy, my stomach is really not liking that smell. Couldn't you roll in something really nice smelling, like lemons or snowdrops?'

She dragged the dog over to where Maddie and Bandit now lay together on the grass, kissing and giggling. 'Here, take your damned dog. He stinks,' Jess announced as she dragged the spaniel towards Bandit, who immediately jumped up and took him from her.

'What the ... wow, Buddy, you really do stink. What you been up to, boy?'

'Dead hedgehog, in fact it's a decomposed hedgehog. It's somewhere over there. Looks like it was hit the last time the sit on lawnmower went through.'

'Bandit ... come, come quickly!' Nomsa shouted, and all three of them turned towards the Hall in concern. Nomsa would never shout, not from the front door, not while they had guests and certainly not unless it was urgent.

Maddie and Bandit jumped up, and all three set off towards the house. They burst in through the front door and took in the scene before them. Bastion was breathing erratically and Nomsa was holding him up.

'He was just sitting outside, he came over all funny, and

by the time he'd gotten himself inside, he almost collapsed, right there in the bar,' Nomsa yelled, her eyes full of concern. 'He needs to be in his bed. I don't know what I was thinking letting him go out there.' She reprimanded herself and Jess could see the worry that was etched across her face.

'He's fine, Nomsa. He's fine. It's just the cold air,' Bandit said as he walked across to Bastion. 'Come on, sir, I've got you.' Bandit quickly and effortlessly put Bastion's arm over his shoulder and within seconds he was helping him up the stairs. 'You've probably just overdone it, my man, being outside and all that, but just to be sure I'm going to get our Nomsa to give the doctor a call. Let's get you checked out, just in case.' He stopped on the last step. 'Did you get that, Nomsa?' He turned to see Nomsa, pale-faced, holding onto the wall.

'I thought he was going to collapse again, I thought …' A sob left Nomsa's throat, making Jess run to her side.

'I think you need a cup of tea.' She walked Nomsa to the kitchen and put the kettle on. Her normal joviality had deserted her, and she looked more than just a little concerned. 'He'll be okay, Nomsa, honest. Now, it looks like Madeleine's taken on the task of calling the doctor and you … you need to sit down.' She suddenly looked around. 'Where's Jack? I thought he was here, talking to Bastion.'

Nomsa took a seat and nodded. 'Oh, he was. But then he ran into the kitchen, said he had somewhere important to go and left your daddy sitting out there enjoying the sunshine.' She looked towards the patio, as her hands continually screwed the edge of her apron round in circles. 'He looks real sick, your daddy does, doesn't he?'

'Do … do you think he's really sick?' Jess paused. 'I mean … what … what if I lose him?' Jess grabbed hold of Nomsa's hands. 'Nomsa, what if we both lose him?' She stifled a sob and then jumped up from the chair. 'Oh my goodness, the girls. Nomsa, please look after him for me. I have to go. The girls, they ran off into the woods, they're still playing hide and bloody seek and probably still waiting somewhere for us to find them.'

'I'll come with you,' Nomsa said as Jess headed out of the kitchen.

But Jess shook her head. 'No, no, it's fine, I'm sure Maddie will have phoned the doctor, he'll be on his way. Why don't you take Bastion some nice hot tea? And while you're at it, get a mug for yourself, you look as though you need it.' Jess held her gaze for just a moment too long, and an understanding passed between them. She wasn't just asking Nomsa to look for the doctor, she was asking her to care for her father, care for him like no one else ever had, and by the look on Nomsa's face, it was an undertaking she was more than happy to take on.

Bandit came back down the stairs. 'Right, he's settled and in his bed, but grumbling and saying that he'd rather get up.' He turned to Nomsa who'd walked through and into reception with two steaming hot mugs of tea.

'Well, if it kills me, I'll keep him in that bed all day,' she said as she headed up the stairs. Bandit and Madeleine caught each other's eye and began to laugh. 'What, what did I say?' she asked, blissfully unaware of the innuendo within her statement.

'We need to go find the girls. They can't have gone too far. Did anyone see which way they were heading?' Bandit asked as he pulled open the door and looked between Jess and Madeleine, who both shrugged their shoulders.

'They could be anywhere by now.' Madeleine zipped up her coat. 'We'll need smelly Buddy's help to find them.'

They all moved through the trees, casually at first. They searched behind bushes and fanned out, each walking in a different direction, shouting both Poppy's and Lily's names, without any of them receiving an answer.

'Where the hell can they have gone?' Bandit strode on. 'There should be noise, they're children, there's always noise,' he shouted. 'You can't take a step without the leaves either squelching or crunching underfoot. Besides, those two are never quiet, are they?' He stopped and once again looked behind a tree. 'Seriously, in the past week, how often have either of them been quiet for more than three seconds at a time?'

Bandit held a finger to his lips and they all stood still. All noise had ceased, not even the birds were singing and Jess held her breath while she listened.

'I don't understand why they haven't come back home,' Maddie whispered, worry crossing her face. 'We only went inside for a few minutes. They can't have got far, can they?'

All three stared at one another. Bandit concentrated on Madeleine's face.

'Oh my God, Bandit, I don't like this, something isn't right. It's ... it's ...' Madeleine suddenly began to run from one tree to the other. Gone were the measured steps, now she ran frantically, anxiously searching for her daughter. 'She knows ... Poppy knows not to leave sight of the house. She knows to come when I call for her.'

Bandit's look was enough to tell them that he too was worried. For a moment he just stood and stared at the ground. 'Okay, okay, what to do. We need a plan.' He took deep measured breaths. 'Right, they ran off in that direction.' Bandit pointed through the trees. 'Chances are that they're hiding and any minute now they'll burst out of the woods in fits of giggles.' He began marching up and down. 'Jess, you go check the summer house, Maddie you phone Nomsa, see if they went back and I'll ... I'll keep heading this way.' He pointed deep into the woods. 'I'll stick close to the road. If they're hiding, they should see me.' He looked determined, and glanced down at where Buddy sat faithfully watching his every move.

'Buddy, go find them, boy, go on, go find Poppy,' he shouted and Buddy set off, sniffing at the ground. 'Poppy, Lily, come on now, time to stop the game, dinner's ready!' His voice carried through the bare winter trees, and almost echoed back at him as he walked further and further through the woods.

Jess ran off to the summer house, but soon returned. 'No sign of them over there.' She walked up to Madeleine who just stood and stared at the floor.

'Jess, I don't like it. How could they just disappear? Surely they wouldn't have gone this far, not on their own, would they?'

Jess stared at her sister. 'I only took my eyes off of them for a few minutes. I saw them run off, they were playing, giggling. I should have stayed with them, but I went to see what Buddy was up to instead.' Her voice shook, and the anxiety rose within her. She began spinning around on the spot in the hope that if she spun fast enough, she'd spot them both hiding. 'They're missing and it's all my fault. I lost them. I didn't watch them close enough. Hell, Maddie, what kind of a mother am I going to be?' Jess began to sob, huge tears fell down her face and immediately Madeleine pulled her into a hug.

'Jess, you'll make a wonderful mother one day, and Poppy won't be far. You'll see.' She picked up her phone. 'I'll call Nomsa again. I bet they'll be sitting in the kitchen eating something good that she'll have cooked up for them. Here, blow your nose.' She passed Jess a tissue in typical mother mode and waved her mobile in the air. 'A signal would be good right now, ah …'

Jess kept searching while Madeleine phoned Nomsa. She

lowered her gaze, realising how close she'd been to blurting out the news, even though she'd promised Jack that she wouldn't. Not till after the wedding. She took deep breaths and listened to Madeleine's call. It wasn't going well. 'Okay,' Maddie said. 'Well, if they do come back, call me immediately. We'll keep looking.'

Bandit had run on ahead. He'd followed Buddy and Jess could see him far in the distance. Then suddenly he began waving his arms in the air. 'Quick, this way,' he shouted. 'Buddy seems to think they're in here.'

Jess spotted him pushing open an old wooden five bar gate, before heading through the garden of an old derelict farmhouse, with Buddy blazing the way.

Both Jess and Madeleine ran after him. The air was cold and their lungs hurt and without a thought for her condition, Jess forged on ahead at top speed. 'Why here? Why would Buddy think they were here?' Shivers went down her spine as the house came into sight. It was obviously devoid of love or inhabitants, and weeds grew through the abandoned clutter that adorned the garden, making it look as though it had been there forever.

'Poppy, Lily, you in here?' Jess shouted. 'Bandit ... Bandit ... where are you, where the hell did you go?' She stopped and looked back. 'They wouldn't have gotten this far, would they?' She held a hand out to Madeleine who inched her way down the path. 'This house, it's quite a long way from the Hall.' She pushed at the back door, which creaked, but surprisingly opened with ease. A plume of dust filled the air and Jess once again shouted for Bandit.

Her stomach turned over and over. The girls were missing and all the terror of the year before flooded back through her as a feeling of impending tragedy, loss, and fear rotated around her mind. She moved from room to room, inching her way forward, careful of her step, all the while wondering what on earth could have happened to make two little girls run into an old abandoned house. Jess ducked to avoid the old units which hung off the kitchen walls, and her hand touched an old, white ceramic sink that obviously hadn't been cleaned for many a year.

'Bandit, Bandit! Where are you?' she shouted, and once again turned to Madeleine. 'Where the hell did he go? How come everyone's disappearing today?' It was like a horror movie, where one person disappeared and then slowly throughout the film, one after the other, the other actors would be gone, until finally just one person remained. Again, she reached out and grabbed Madeleine's hand. There was no way she was allowing either one of them to disappear, not again, not today, not ever.

A sudden noise came from deep within the house, a soft rumbling that sounded like thunder. Then there was a bang, followed by the sound of sobbing. 'They're here, I've got them.'

A loud gasp came from Maddie. 'Where are you?' she shouted as she followed Bandit's voice and a barking Buddy.

'We're here, good boy, Buddy. Good lad.' The spaniel seemed to have appeared from a door beneath the stairs. He was happily wagging his tail, bouncing around in the hope of treats, but still smelling of the decomposed hedgehog.

'They were in the cellar. No idea how, but the door had slammed shut and locked them down there,' Bandit said as he emerged from the staircase covered in dust and carrying a pitiful, sobbing Poppy in his arms. 'They'd gone down there to hide. I found them right down at the bottom, behind a load of old boxes.'

'But they're both okay ... please tell me they're okay?' Madeleine's voice was barely a whisper, her eyes searched Poppy's frame, but she was fixed to the spot, her body shaking, and Jess knew that she'd been fearing the worst.

She was reliving the horrors of the past as her eyes became fixed on Bandit.

'They're fine, honestly. Aren't you, honey?' Poppy's face was hidden in the nape of his neck and Jess could see Lily creeping up the stairs behind them. Her face was ashen, her eyes puffy and full of tears and a deep sob came from within her.

Bandit transferred Poppy into her mother's arms. 'I'll phone Nomsa. Tell her the girls are safe and ask her to organise baths. It's filthy down there and God only knows what they might have touched.'

'Poppy, tell Mummy what happened?' Maddie hugged the little girl to her and waited for a reply. But she didn't get one. 'Poppy, talk to me. Haven't I told you about going out of sight of the Hall?' She held the child away from her so she could look into her face. 'You know it's naughty, don't you?' Madeleine's voice was calm but shaking as she automatically pulled Poppy into an embrace again and began rocking the sobbing child. 'How did they end up locked down there?' She directed the question at Bandit, who shook his head.

'I don't know. Something to do with the door. We'll get to the bottom of it later.' Bandit fussed the smelly dog. 'It was our Buddy that found them. Didn't you, boy, you good boy?' he said as Buddy immediately rolled on his back, his whole body bending in two as he wagged his tail.

'Poppy.' Once again Madeleine held the child from her and looked directly into her eyes. 'I need you to tell Mummy what happened.'

Poppy shrugged and Madeleine continued, 'Why did you hide down there? I've told you before how dangerous it is to go into old houses, haven't I? We're always telling you not to leave the safety of the Hall, honey, aren't we? So why did you?'

Poppy's eyes went to stare at where Lily stood.

Madeleine turned to Lily. 'Lily, do you have any answers? Do you want to explain? This is not your house and I need to know why you came in here. What on earth were you both thinking?'

Jess watched as Lily physically shrank into herself and she felt her heart go out to her. 'Come on, sweetie.' Jess held her arms out to the child, who immediately fell into them and Jess could feel her whole body shaking with fear.

'We were just playing, wasn't we, Poppy?'

Poppy nodded. 'We ran away when Bandit was tickling Mummy. We ran and we ran. But then Lily screamed, she grabbed my hand and we ran to the house. She said we needed to hide, didn't you?' Poppy sobbed and clung onto her mother, as both Madeleine and Jess caught each other's eye.

'Lily, why did you do that, honey?' Madeleine continued to look at Lily. 'Why did you scream? Did something frighten you?'

Jess felt torn; she loved Poppy with all her heart and would always protect her, but now she felt responsible for Lily too. After all, it was almost certain that they were sisters and she was probably far too young to know how dangerous an old house might be, or did she? Jess knew that Lily had grown up in squalor; they'd had a shared toilet down a corridor or a bucket in the corner, old houses were probably normal in London, which made Jess wonder how many other awful things she'd seen or had to endure while growing up there.

Poppy sobbed again and turned in Madeleine's arms. Her eyes were now fixed on Lily, who shook her head, and for just a moment Jess wondered if the girls were using telepathy to communicate, just as she and Madeleine had done as children. Especially when their mother had been looking for answers that neither had wanted to give.

'We were looking for a hiding place.' Lily clung onto Jess. 'I'm so sorry … it was just a game. Wasn't it, Poppy? Tell them, Poppy. Tell them it was just a game.'

Poppy nodded, but Jess was not convinced. The shaking of heads, the staring, and the way that Lily was physically shaking didn't ring true, but Jess wasn't sure what she should ask or do to get to the truth.

'Honestly, Jess. The door, it just slammed shut. It locked on us and I couldn't open it; it was too heavy. I tried and tried, but it wouldn't open.' Lily's eyes searched Jess's. 'Go and try it if you don't believe me.'

Jess sighed. She knew she had to give the girls the benefit of the doubt, but still felt sure that there was more to the story than either was willing to tell.

'Lily said you'd come. She said you'd come and find us, but we had to hide. It was a game of hide and seek and that means being quiet, Mummy, right?' Huge sobs continued to leave Poppy's throat. 'So I just did as I was told.' The irony of the statement didn't go past anyone in the room. Even if bribed, Poppy was the worst person at keeping quiet ever and Jess saw the disbelieving look that went between Madeleine and Bandit.

'Am I still allowed to stay with you till after Christmas? Or … or are you going to send me away now?' Lily questioned. 'Because … because our Daddy really wants to stay and I'm so so sorry that I've been so very naughty.' She stood back and wiped her eyes, distancing herself from Jess before going to stand and face the wall. It seemed like an act of learned behaviour and Jess felt heartbroken as she wondered how many times Lily had been punished this way in the past.

'My school teacher always makes me stand against the wall when I've been naughty,' Lily whispered.

'Oh, Lily, please don't do that. Come here, of course we

want you to stay. Don't we, Maddie?' Jess looked at her sister for help.

Madeleine nodded. 'We wouldn't send you away, Lily. Come here. It's okay, honey. It's okay,' Maddie said as she passed Poppy to Bandit and grabbed hold of Lily. Jess watched as they held onto each other tightly. 'I'm sorry if I sounded angry with you, I was scared too. It was an accident. I know that and ... and ... Poppy knows that too, and you're both okay ... so lessons learned. Okay?'

Jess could hear the fear in Maddie's voice. She could have lost her daughter, she could have relived the hell she'd gone through the year before and she'd obviously feared that the girls could have both been hurt, or worse.

Jess left the room and went back into the kitchen. She shook her head and with it her whole body trembled. Was this what it was like to be a mother? Was it a constant battle to keep your child alive? Would every day be like this? And was it compulsory to show care and empathy for another child, even though your own daughter's life could have been in danger? Her head spun with questions that she couldn't answer. A child was a huge responsibility, a responsibility that lasted a lifetime, not just for the first years. It was for always.

Jess let her mind go to how her own mother used to react and she remembered how she'd shouted at both her and Maddie repeatedly. They'd always been in trouble for messing around, and for playing games that she didn't agree with. She'd always felt like her mother was picking on them, telling them both to walk slowly, to sit still and to be careful in everything they did. But now she understood. Now she knew what constant fear her mother had had to live with. Especially as her mother had been on her own for so many years, with not one, but two of them to keep safe and alive.

Jess looked around the kitchen. It had an old wood-burning stove, along with a bread oven that had been built into the wall many years before. She stopped and ran her fingertips through the inches of dust that covered the units. The room was stuffy, dusty and the whole place was dirty and cold, but for some reason it felt homely. It felt like she belonged and she took a moment just to close her eyes and wonder what it would be like to live in a house like this.

She left the house by the back door, and went to stand in the farmyard where rubbish, bits of wood and old pieces of machinery lay everywhere. It had all been abandoned. And to Jess it looked as though the farmer had come back from the fields one day, put his tools down and left, never to work the farm again.

Had the farmer lived here alone? Did he have a family or could he have died? Jess spun around; she could hear the noise of a vehicle, but couldn't see it until she jumped up onto the old, rusty tractor and caught a glimpse of an old van, which had taken off at speed. It was heading away from the farmhouse and past the Hall, making Buddy dance on the spot. He barked and for a moment he looked as though he were about to give chase. 'Here, boy,' she shouted as she got down. 'Stay here, boy.' She wondered where the van had been. The only house for miles around was the Hall and this derelict farmhouse. 'Rustlers?' She pondered the thought and it occurred to her that she should mention the van to Bandit, just in case.

Jess held onto the wooden gate, staring at the Hall. It rose up in the distance like a fortress. Everyone she loved lived here on this estate. Everyone she loved seemed to have someone, even Nomsa who now had Jess's father. Everyone else seemed to know what tomorrow would bring, or what they should be doing today. Yet she had no idea what to do in the next ten minutes. Did she take Lily to their father? Did she insist on the truth or, like Maddie, did she appear to let it go in the hope that the truth would come out on another day? Was that what a mother would do? She shrugged.

Some days her life felt like a fairground ride with everything whizzing around. It was as though she was caught up in a bubble, standing on the inside looking out. She closed her eyes and took in a deep breath. She tried to concentrate, tried to make sense of all that was happening and suddenly realised that the whole world was spinning around her, spiralling on its very own axis, and she was floating above it, watching it turn.

Chapter Twenty

'So, where's the fucking brat?' Griff growled as Annie snatched open the door and scrambled into the van. She looked over her shoulder and immediately shrunk into the cluttered seat beside him as he grabbed at her shirt.

'Get off of me, Griff, and drive, for God's sake, just drive, before they see us,' she shouted as she kicked out at him with her foot, then rummaged for the seat belt.

Griff looked into the back of the van as though the child would miraculously appear. 'But she was there, right there, running through the trees. I saw her. So what the hell went wrong? Don't tell me you let the little brat get away?' The van started, the engine revved and Griff drove off at speed.

'Sod off, Griff. What the hell do you think I've done with her, stuffed her up my bloody skirt? Of course she got away, stupid.' Annie pressed herself into the side of the vehicle, wishing there was more space between her and Griff. She didn't like him being so close, and she inched her way over the seat until she found herself sitting on the edge, just far enough away that he couldn't reach her without swerving the van. 'And yes, you're right, the kids were both there, they were playing in the woods.' Annie pushed the sleeve of her denim jacket up, scratched at the blisters on her arm and studied the track marks.

'So what happened?' he yelled.

'I hid behind a bloody tree. I was hoping that Lily would run off on her own, but she was with the little 'un, a kid younger than herself. Then Lily saw me. She's never liked me. It's all Bastion's fault, he turned her against me, must have told her all sorts of crap. As soon as she saw me, she ran off.' Annie grabbed hold of the door handle as Griff raced round a bend. 'Took the little one with her and they ran through the woods and into the old house we were parked behind.' Again she looked over her shoulder as they left the grounds of the Hall, trying to make sure they were not being followed.

'So why didn't you just go into the house and bloody well grab her?' he barked out as the van swerved out of the junction and onto the main road at speed.

'I tried, but I couldn't run in these, could I?' She lifted her foot to show the scuffed, dirty, bright red stiletto.

Griff raised his lip at her and growled like a dog.

Once again Annie tried to move as far away from Griff as she could, but her arm was already pressed against the door. She used her other hand to keep scratching; her whole body itched and she felt nervous and fidgety, and the shakes had begun. She watched his hands carefully, wondering if he'd strike out without warning, like he normally did.

'You should have grabbed her.'

'Griff, don't be stupid, I couldn't. She had the kid with her and I couldn't grab her while she had the little 'un with her, could I?'

Griff suddenly lashed out with a fist to the side of her head. Annie screamed and clutched her jaw as she shrank even further away from him towards the door. 'That's the second time you've called me stupid. Don't try a third.' He glared at her and Annie nodded. 'You should have grabbed that little shit too.' He wiped his nose on the back of his sleeve, wound the window down, cleared his throat and spat at the road. 'We could have held onto her for a while. Groomed her for a bit, you know, till she bloomed, till she was ready to use.'

'I'm not kidnapping someone else's kid, Griff. We agreed on Lily, no one else and I wanted to get Lily on her own. I followed them into the house, but they'd run on ahead and the little buggers must have hidden somewhere real good, 'cause I couldn't find them, and then there were voices coming from the woods, people shouting their names. I had no choice but to leg it before they saw me.'

Annie looked at Griff. He wasn't happy, in fact he was downright furious and she didn't like the way he'd suddenly begun pushing the air out of his flared nostrils. She needed to stay out of range of his fists.

'Why the hell did it matter if people were shouting? You're her mother, for fuck's sake. You should have told them that you were visiting, that you'd come to take her with you. Most kids go to their mother's for Christmas, don't they?' He slammed his hands against the steering wheel, making Annie scream as the van swerved to the right, narrowly missing an oncoming bus. 'We'll go back to the hotel and this time you'll go in and tell them who the hell you are. Tell them that you're taking her. You have rights.'

Annie began to shake. 'That's where you're wrong, Griff. I've got no fucking rights. I left her, didn't I? Took all that they had, every bit of furniture and now he won't let me see her and what's more, she hates me.'

Griff slammed his foot on the brake, stopping the car, and turned towards her. 'If you support her, like you reckon you do, why the hell would he stop you from seeing her? Why would he turn her against you, eh? Unless you're lying your fucking arse off.' He leaned across, his face almost touching hers. His breath smelt of alcohol and she could see the bloodshot whites of his eyes, and she began to fear what he'd do.

She had to think quickly. 'You have to understand, Griff, I haven't been able to pay him this week, have I?' She looked out of the window. 'Been saving up to pay you off, haven't I?'

Once again Griff moved closer. 'So how the hell did you know where the kid was?'

''Cause I went to the flat, where Bastion used to live with

the kid. He … Bastion … he told the neighbour he was coming here, coming to find some damned daughter I've never heard of.' She lifted her hand and pushed at Griff's shoulder. 'Do you mind getting out of my face?'

Griff moved even closer to her, until he was almost sitting on her knee. 'We came for the girl, Annie, and we're not going home until we've got the girl. I've done a deal up here and they are dangerous people to piss off. And until we get the girl, there'll be no drugs, you got that?'

'But, Griff. Look, come on … I'm sorry. Can't we forget about her? Take me back to London, eh? It's still early in the day, we have time to get back, and once Christmas is over, you know, business will pick up again, the punters they'll start coming back and then I'll pay you, you'll get the rest of your money, you know that.'

She thought of the money she'd stolen from Bella and smiled. There had been just over five grand and her eyes had lit up as she'd pulled the floorboard back to expose the find, but it had been the stash of heroin that had really excited her and she'd taken the lot. She'd gone down to the cellar and hidden the majority of the drugs before going back to her room, where she'd counted the money, before falling into a heroin-fuelled stupor for the rest of the night.

She'd woken the next morning to the sound of screams, to Bella pleading and crying and Griff shouting. But her mind was still in a haze and she hadn't cared what Griff was doing, not to Bella, not to anyone. She had the money and she lay on the bed, staring at it, trying to decide what to do. Should she take the money and the drugs and run? Should she leave town, the country and go somewhere Griff would never find her? She'd rubbed her nose on the back of her hand and had just begun folding the cash when Griff had burst in. He'd immediately pounced on the money, even though Annie had tried to hide it by lying on top of it in the hope he hadn't seen it. But he'd been fast; he'd grabbed the cash and she'd watched him nervously as he'd counted it.

'It's not enough, is it?' he'd screamed at her. His fist had lashed out and had caught her under the jaw, sending her flying across the bed. 'You ought to be glad you have more to offer than Bella did,' he'd shouted as he'd pointed to the door, pulled the flick knife from his pocket and wiped it clean of blood on the edge of Annie's dark blue bed sheet. 'She'll not be working for a while and neither will you if you don't hand that kid over.'

It had been then that Annie had realised that Griff had liked the idea of having Lily so much more than he'd wanted the money, and he didn't care who he hurt to get her.

And now, in the van, he seemed even more determined that he'd get his own way. But she couldn't go back to the hotel, not today. Bastion seemed to have made himself at home there. They'd hidden in the car park and watched the comings and goings and she'd spotted him, sitting on a bench talking to a handsome young man. Annie knew that Bastion would walk over burning coals before he'd allow her to just waltz in and take Lily with her. It had been pure chance that a while later she'd been taking a look around and seen Bastion stand up and almost collapse. Watching him Annie hoped that he would. At least if Bastion died, she'd be the only parent left and no one else would be in a position to challenge her. She'd held her breath for a while in the hope that an ambulance would arrive and that Bastion would leave.

But a woman had run out of the hotel and shouted to the others, which had given them the chance to grab Lily. Griff had driven them out of the car park and they had followed the road in the direction the girls were taking through the woods. Griff had parked behind an old farmhouse and Annie had jumped out of the van and gone to get her daughter. But Lily had run off and grabbing her as Griff had suggested had been more difficult than she'd initially thought. She had to find a better way. She needed a plan. But she couldn't think, her mind was spinning, and after the high of the night before, she was now hitting a massive low. She felt sick, her hands were shaking and she could feel herself bouncing up and down in the seat, like an agitated child. She wished she'd had time to retrieve some of the drugs and bring them with her.

'Stop fidgeting. We're getting some food and then you're going back to the Hall to get the kid.' He started the van and hit the accelerator and Annie felt herself grab hold of the seat.

'Griff, I'm going nowhere. I need a fix. Now ... take me home.' All she could think about were the drugs that she had hidden in the cellar.

'Do you know how far away from home we are, bitch? Do you?' He looked from her to the road, then back again. 'Two hundred and fifty miles, that's how far. Or should I put it another way? Four and a half frigging hours, if the motorway isn't standing still.' He swung the van around a corner.

'We didn't need to come, did we? You could have left it, could have waited for the rest of your money, but no, no, no, you insisted that you wanted the kid.' Annie wound her long, greasy auburn hair around her finger and tugged at it with frustration.

He crunched the gears, making the van lurch forwards. 'You're still at least five grand down, Annie, and I've promised her now.'

She kicked at the dashboard. 'I said I'd pay you the rest.'

'And just where did the damned money come from, eh?' Griff looked at her, his lip curled up on one side and Annie sensed his mood and once again inched as far away as she could. 'Seems a bit of a coincidence to me that Bella's money got nicked last night and suddenly you've got some.'

Annie turned and tried to look shocked. 'Well, it wasn't me, I didn't take it,' she lied.

He nodded. 'You must think I fell off a bus, Annie. You know exactly what happened to Bella's money,' he sneered. 'Well, it's a shame poor Bella had to pay the price for your damned thieving.'

'Look, Griff, please, stop having a go at me. I need to score, you got anything?' She sat forward and began rummaging around in the glovebox, then scoured the floor. She kicked at the rubbish, picked up the empty beer cans, shook them and then tossed them back down, before moving onto the fast food cartons, paper bags and remnants of tin foil. She thought of the stash back at the brothel, and wished she'd thought to bring just a few packs with her, but it'd been too much of a risk. If Griff had seen it he'd have known for sure that she'd stolen it all from Bella.

'Annie, you don't give a shit about Bella, do you?' he snarled. 'Even though you saw the fucking blade, you don't care, do you?'

'She knows the game, she can look after herself.' Annie knew that Griff could be cruel, he always took things to extremes, and for a split second her thoughts did go to Bella, the blade, the blood and the fact that the screaming had stopped abruptly. 'Did you kill her?'

'You're some nasty piece of work, Annie.' Once again he spat out of the window. 'No, I didn't kill her, but she won't be working for a while, will she? Not good for business when your face has been slashed, is it?'

'So you cut her?' She resumed rummaging through the litter.

'Annie, stop doing that, you're really pissing me off.' His hand shot out and caught her on the arm.

'Ouch … you bastard … I can't help it, can I? I need some gear.'

Annie could see the way his lips were pursed, that he was

angry with her and she knew that her chances of him buying her drugs were as remote as him taking her out for a fancy dinner. 'Griff, come on, baby, please. I said I was sorry ...'

Griff suddenly stopped the van, reached across her to open the door and with one swift movement the seat belt had been unclipped and Annie felt herself being pushed out the door.

'Do you know what? I'm sick of fucking hearing you. If you want a fix, go earn a frigging fix, Annie. Go get some business. I'll be back here for you at midnight, gives you a good twelve hours to earn some damn coin and it'll give me some time to decide what we do next.'

Annie winced as she stumbled, her ankle twisted, her stiletto left her foot and she landed heavily on the pavement. Everything suddenly hurt; her backside, her arm and her hip had all hit the cold concrete, all at once, which was where she now sat, in a heap on the ground.

'You can't leave me here,' she shouted. 'Oy, are you listening to me?'

The van door slammed shut, but the window came down.

Griff laughed. 'Why, Annie? Why the hell can't I leave you here? Truth is, bitch, I can do what the hell I like. You owe me.'

She sighed, and watched as the van drove away. She was on the edge of a town that she didn't know, with no safe house to go back to, no money, no condoms and no regulars. She knew the dangers of being on the street, especially working a patch that wasn't her own. But the need for the drugs took over and she stood up, dusted her skirt down and pushed the stiletto back on her foot.

'You don't think I can do this, do you? I'll show you. I'll score and don't think I'm sharing the profits, no way, this is not your patch,' she shouted at the back of the van and Griff who could no longer hear her.

Chapter Twenty-One

It was beginning to get dark as Jack sneaked back into the hotel. He crept through the corridors and towards the room he shared with Jess, all while carrying a Moses basket in one hand and its frame in the other. The basket was a wicker one. He was sure it was almost identical to the one Poppy had had as a baby and after hearing Jess speak of how happy and proud she'd felt as she'd watched Poppy sleep, he'd known she'd want one for their baby too. He hoped she'd love the fact that he'd spent the last couple of hours in Scarborough choosing it for her.

Jack wanted it to be a surprise and hoped that no one had seen him entering the hotel by the side door. The last thing he needed was to have been seen and for someone to tell Jess where he was and what he was carrying. He headed along the corridor that led to their room, which was at the back of the house. The corridor was narrow and not particularly easy to negotiate, not with his arms full, but he didn't care and couldn't wait to see the look on Jess's face when she walked in.

Jack stood outside the door, and for a moment he just pressed his hand to it, wondering if Jess might be inside. He looked at his watch. She'd been off duty the whole morning and a few weeks ago he'd have known exactly where to find her. She'd have been with Emily, in her room or sitting with her in the garden. But today Jess could be anywhere, and if she wasn't in their room, then he'd guess that she was sitting in the warmth of the kitchen, maybe chatting with Nomsa or perhaps helping Madeleine with all the Christmas preparations.

He turned the key in the lock. He'd always loved their

room. It didn't particularly have the best view, but it was a room he liked, a room he'd always felt loved in and a room where he and Jess had shared their most intimate moments.

He hoped that Jess would be inside. They really needed to talk; he wanted to tell her how he felt, how much he loved her. He had wanted to tell her all of this for the past couple of days, but the only chance he'd had to speak to her was when she'd been clearing Emily's room. It seemed that every time they got a moment to themselves, someone had walked in, interrupted them or needed one of them to do something else. And why wouldn't they? It was a hotel, it was Christmas, the rooms were public and the guests were there to enjoy their stay, not to overhear a conversation that really should have been kept for a private moment. But with all that had been happening, private moments had been rare. Their shifts had been opposites, which had meant that he'd worked through the nights, and Jess through the days, so even at bedtime they'd simply not been together.

Jack thought of the DNA test, of Bastion and although he still felt that the DNA test needed to be done, after the story he'd been told that morning, he now had no doubt that Bastion really was Jess's father. He knew too many details and the man had far too much heartache for it not to be true.

Opening the door, Jack hesitated before entering and heading to the window. He looked out, took in the limited view and then placed the wicker basket on the floor, while he erected the stand, and then stood back to see the Moses basket in all its glory. He nodded; it was beautiful, he knew that Jess would like it and he felt pleased with his choice.

He took in the familiar surroundings of their room and smiled. He and Jess had chosen everything in the room together, from the red tartan bedspread to the picture that hung above the bed. It was a picture of the two of them, taken the year before during a holiday in Italy. They'd been sitting in the main square on the island of Capri, hooking arms and sipping out of each other's glasses, their lips just millimetres apart and their eyes locked together. The look on their faces was one of pure love. He laughed as he remembered the cost of the kir royales, thirty-two euros for the two, but so worth the look on Jess's face when he'd ordered them.

He sat on the bed, but then stood up and moved to the chair and sat, tapping his fingers on the chair arm. He wanted to be there when Jess came back, he wanted to see the look on her face. He looked up at the clock, then closed his eyes and breathed in deeply to take in the familiar smell of the room. A soft, citrus smell surrounded him; it was the smell of Jess, of her perfume. He smiled and looked over at the basket and wondered how long it would be before their baby would be in there, cooing and gurgling and melting their hearts. The basket was pure white, and now he wished he'd bought a Babygro, a blanket or something that would make it look just a little less sterile. He made a conscious decision to call back at the shop and buy something of colour, maybe in a lemon or ivory.

He'd sat for what seemed like hours and again he looked at his watch. It was just after three. He rummaged in his trouser pocket and pulled out his mobile. 'Do I text you, or just wait?' he asked himself, but then dropped the phone on the bed. 'No, just wait,' he whispered, after deciding that a text might worry Jess, or put her off coming to the room altogether.

He glanced at where the television hung on the wall, and then at the bedside table, where his eyes fell upon the letter that Emily had written to him, a small white envelope with a Post-it note attached and in Jess's handwriting, the words, 'Jack, you still haven't read your letter.'

He stood up, went to the door and listened. But the corridor beyond was silent. He came to the conclusion that Jess and the children must have gone to the kitchen for their tea. Meaning that all he could do was wait. He went back to the chair and sat down. Once again he looked at the envelope, then picked it up and tore it open. An old metal key fell out and he picked it up and studied it. The key was similar to one that you'd see in a museum. Big and clunky, with a scrolled shaft. He smiled and placed it on the bed where he could see it as he read.

My dear Jack

Secrets, secrets, secrets, every person in this house has far too many of them. The secrets have always been there, they've always surrounded us, both in the past and in the present. But for the sake of this house, and the love you have for Jess, you all need to start talking to one another, and once and for all, the secrets need to end.

I always found that secrets breed lies and lies are not good, not for any of us, least of all for an old lady who has struggled for most of her life trying to keep far too many, not only the secrets of her own, but also those of others.

If you're reading this letter, then I will have already left this earth and although some people may be sad at my passing and feel that my life has been one dedicated to others, I really don't want anyone's pity. You can be assured that my life was exactly as it should have been. I had everything I could have wished for and I had no desire for it to have been any different. You see, I love the Hall with all my heart and even though, whilst growing up, the winters here were harsh, I still loved it above everything else. My happiest memories were made here, from a time that surrounded my childhood, a time when I still had my mother and father, along with my brother and sisters. But it was Mary, my twin that I was closest to. We'd spend the nights together, snuggled up, chatting in one another's bedrooms, all in secret without our parents' knowledge. It was here we spoke of our first loves, where I told Mary all about my Eddie, how I hoped to have a love and marriage as good as the one I thought our parents had. And if it had been up to me, my marriage would have been good. I loved my Eddie with every piece of my heart and I know that he loved me too. With that love came our son, Arthur, who was born out of wedlock; the pregnancy had been another secret that I'd held until after his birth. But my Eddie had gone to war before he knew I was with child. A war that brought him back a different man; his mind was broken, his body ruined and he came home a man who needed me to look after him, even though he had no idea who I really was. But to me, that didn't matter. I loved him, just as I loved our son.

This house, Wrea Head Hall, my family home, was the place where my son, my Arthur, was born. His memories of being close to this house as a child were good, although because of the war he was brought up by his grandmother and lived in the gatehouse where Madeleine and Bandit now live. But now as an infirm adult, his being back here gives him the calmness and continuity that he needs, and because of that I'm grateful that we returned and that as I leave this earth, he has people around him who can love and care for him in my absence.

For me, I could never imagine bringing up my child anywhere but here. But for you, it's different, and I know that. Forgive me, Jack, but Jess told me that you're about to become a father. It should be a time of happiness, of new life, but I know the events of last year have left a sadness within you, a need for stability and security that lies at your very core.

I know you need a future, Jack, a life away from Wrea Head Hall, however I hope you'll not want to be too far away and that the responsibility of becoming a parent will come naturally to you. It's certainly a responsibility that I know you'll take seriously, because you're a good man. Jess chose her life partner well. And even though I know that right now you'll be confused, please be assured that every person who finds out they're about to become a parent goes through all of these feelings. I know that I certainly did. But I also know that both you and Jess will be the best at everything you do. You'll be the best father and husband that she could wish for and vice versa.

As I said before, this house has held far too many secrets and even though you are not aware, it's held one for you too. One that your mother has chosen not to tell you in life, but one that I feel you should know after my death, for if I don't tell you, then who will? There will be no one left who knows the truth, except for your mother, and she must have her own reasons for keeping the truth from you.

I kept a secret for many years before you were born, a secret that should never have been mine to keep. I would have been almost twenty when I found out that my father was having an affair. No one else knew the truth. Not my mother, nor my siblings. You see, my father was a man of discretion. He was very careful in his actions and the affair was a secret he'd kept for many years, even after the birth of my youngest sister, Rose, a time when my mother seemed to love him the most.

Our childhood nanny, Pamela, lived in the farmhouse that stands just down the lane within the national park. We were told that she'd chosen to stay close to the Hall because of her love for it and for us. But the reality was that our father had built the property for her, in order that he could continue his affair without our mother's knowledge.

Pamela would have been in her late thirties when she bore a daughter, Ingrid, a daughter that would come to visit us at the Hall and play with our sister Rose. Little did we know at the time that she was our half-sister, a product of my father's love for Pamela. But then one Christmas, Pamela took sick. She had the fever and my father stayed with her until the end. Ingrid came to live with us at the Hall. But she rebelled and as soon as she could, she left and my father had no idea what became of her. Therefore when he died, I inherited the farm, even though it was a property I never wanted.

In short, Ingrid came back some years later, with her son, William. I was happy to see her and gave her the farm to live in and she stayed for a number of years, but a traffic accident took her life and William went a little wild. He got drunk daily and took many women to his bed, one of whom was your mother. But the idea of fatherhood was not in his plans and one day he just got up and left, never to return, and none of us have seen or heard of him since.

So you see, Jack, you are a direct descendant of my father. You are my great-nephew and in order to settle the secrets of the past and with the knowledge of your heritage, the farm should rightfully be yours.

So, Jack, I hereby bequeath it to you. I want you and Jess to make it your home. But it's old and it's been empty for twenty-five years. You'll have a lot of work to do, and for that I'm so sorry. But you're young and you're strong and you could make it a good home for you both. It's close enough to the Hall for Jess to be near to Madeleine, but far enough away to give you a little independence.

Also, I give you a key. The key is only a symbol, because in reality the locks have not worked for years. But you, Jack, need to provide the locks, you need to make this house a home where your child will flourish, a place of *safety for Jess, and ultimately the key should be one to both of your hearts.*

Make your home a happy one and make many good memories there in the years to come.

All my love for both of your futures.
Emily x

Jack took in a deep breath, stood up, walked to the window and opened it. He needed the air, needed to think, needed to breathe and he used his hand to waft the air towards him as he gulped in the breaths, one rapidly after the other. He felt as though he had been submerged in water for the longest time, only to be allowed back to the surface to breathe at the very last moment.

'Why ... why hasn't my mother ever told me?' he asked himself and then glanced back down at the letter, and re-read it. He looked out of the window, and towards the farmhouse. The trees were bare and he could only just make it out in the distance. Of course he'd known it was there. Everyone did. But he'd never been to it. Why would he?

The sound of children's voices could be heard through the open window, along with those of Madeleine and Bandit and the bark of Buddy. He grabbed the letter and pushed it deep in his pocket.

Emily had spoken of secrets, how the house had had too many. But now, with this gift she'd given to them, he didn't know what to do. Should he tell Jess, or should he keep this information to himself, keep the secret for a little while longer, even though Emily had indicated that he shouldn't?

Sitting back down in the chair, he crossed his legs, tried to look relaxed. But inside his mind was spinning, his legs felt like jelly and his heart pounded like a bass drum. Emily had given him a house. No, not just a house, but a house that would become their home. He couldn't comprehend what it all meant. His father was the grandson of Emily's father. But if this were all true, why had his mother struggled for all those years? Why hadn't she made it public? Surely she would have been entitled to something. He thought of how she'd lived, how proud she'd always been, how she'd always paid her way, even at times when she could least afford it. She had so little, yet here he was now with so much. He had a house, he had somewhere that he and Jess could call their own. It was somewhere that wasn't the Hall, but as Emily had suggested, it was somewhere just close enough to Madeleine that Jess would be comfortable.

He wiped his brow. He felt hot, even though it was winter; his hands were clammy and he wiped them down his jeans. He had to make a plan. He wanted to go to the farmhouse before it got too dark. He looked out of the window as the dusk pulled and cursed. He wanted to see where and how his father had lived, and he needed to see what Emily had meant by 'have to do a lot of work'. Was the work something he could do by himself, or not? He quickly decided on the latter. After not being used for twenty-five years, the electrics and the plumbing would all need replacing. He thought of his savings, the money he'd inherited from his maternal grandmother and for a moment he closed his eyes and calculated whether the money he had would be enough. It would probably be tight, especially if they had to replace everything.

He heard footsteps in the corridor and knew that someone was about to walk past, and he stood up and paced around the room, waiting to see if the door opened. A key could be heard in the next door room and Jack felt the air unexpectedly expel from his lungs. It was at that point that he realised he'd been holding his breath and he had to make a conscious effort to breathe before walking to the door. His hand rested on the doorknob and a few moments later, he opened it, only to hear the sound of Christmas carols as they drifted up the stairs and into the corridor.

He left the room and made his way to the top of the stairs, where he leaned on the balustrade and looked over to where a small group of five-year-old schoolchildren stood by the twenty-foot Christmas tree, which now twinkled brightly in the dimming light. All the children were dressed in identical red jumpers, white shirts and grey trousers or skirts. Their parents were all nervously watching, their mouths silently making out each word as their children sang and their teacher stood, his eyes wide open, waving a baton in the hope that he'd keep them all in time with one another.

To one side of the group stood Jess, who was leaning against the library's doorway. She listened to the carols with a soft, loving smile on her face, while in her arms was a dishevelled looking Poppy, who she rocked back and forth. He leaned further over the balustrade to see young Lily, who sat on her father's knee, her arms curled tightly around his body and her face nestled into his neck.

Jack smiled at the sight, just as Jess looked up and in his direction. He turned away and ran down the stairs, taking them two at a time, then walked across the grand hall until he stood beside Jess. His arm automatically went around her waist and he caught her eye, before pulling her towards him and kissing her gently on the cheek.

'I love you so much,' he whispered as Jess momentarily closed her eyes. 'You have to trust me. It's all going to be okay.' His words were almost lost in the music, but he knew she'd heard him and he now knew exactly what he needed to do to make her happy.

'Here you go, my lovelies,' Nomsa said as she passed glasses of eggnog around to the adults, and warm chocolate milk to the children.

Jack took a glass and went to pass one to Jess, then halted. 'Oh, maybe we shouldn't.' He winked at Nomsa and placed the glass back on the tray, as Jess put Poppy on the floor. 'Honey, stay with Lily, won't you?' she said as Poppy smiled and took up residence on the settee beside Bastion.

'Jess, why don't you go and get changed?' His eyes locked with hers. 'It's about time I took you out to celebrate,' Jack whispered as he took Jess's hand and led her towards the staircase, and towards the room where he'd left the wicker Moses basket.

He was desperate to see the house, but it would still be there in the morning and viewing it would just have to wait. Now he needed to be with Jess and he curled an arm around her waist as they headed up to the bedroom.

Chapter Twenty-Two

Jack turned over in bed. Daylight had only just broken and he pulled the quilt up and over both Jess and himself as he snuggled in with his hand on her stomach. He'd lain awake for the past hour, just watching her sleep.

He loved the way she curled into him like one part of their very own jigsaw, the way her hand went under her cheek like she had a home-made pillow and the way the corners of her mouth were turned up in a half smile, making him wonder what she might be dreaming of.

'I love you so much,' he whispered as his chest filled with pride. 'I'm going to look after you.' He moved his hand over her stomach. 'I'm going to look after you both,' he promised as he caught sight of the jeans that he'd abandoned the evening before. Emily's letter was still on his mind, the words repeating themselves over and over. Had it been a dream? Had he dreamed that Emily had just given them a house? It all seemed too surreal. Not only had she given them the answer to his prayers, she'd given them a home, a place to be where they could live independently, away from the Hall, but close enough for Jess to be happy. She'd also given him the answers to many of his questions. For years he'd ached for information about his father, he'd wanted to know who he was, where he lived. He'd been shocked to find out that the answers really hadn't been that far away, and that in the end his whole history was here, at the Hall.

'I don't want you working there,' his mother had said when he'd first been offered the job. 'Can't you refuse, find a job somewhere else, in fact anywhere else?' His mum had challenged his decision for days and had made it very clear that she hadn't wanted him working at the Hall. The problem was he'd had no idea why and, like any young man, he'd gone his own way and had taken the job against her wishes.

'Are you awake?' Jack kissed Jess's cheek as his hand caressed her stomach.

'Mmmm, I am now.' She smiled and turned to him, her eyes sparkling in the early morning light as her lips gently brushed against his.

'I love this baby already,' Jack said as his hand moved from her stomach and went up to touch her face. He returned the kiss. 'I love you both so very much.' And he did. While watching her, he'd realised how much he was looking forward to the birth, to nurturing his baby, caring for it and protecting it. He tried to imagine what it would be like to decorate a nursery, a place where a rocking chair would stand, with Jess sitting in it, rocking his own son or daughter to sleep.

Jess jumped up and out of bed. 'Oh dear, this is the trouble with pregnancy, you need the loo far too many times a day.' She opened the door to the en suite. 'What are your plans today?' she asked from behind the door.

Jack thought about his answer. He didn't want to lie, but he wasn't ready to tell her about the house, not yet. He needed to keep it to himself, for just a day. He needed the time to digest what had happened, what Emily had given them and he wanted to go to the house alone, to see where his father had lived, to see if there was anything at all that had been left behind, something, anything, that would give him a clue as to who William had been.

He pursed his lips. It wasn't that he didn't want Jess to see the house; he knew she already had. The night before she'd told him about how the girls had used it as a hiding place, how they'd been locked in a cellar and how after they'd been found she'd walked from room to room admiring it.

She'd also told him how dirty it was, that it looked close to derelict and he felt the need to clean it a little and make it homelier before she went back.

'Jack … you okay?' Jess was standing by the bed, undressing. 'I'm going to take a quick shower. I'm on reception this morning, need to be down there in an hour.'

'Yeah, I'm fine. Sorry.' He looked her up and down, took in her shape and gave her a cheeky smile. 'You are so beautiful, Jess. I'm so lucky to have you.'

She swiped at him with the satin nightgown. 'Get away with you,' she said with a laugh.

'Hey, behave.' He grabbed her hand and pulled her towards him, making Jess land on the bed beside him, naked. She immediately curled her body into his and he threw the duvet back over her.

'It is going to be all right, Jack, isn't it?' She looked up and into his eyes. 'I so want everything to be perfect and I think … I think we kind of deserve something good to happen, just for a change, don't we?'

He sighed. 'Oh, Jess. You deserve it to be more than perfect and it will be, I promise.'

'Really?'

'Yes, really. You tell me what you want and I will do everything within my power to provide it for you.' He lowered his lips to hers and kissed her gently. 'You're going to have everything you want and more.'

She smiled. 'I just want you. You'll be the best father, Jack. I just know it.' She moved onto her side. 'I've got my first scan at four o'clock. You will come, won't you?' She put her hands together as though in prayer. 'We can meet our baby together.'

Once again, Jack's hand went to her stomach. 'Of course, I will. I wouldn't miss it for the world.'

Chapter Twenty-Three

'Yeah, I'll be needing a skip, the biggest you've got.' Jack pulled at the rotten architrave and watched as it practically disintegrated in his hand. 'In fact, I could most probably do with a couple.' He walked from kitchen to living room while holding the phone to his ear. Emily had been right, there was a lot to be done. Everything needed ripping out and tearing down. Emily might have said that it'd been twenty-five years since anyone had lived there, but he guessed that nothing had been repaired, altered or replaced for at least sixty or seventy years, maybe even since the house had been built by Emily's father, his great-grandfather.

'What … really?' His shoulders slumped. 'Two days? But that'll be Thursday, what's that?' He thought for a moment. 'The twenty-second?' He sighed and walked back into the kitchen. 'Yeah, sure. It'll just have to be okay, won't it?' He reeled off the address, put the phone down and looked at his watch. It was still early, not yet ten and he calculated that he'd have around five hours before it got dark and he'd have to leave and get ready to go with Jess for the scan. He started walking back and forth, all the while looking around and wondering about his father, trying to imagine him living in this house. He rummaged through a kitchen drawer that was full of old letters, pieces of paper, old faded photographs, a more than healthy quantity of spider webs, and what seemed like dozens of dead spiders, along with the remains of other odd looking insects.

One of the photographs was of a man, sitting at a kitchen table. Jack held it up to the light and tried to make it out but the colour had all but faded and the image was hard to fully distinguish. Jack turned in the kitchen; he could just about make out the same shapes and decided that the photograph could have been taken in this very room. He looked to the corner where the kitchen table would no doubt have previously stood. Is that where his father had sat? Was that where he ate his breakfast and dinner while growing up? Did he sit in the lounge, and watch television – did they have one back then? Jack stared at a patch of dust on the work surface that had been disturbed and he allowed his fingers to trace the same path. Was this the exact spot that Jess had touched the day before? He now wished he'd brought her with him, wished she was here to help him make plans. He dug in his pocket for his mobile and thought about calling her, but shook his head and dropped it onto the counter, making a plume of dust fly up and into the air.

He needed to find a way to turn this house into a home for Jess and the baby. But where to start? 'Skirting boards, architraves, and the wood chip wallpaper all need tearing out, along with the kitchen cupboards,' he said to himself as he walked through what he thought might be a utility room and into the downstairs bathroom. 'And you are definitely going.' He directed his statement at the bath and the toilet; both were old and stained beyond belief and neither looked like they'd ever been cleaned in the whole history of the house. His hand went out to flush the toilet, but he thought better of it, and decided to get a plumber in first, just in case the flushing caused a flood. 'Electrics.' He flicked a switch on and off, and pulled open the cupboards looking for the fuse box, but couldn't find it. 'I guess you'll need replacing too.'

He began making a checklist as he walked up the main staircase, treading carefully on each step as he went. At the top of the stairs were four bedrooms, three that looked like doubles and one that was smaller and obviously a single. The single room sided onto what he thought to be the main bedroom and he decided that he'd speak to Jess and ask if she'd like to have an en suite for themselves and then keep the downstairs bathroom for everyone else.

For a moment he stood in the centre of the main bedroom. It looked out over the back of the house and had views across the fields for as far as he could see. He tried to imagine living here, going to bed and making love to Jess right here, in this room, just as he'd done the night before. A huge smile crossed his face as he remembered how happy Jess had been when she'd seen the Moses basket, how they'd chatted over dinner, and then afterwards had gone back to the Hall and made love, repeatedly, before laying together, and chatting endlessly about the future, and about the baby, until Jess had fallen asleep in his arms. It had been a feeling of being home, a feeling of knowing how much he loved her. They'd spoken of how everything would change, but in the end they'd both been convinced that it would change for the better.

He'd pushed aside his own worries about his father. He'd obviously had his reasons for leaving and although Jack had taken it personally for years, he couldn't take it that way, not any more. After all, his father had never known him, and by the sounds of it he'd barely known his mother either. They'd both been very young, reckless and scared. And although his mum had had no choice but to deal with the situation, to bring her baby up the best she knew how, his father had been nothing more than a child himself, with no real family to help him, and Jack could almost understand why he'd have turned tail and run.

'You're going to be the best home ever because I'm going to make you the best,' Jack said smugly to the house as he stepped out and onto the landing, where he looked up at the loft door. 'And I'm not even going to think about what could be up there.' He laughed and went back down the stairs and into the kitchen, where a door led off under the stairs. He opened it to see a set of old, rickety downward wooden steps. 'So that's where the cellar is,' he said as he remembered what Jess had told him about Poppy and Lily getting trapped behind the door. He looked at the lock, picked up a screwdriver from his tool bag and forcibly removed it. 'There, that'll stop you frightening any more little girls, won't it?'

The farmhouse was very quiet, almost nothing could be heard and even though the trees were bare, no matter which window he looked out of, nothing could be seen of the Hall. Had it been built that way intentionally? He smiled as he realised that every window ironically faced away from the Hall, making Jack think of the years gone by, when Emily's father, his great-grandfather, would come here to visit his mistress, knowing full well that wherever he'd been in the house, he couldn't be seen. It had been the perfect place to escape to.

'There will be no secrets here. This won't be a house of secrets. This house will be a home, a place of love, and of family,' he announced to the walls. 'I'm going to make you all cosy and warm.' He poked at the wood burning stove, got down on his knees and looked inside. 'Oh yes, you'll need cleaning.' He sat back on the floor and leaned against the wall. 'So many things need to be done. So, what do I do first?' he whispered. 'Do I go and get Jess, bring her here, tell her everything and let her see how bad it is?' He knew she'd already been inside and, without knowing the house was theirs, she had described it in detail the night before. All the time she'd spoken, he'd listened with interest and on more than one occasion he'd almost told her of Emily's gift. He nodded his head. 'I could work over Christmas, and strip the place out. At least then it will be free of the past and when Jess sees it again, it'll be clean and the rooms empty, devoid of its history and free of the past.' Again he nodded. 'It could be a wedding gift for Jess, a New Year surprise.' He stood up. He thought about how after the wedding he could bring Jess here and carry her over the threshold and show her what he'd done. And then, together, they could plan how to transform the farmhouse. They could choose a kitchen – he could imagine it now, a real homely one, with a long oak table in the corner where Maddie and Nomsa would turn up and perch while they all cooed over the baby.

Jack thought of his plans for the next few days, his work rota and all the times he could escape without Jess becoming suspicious. Again he looked at his watch. Jess had the scan appointment at four and he'd promised he'd be there. A smile crossed his lips. 'I'm going to meet my baby,' he whispered to himself. 'But I have to be back and at work by six.' He knew that for the next week, at least, he was scheduled to work evenings. He sighed. 'So, you house, you will have to be worked on during my mornings.'

He began picking up pieces of old left over furniture and dragging them outside. The skips would be a couple of days, but that didn't mean he couldn't begin the emptying, pulling out the old and getting it ready for the new. He also thought of the contractors who had worked on the Hall and he was sure that he knew at least one electrician, plumber and plasterer who'd be happy to work for the extra money over Christmas.

He thought about Jess, about what kind of kitchen or bathroom she'd want. Whether she'd want carpets or wooden floors. He was determined that everything had to be perfect, everything had to be just as Jess would want it and once it was transformed, it had to be safe and ready to move into, as a family.

Chapter Twenty-Four

Jess furiously paced up and down the hotel reception. She looked up at the clock, whilst repeatedly flicking the top of a pen, up and down, up and down.

'Where is he, Maddie? We've got a very important appointment and he promised he'd be here.' She dropped the pen down and onto the diary.

'Jess, he'll be here, Jack's never late. In fact, he's normally twenty minutes early to go anywhere, you know that.' Madeleine walked from reception and into the dining room, where she picked up a handful of salt and pepper pots, before carrying them into the kitchen.

Jess once again looked back up at the clock. Maddie was right. It was almost three o'clock, and during the past eighteen months, she'd never known Jack to be late, not once.

So where was he?

Jess turned, went to the dining room and picked up the remaining salt cellars and followed Madeleine into the kitchen, where Nomsa stood with her hands on her hips.

'There you are, Maddie. Now all the starters are organised. Soups in the pots and Bernie's preparing the mains. The majority of the desserts are either in the fridge or on the side waiting to go in the oven.' She untied her apron and, with a tray in her hands, she walked towards the door. 'Now, it's my afternoon off and if you'll excuse me I have a game of Scrabble planned with Lily and Bastion.' She blushed. 'Oh, they both think they'll beat me, but do you know what, I'm planning on whooping their asses.' Her Caribbean tone sang out. 'Oh, Maddie, you don't mind me taking a tray up, do you? I promised I'd take up some hot drinks for me and Bastion, and a glass of lemonade for our little Lily.' She indicated the tray. 'That is okay, isn't it?'

Madeleine nodded and started to fill the salt and pepper pots. 'Of course, Nomsa. You're more than welcome to anything you want, you know you don't have to ask.' She pointed to the fridge. 'If I'm right there were some of your lovely mince pies in the chiller. Why don't you take a few of those up with you too?'

Nomsa put the tray down, opened the fridge and put half a dozen of the mince pies on a plate. 'Well, I know Bastion likes my baking and he'll appreciate these, that's for sure.' She gave them both a knowing smile and then turned, picked up the tray and made her way to the back staircase.

'Well, what do you think about that?' Madeleine asked Jess. 'They're getting a bit cosy, aren't they?'

Jess wasn't sure whether to mention the kiss she'd witnessed and shrugged her shoulders. 'Maddie, I really don't care if my dad's having it away with half the Women's Institute. I'm too busy being annoyed with Jack.'

Madeleine turned. 'Jess, give him a break. Have you tried his mobile?' She began placing a selection of linen napkins on the table. 'Anyhow, what is it with you at the moment? You seem a bit distant.'

Jess stared at the floor. She and Maddie had always been close, and it was becoming more than obvious that she couldn't keep the news of the baby to herself for much longer. After all, since they were very young, they'd always told each other everything, and even though she'd promised Jack, he'd let her down. And now all she really wanted was to tell her big sister about the baby.

'Maddie, I'm … I'm pregnant.' A long, shrill squeal came from her sister's lips. 'I'm … I'm ten weeks pregnant,' she tried to say, but felt sure she hadn't been heard until Madeleine spun around on the spot.

'Oh my God, Jess. How could I have been so blind? I mean, I should have guessed, you've been a real moody cow for weeks now. When did you find out? Why on earth didn't you tell me? Look at you, there's nothing of you. What did Jack say?' Madeleine threw out questions one after the other, as her hand went straight to Jess's stomach. 'Hello, little baby, hello in there. Hello. Can you hear me? I'm your Aunty Maddie.' The words came out as more of a screech and for a few moments Jess enjoyed the closeness of her sister's hand. 'I'm going to spoil you so much. I am. Do you know that?' She leaned over and planted a kiss on Jess's stomach. 'Oh, Jess. I'm so in love with her already.' Madeleine sat up, but her hand remained on Jess's stomach. 'She'll be beautiful, just like you.' Tears of joy sparkled in Madeleine's eyes.

'It could just as easily be a boy,' Jess stated. 'And it's still early days. It's my first scan, Maddie and it's in less than an hour, and Jack should be here. He promised he'd go with me.' Jess felt herself being hugged and squeezed by Madeleine, before being pushed towards the kitchen bench and forcibly sat down.

'But you're only ten weeks, isn't it early for a scan?' Madeleine looked concerned. 'Is there something wrong?'

'No, not really. The doctor is just being cautious because of all the trauma. I only found out just before Emily died.' Jess knew her own body well; she remembered how she'd picked up on how she'd felt different immediately, and the moment she'd missed her period she'd known. She'd only waited a few days before she'd bought the test.

'Well, that proves that Jack's just running a bit late. He'll be here. You know he wouldn't miss something like this, not Jack.' Maddie continued to hold her hand to Jess's stomach.

'Do you know what, Maddie? He really didn't take the whole idea of pregnancy and our having a baby too well, not at first.' Her voice broke as she looked up at her sister. 'But ... last night, he apologised, he said everything was going to be okay. He promised.' She put her hand over Maddie's. 'He's even bought a Moses basket, like the one you had with the pretty white broderie anglaise interior. I know it's a bit soon, but when we went back to the room last night, it was there, all set up, all ready and looking so beautiful,' She looked out of the door and into reception. 'But now, he hasn't turned up and ... What if he's had second thoughts?'

Maddie sat back on the bench. 'Oh, Jess, you know Jack better than that. He wouldn't take off.'

'I don't know any more. Last night everything was perfect. Jack was so loving. We went out for dinner, came back here, went to bed.' A sob left her lips. 'I thought he was happy.'

'Hey, come on, this is your pregnancy hormones that are screaming. I'll try his mobile and then I'll try his mum, see if he's up there. He's probably gone to his mum's and will be telling her all about the baby. He'll have lost track of time.' Madeleine looked at her watch. 'Now, you go and dry those gorgeous eyes of yours, and get ready to go. You can bet he'll be here any moment and we'll have worried for nothing.'

Jess stood up and nodded, just as Lily burst into the room and fell onto the kitchen floor in fits of giggles.

'Hey there, sister, what you doing down there?' Jess walked towards her and Lily jumped up and ran to give her a hug. Her hair was in bunches, making her look even younger than she had before.

'Well, I was upstairs with Daddy and Nomsa, and we were playing Scrabble and I was drinking lemonade, when they both went real quiet. They do that a lot and then our daddy said to me ...' She jumped up onto the kitchen bench, put her hands on her hips and began to emphasise the Caribbean twang to mimic his voice. '... Lily, my girl, you run down them stairs and ask our Jess for a looooong wait, and while you're gone, I'm gonna give this fine woman a kiss.' She smacked her lips together and continued to giggle. 'I think they're snogging.' Her hand went over her mouth and both she and Jess laughed together. 'Do you think she'll be our new mummy?'

Jess took a step back and glanced at Madeleine who stood in the corner of the room with the phone to her ear. 'Well ... oh ... err, I don't know ...' She hadn't really thought of Nomsa becoming her step-mum. She smiled and it occurred to her that she quite liked the idea. It was early days, but Lily was right in her observation, Nomsa and her father were getting closer. 'So did they say how long you've got to stay down here?' Jess asked Lily, who now sat on the bench with her hands under her chin.

'Till you give me the long wait ...' Her reply was innocent, she had no idea what her father had told her to do, but all of them began to giggle.

Chapter Twenty-Five

Jack was in the cellar taking a look at the heating system with the light from his torch when a noise in the kitchen above stopped him in his tracks and he headed back up the stairs, stopping two from the door.

'I've told you before,' a man shouted as he stamped through the empty house, 'it's not my job to grab the kid, it's yours. You're her mother. Now you need to get your backside up to that bloody Hall and get the girl, just like we agreed.'

Jack held his breath. He didn't like the sound of the voices that came from within his house. He stood still, watching through a crack in the door, waiting and listening.

'They can't stop you from taking her, Annie. She is your fucking daughter, for God's sake.' The man moved through the empty rooms, his steps echoing, the floorboards creaking, and a thudding noise came from the window as he pushed it open, whilst taking long, deep drags of nicotine from his cigarette.

A woman, presumably Annie, stumbled into the room behind him. 'Shut the bloody window, Griff. It's the middle of winter, for Christ's sake.'

Annie's heel dropped down between a gap in the wooden floorboards and as she stepped forward, her shoe was left behind. 'Damn shoes, why can't prostitutes wear sneakers? I'm sure the damned punters wouldn't give a shit,' she growled, and grabbed the shoe. She pulled as hard as she could and finally fell backwards, landing heavily as it freed itself from the boards. 'It's a wonder I'm not covered in fucking bruises.' She rubbed her leg, looked down at the shoe, which was now minus a heel, replaced it on her foot and pulled herself up.

'Another pair of bloody shoes I'll have to replace. They're sick of seeing me in that damned charity shop.'

'Bugger the charity shop, Annie, and if you haven't noticed, you're not only covered in fucking bruises but also scabs and bloody puncture wounds where you keep injecting,' Griff yelled as he turned from the window, flicked the ash from his cigarette on to the floor and walked to the wall, where he tapped at the light switch. 'Damn it, no bloody electric? Try in there.' He paused, and waited. 'Annie, I said try the damned switch.'

'All right. Don't shout, I heard you.' She stomped across the room. 'This place has probably been empty for years so if it doesn't work in there, what the hell makes you think it'll work in here?' She flicked the switch with no effect and continued to stand in the darkness. 'Besides if you put the bloody lights on, it'll be like sending out a beacon and you might as well just shout out that we're here to kidnap the girl.' She walked over to where Griff stood. 'Give us a drag, I could murder a fag.' She took the cigarette from his mouth, placed it between her lips and closed her eyes as she inhaled.

'Don't be stupid. It's not kidnapping, not when she's your own kid, is it?' Griff grabbed the cigarette back and kicked at the walls. 'Now just go and get Lily and let me sell her to the highest fucking bidder. Your debt'll be just about paid and then I won't have to go and kill either of you, will I?'

His tone was menacing, aggressive and Jack was sure he was capable of doing what he'd threatened. His mind began to race and his heart pounded as he took in a deep breath. What could he do? He couldn't, no he wouldn't allow him to go after Lily and he knew he had to do something, he just wasn't sure what. He began looking around and down the cellar steps in the hope he'd find something he could use as a weapon.

'What do you mean just about? If I give you the kid, we're done. Is that clear?' Annie leaned against the wall, pulled the stilettos back off of her feet and shook them free of gravel. 'Griff, is that clear? I want free of you. I want to know that I'll never be owing you any more bloody money. Not ever.'

'Oh, you'll be free of me all right, you dirty old slut.' His hand shot out, making Annie duck. 'You're a good for nothing dirty addict, do you know that? You stink, you need a bath and I'd do better with you out of the house anyhow. Men only come for the other girls, you never get picked, not unless there's no one else left to shag or they're old, fat or bloody stupid.' He spat at the floor and looked her up and down, 'Look at you, what makes you think a bloke'd even want you?'

'Fuck off, Griff. I had a bath on Sunday.' She stroked her hair down flat, and pushed it behind her ears. 'And I'm not an addict. I can do without it. I … I just like it, that's all.' She stamped across the room and towards the cellar door making Jack hold his breath.

'Annie, you talk bollocks. In an hour or two, you'll be on your damn knees and you know it.' Griff paced back and forth. 'But by then I won't give a toss. By then, I'll have the kid. Won't I?'

'You will if I give her to you.' The woman looked defiant, and Jack guessed that any drugs that were still in her system were making her brave. 'You're not treating me how you do the others, Griff. I want assurance, I want to know that the damn flick knife will be staying in your fucking pocket, where it belongs.'

'Ah, so you finally thought about poor Bella, did you? Finally realised what a fucking mess I made of her face, did you? Well, I'm telling you now, Annie, you do what you're told or you'll come up against more than my blade, you got that?'

Annie moved as far away from Griff as she could.

Griff laughed. 'Well, if you don't give me the girl, you're as good as dead, anyhow. You got that?' He pulled his van keys out of his pocket and moved across the room towards where Annie stood, his nose almost touching hers. 'Now, what are we doing hiding out here anyhow? We need to go into town and find a charity shop to get you some decent clothes to wear and make you look respectable, then we can get down to the hotel and get Lily and get out.'

Jack felt his stomach turn. Griff was twice his size and according to the woman he had a knife, making Jack wonder what he could possibly do. He had to think and fast. The couple were about to leave, about to make an attempt to kidnap Lily and, right now, he was the only one who could stop that from happening. She was so sweet, so funny and so terribly innocent. He'd heard their plans and there was no way he could allow them to go near her. He needed to warn the Hall and get them to call the police. He felt in his pocket for his mobile, but the phone was not there. He went over his movements. He'd been clearing the rubbish, cleaning up the dust and then he remembered the moment he'd taken it out of his pocket. He'd been standing in the kitchen thinking of calling Jess, but had changed his mind and had thrown the mobile on the kitchen worktop while he'd worked. What now? Confront the pair or wait till they had gone? They had spoken about going to a charity shop so he knew he had time before they'd get to the Hall. In seconds, Jack weighed up his best course of action and decided that inaction was by far his best bet, especially seeing as Griff had a knife.

At that moment he heard the kitchen door bang shut and looked back through the gap in the door to see that the pair had gone. Jack started up the last two steps that would take him to the kitchen.

Chapter Twenty-Six

'Not a chance, Maddie. I don't care what excuse he might come up with.' Jess looked at her watch. 'And what's more it's almost four o'clock, we'll be going in soon.' She shuffled in her chair, moved her hair back from her face and sipped at the glass of water. 'How much of this do I have to drink?'

Maddie turned and smiled. 'You need to drink all of it.' She pointed to the jug, just as a heavily pregnant woman walked into the room, sat down, crossed her legs and then thought better of it and uncrossed them.

'You here for a scan, my darling?' she asked as she dug around in her handbag, pulled out a tissue and noisily blew her nose.

Jess nodded politely. 'Ten weeks, how about you?'

'Ha ha, really, wow, you're barely pregnant.' She laughed at her own words. 'I'm thirty-six weeks, love, about to pop. Is it your first?' The woman was huge.

Jess answered, 'Yes, my first.'

The woman nodded. 'You wait till you've got six of the little buggers, like me. Then you'll know about it.' She laughed, picked up a magazine and began flicking through the pages. 'See this magazine?' She looked up at Jess. 'No way I'd get time to look at this at home, always one of them wanting my damned attention. Can't even go to the bloody toilet on my own.' She turned back to the magazine and continued to read.

Madeleine moved closer to her sister and whispered, 'Now, if that doesn't put you off having six of them, I don't know what will.' She pursed her lips and both sisters tried not to giggle.

Then Jess's expression turned serious again. 'Maddie,

Jack promised. He said he'd be here.' She allowed the toe of her boot to graze the edge of the table that was littered with newspapers, magazines and empty Styrofoam coffee cups. 'He said he'd be here today. What kind of a father will he be if he can't even do that?' She knew she was being unfair. Jack would be an amazing father. She looked over her shoulder in the hope that she'd see him, running in through the main door, bunches of flowers in his arms and that cheeky half smile that normally crossed his face when he'd done something wrong.

'Jess, you said it yourself, Jack doesn't do this,' Maddie replied. 'He never just disappears and, what's more, even if you two have had a spat, he always turns up.' Her hand rested on Jess's knee. 'Come on, sis, we haven't seen him, his mother hasn't seen him, his friends haven't seen him … don't you think it's all a bit odd?' She stood up and hovered over where Jess sat. 'Honey, most people would wait, but with our history, someone disappearing concerns me. Don't you think we should report him as missing, go look for him or something?'

Jess stared at the sanitised flooring of the waiting room, looked up at the signage and once again read the word, 'Ultrasound' that was etched into the glass partition. She watched as a doctor entered the room, shouted a name and the heavily pregnant woman stood up and left.

She glanced down at the newspapers and began to read the headlines. A man was missing, another had been attacked with a hammer and a woman had been given a record insurance payout when her husband had been killed doing his job. One headline after the other spun around in her mind, 'attacked, killed, missing … attacked, killed, missing.'

'Oh my God, Maddie, you really think he could be missing?' Her breathing suddenly became short and sharp.

She leaned forward to grab hold of the edge of her chair. 'What if …' Jess turned and grabbed Madeleine's hand. '… what if he's been hurt? What if he crashed his car, you hear of it don't you, buried in the undergrowth for days on end, while he dies because no one found him.'

'Jess, you need to drink.' She felt the glass being pushed back into her hand.

'Maddie, we have to start looking for him, don't we?'

Madeleine nodded. 'It really is unlike him. I've never known him to be late for anything, and I know it's not been long, but we both know that Jack would never willingly miss this scan and seeing his baby for the first time. I do think we have to consider that something must have happened to make him late. But you can put the car crash idea out of your mind. If he'd crashed his car, the police would have come to you, to the Hall, it's where Jack is registered as living.' She gave Jess's leg a reassuring pat. 'After the scan, I'll phone around again. I'll make sure he hasn't turned up at his mother's and then, let's say he hasn't turned up by …' She paused and thought. '… say six o'clock tonight, that'd be three hours after we'd expected him, that's when we'll phone the police. That will have given him loads of time to get in touch, wouldn't it?'

Jess nodded. 'But they'll think we're nuts. He could have just gone to the shops and lost track of time. Do you think we're getting a bit ahead of ourselves?' She smiled and tried to convince herself that all this was true. 'Besides, would they respond that quickly?'

Madeleine sighed. 'I don't know, hun, normally with an adult, they'd wait until someone has been missing for at least a day, but with what's happened in our past, they'd expect us to worry and I'd hope they'd respond quickly. After all, I'd only been missing a couple of hours last year, but if they hadn't come when Bandit had rung them, Liam would have killed me. It was all down to their fast response that I'm still here.' She squeezed Jess's hand. 'But, first and foremost, we need to get into this appointment, see that your baby is doing okay in there and then, we need to get back to the Hall.' She looked at her watch. 'We should be back by five, half past at the latest, which gives us time to look for Jack ourselves before we even think about the police.' She began to rummage in her bag. 'Here,' she said as she passed an old white envelope and a pen to Jess, 'start making a list. Let's write down the names of his friends, his associates, of places he normally goes to on a daily, weekly or annual basis. Favourite pubs, gyms, or shops and, if you know it off the top of your head, his mobile number.' Jess watched as she moved into action. 'Actually forget that, I have his mobile number.'

Both sisters locked eyes in a determined stare. 'He won't be far, Jess. I promise you, we will find him.'

Chapter Twenty-Seven

Jack drifted in and out of consciousness. Each time he became aware of his surroundings, he held his body as still as he could. The pain that travelled through his legs made him gulp for air and grit his teeth. He tried to move, but the more he tried, the more pain he felt. Shooting pains went through his ankle and up his leg. He swallowed hard, and began taking short measured breaths in an attempt to ease the pain.

He was trapped and had been since the moment he'd put his weight on the top step and the old rickety steps had collapsed beneath him, leaving him unconscious on the cellar floor amidst a pile of joists and balustrade. He moved his right foot to the left, but the sharpness of splintered wood felt as though it was about to penetrate his skin; then he moved to the right and the pressure became immense. He tried to concentrate on which part of his leg the pain was coming from the most, but couldn't. Every part of him hurt. Every inch of his leg was agony from the knee to the toes. It felt cold and damp and he presumed that the moisture was either blood or water. But the cellar had been dry and if it was water, he couldn't work out where it would have come from unless a pipe had burst as the staircase collapsed. He closed his eyes and tried to wiggle his toes, but they felt numb and detached as though they didn't quite belong to him.

'Oh, man, this is bad,' he whispered to himself. He turned his head from side to side, mentally checking his neck and spine as he tried to concentrate on the sound of his watch. The constant ticking kept him aware and conscious, although with the darkness that had now surrounded him he had no idea how much time had passed since he'd fallen.

A sudden thought passed through his mind. No one knew where he was. No one was coming to find him. Which meant that it was up to him. He had to save himself. He had no choice. He had to move, he had to get out of the cellar and he had to warn the others about what Annie and Griff were planning. But the more he tried to move, the more he began to panic. His arms lashed from side to side, he pulled at the lumps of wood in an attempt to free himself. 'What if I can't do it? What if I can't get to the Hall in time?' He felt bereft, he felt angry, but most of all, he felt alone. Would anyone look for him? Would anyone notice his car where he'd parked it beside the barn?

'Nooooooooo!' he screamed as he pulled at a piece of wood and dropped it. 'Damn you.' His frustration was building, and once again he grabbed at the wood without success. His body slumped in a heap and he felt the energy leave him. Was this how it ended? Would he be trapped here forever? He tried to run his hand down his leg, feeling for the wetness. Was it blood, was he about to bleed to death? Or would he simply die of starvation, in a place where no one would have ever thought he'd be? A hundred different images ran through his mind, each one worse than the last. But he couldn't think about any of that now, he had to put all those images to one side and be strong. He had to help Lily.

'Why? Why now?' he screamed as he realised that nothing made sense, life didn't make sense. He'd just realised what he really wanted in his life. He wanted Jess, he wanted their baby, he wanted Bastion and Lily to be family and more than anything else in the world, and with thanks to Emily, he'd wanted this house to be their home. So why did it feel as though it was all about to be snatched away?

A determination went through him. He had to get out, he had to get to Jess and he had to ensure Lily's safety.

He needed something to help him, something to use as a crutch, something to help him get back up what was left of the stairs and to where his mobile lay on the kitchen worktop. He turned his head in an attempt to look around the cellar. He felt all around him in the hope that there would be something he could use. Then he felt his torch, and breathed a sigh of relief when it lit up the room, giving him the chance to assess the damage and to look down at his leg. 'Shit.' He could see the blood, the shape of his leg where it no longer looked straight and surmised that it was not only badly cut, but more than definitely broken. 'Great,' he shouted. 'That's just fucking great.' He took in measured breaths. Now he'd seen the damage, it hurt even more. The torch began to flicker; the batteries were dying. He used what was left of the battery to look around and noticed several piles of boxes, the word 'Christmas' clearly marked on the side of one, making him wonder if he'd get to see the one that was now only a few days away.

'Oh boy, you sure left plenty behind, didn't you?' he said to the ghosts of the past and shook his head as his torch flickered and, with the last remaining moments of battery, he pointed it one last time at what was left of the staircase, only to watch the light extinguish itself and once again leave him in the darkness.

Taking a deep breath, Jack pulled himself to one side and then to the other, while using his arms to control his weight. The last thing he wanted was for any more of the staircase to break or fall upon him. But he knew that if he had any chance of saving Lily, he had to free himself and he had to do it now. He had to move, he had to release his legs and somehow he had to climb what was left of the stairs and get back to the Hall.

His eyes focused on the outline of the cellar door. It was the same door that he'd torn the lock off earlier, and now it blocked his view, leaving only a shard of dim fading light around it's edges. He'd hung his coat on the back of the door, while working. He'd worked up a sweat and had taken it off for a while, but now the cold was becoming unbearable as the dampness of sweat dried on his skin and his temperature dropped, making him shiver relentlessly. He could just about make out the shape of the coat. It looked like a person standing at the top of the stairs, and he imagined that someone was there watching over him, taking care of him in the darkness, willing him to go on. It was a nice thought, but what he really wished for was that he'd kept the coat on, that he'd left the cellar for another day and that right now he was at the hospital, with Jess, meeting their baby.

As the pain became more and more unbearable, Jack once again began drifting in and out of consciousness. Each time he came around, he tried to pull the air into his lungs, and he tried to look at his watch; even though the numbers shone out, they appeared blurred and he couldn't make out the time, but he knew it was late. He knew Jess would be worried. 'Are you looking for me, Jess?' he whispered, with the hope that she'd begun to search. 'I'm so sorry I've let you down.' He began to curse at his own stupidity. Because of him Lily was in danger, they could have taken her by now and if they hurt her he'd never forgive himself.

'Help, help … can anyone hear me?' he yelled, knowing that no one could. He'd already worked out how far away the farm had been from the Hall. He'd originally thought it a good thing, but now, now he wasn't so sure.

He kicked himself. What had it been that Emily's letter had said? 'There had been too many secrets.' Well, she'd been right and now, because of him there were even more of them and on top of that Lily was in danger and he had no way of letting Jess or Bastion know.

Chapter Twenty-Eight

Jess arrived back at the hotel. 'He's bound to be back by now, Maddie, and if he is, boy is he going to get it.'

'For one, I hope he is back and for two, I wouldn't want to be him if he is.' Madeleine pushed open the large wooden door and stepped inside the warmth of the hotel. 'Always nice to be home on a winter's night, isn't it?'

Jess followed her sister in and nodded as she tore off her gloves and scarf. 'Okay, I'm going to head on up, see if he's in our room.' Jess began climbing the stairs. 'If he's in the kitchen with Nomsa, tell him to come up, I need a word.'

Jess knew that the room would be empty long before she reached it. An overwhelming sense of loss filled her heart as she realised that if Jack were capable of getting to their room, he'd have been at the hospital. He'd have kept his word and by now they'd have both met their baby for the very first time.

Placing a key in the door, she hesitated before opening it. 'What if he really isn't here, what will you do?' Her stomach began to turn, her heart beating heavily and she had a sudden need to throw up. Running into the room, Jess ran straight to the en suite where she sat on the side of the bath with her head over the sink and splashed cold water on her face.

She stared back into the bedroom where the Moses basket stood, empty and waiting. Jack had said that he was going to buy some blankets and Babygros, one of each in lemon and cream, just to add a little colour. At the time she'd smiled and Jack had spoken about the scan. He'd been excited and had really wanted to find out whether their baby was a girl or a boy. Jess remembered how she'd explained that it was far too early and that at just ten weeks it was impossible to tell. He'd been disappointed, but had talked about going into town together after the appointment and buying the biggest teddy bear they could find.

Jess sighed. 'He was so excited,' she whispered. 'So why wouldn't he turn up?' She thought of Jack, of his punctuality, and how he was always early to go everywhere. And deep in her heart she knew that he'd never abandon her, which meant that something had happened, or that someone was stopping him from coming home. 'Where are you, Jack?' She closed her eyes, causing a flashback from the year before: the cable ties, the pain in her wrists, the cage. She could vividly see Liam's burnt face glaring at her while he poked her with a stick and the way he'd threatened to cut the rope from which the cage hung. She jumped back into the present, her skin hot and clammy. If Liam had cut the rope, she'd have plunged to her death. Jess gasped and splashed more cold water on her face.

'I have to do something. He can't have gone far and he wouldn't have left me, so … so he must be hurt.' She pulled her mobile from her pocket and once again tried to call him. 'Come on, Jack. Answer.' But the phone rang and rang, before going to voicemail. She listened to his voice, to the message he'd left and smiled. 'Oh, Jack. I don't know where you are, but I am going to find you.'

Jess headed down the stairs and entered the kitchen where everyone was congregated. Bandit stood talking to them all. 'I'm going to search the woods, and the summer house. Madeleine, could you check the hospitals, and accident and emergency? Len, if you could drive the roads between here and Jack's mum's house, look for any sign that a car could have left the road. Ann, if you could phone the list of his friends that Madeleine gave you. Someone has to have heard from him. Bernie, I'm afraid evening service will be left to you to run.' He turned and acknowledged that Jess had walked in. He held out his arms and pulled her towards him. 'Nomsa, could you look after Jess? And Bastion, could you keep an eye on the schoolchildren who are starting to arrive for their rehearsal and, of course, on the girls?' He kissed Jess on the forehead. 'We are going to find him, I promise.'

The words made Jess crumple in a heap. Suddenly it was real. Jack really was missing and even Bandit was taking it seriously and throwing his military training into finding him. 'The police, do you think we should call the police?'

Everyone shook their heads. 'Jess, it's too soon,' Madeleine said. 'He's a grown man, and unless we have proof that he's missing, the police won't do anything. Not yet.' She paused and looked at Bandit as though searching for the words.

'Maddie's right. Let's wait, do a few searches ourselves, and if he hasn't turned up after dinner, then we'll call them.' Bandit looked at the others. 'Right, has everyone got a mobile phone?' he asked and watched as everyone rummaged for phones.

Chapter Twenty-Nine

'Griff, come on, I'm cold and what's more I don't like these clothes, they itch like hell and they're too fucking big. Hanging off me they are. Look.' She pulled at the oversized wool skirt and jacket that Griff had bought from the charity shop and pulled a face in his direction. 'God knows who wore them before me, they've never heard of fabric softener, that's for sure.'

'Shut up, Annie. You're doing my head in and I'm trying to sleep. And stop talking bollocks. When have you ever used bloody fabric softener?' He lay back in his seat with his eyes closed, while the rain battered the rusty old van. It sounded like a million drummers all tapping all at once, and Annie wondered how on earth he could even think about sleep during such an onslaught.

'I don't think tonight is a good night, Griff. I can't grab her in there. There's far too many people about.' Annie fidgeted with her skirt. Her head was bowed and each time someone ran past with umbrella in hand, she made an attempt to hide her face with her hands. They were parked right next to the hotel, where anyone who passed could see them, and she was feeling more than nervous. 'Griff, can't we move the van? What if Bastion comes outside? What if he sees me?'

Griff sighed. 'Annie, if you hadn't noticed, there's a goddamned storm going on out there, so why the hell would he come outside?' He moved around in his seat, kicked his boots off and put his feet up on the dashboard to show his moth-holed socks. 'Anyhow. It's not all about what you want, Annie, is it? It's about what you owe me, what's rightfully mine, and what you've gotta do to put that right.

Have you got that?' he growled as he pushed his feet harder against the dash making it creak. 'And I don't give a shit if you're cold or not, we ... we are going to sit here all fucking night if we have to, so why don't you get your arse in that hotel and get her?'

Annie began to tremble. She wasn't sure whether the trembling was with the cold or with nerves and once again she leaned forward to look at the front door of the hotel, where a group of young children were all running in, hand in hand with parents and siblings. She moved uncomfortably in her seat, knowing that Griff wouldn't give her much more time to make her move, but she still wasn't sure that their plan would work. Could she really walk in there, dressed like this, dressed in a suit, pretending to be just one of the other children's mothers? Was this how a mother dressed? She shook her head as she took note of the other women who were entering the hall. Most looked as though they wore jeans, and big coats, with scarves, hats and gloves, and without exception, none wore two piece woollen suits.

'Look at them, Griff, they're not dressed like this ... and if I go out there, I'm gonna stand out a fucking mile. Besides I'll get wet, won't I?'

Griff leaned across to her and stared into her eyes and for a moment Annie thought he'd softened, that he was about to kiss her, but then she saw the flash of his flick knife as he held it up in the air. 'Get out of the fucking van and go get the fucking kid, and do it now!' he screamed and Annie scrambled to throw the door open. She had to get away from the blade and she jumped out of the van and into the pouring rain.

For a moment Annie just stood, the rain coming down in torrents, and within seconds both the wool suit and her hair were soaked. Her blouse clung to her skin and her lack of underwear became very apparent, very quickly. She took a step towards the hotel and looked up at the big oak door. It was closed and she began to wish that she'd jumped out of the van earlier while the others were going in. At least then she'd have had the opportunity to enter the hall with the other children and their parents. She placed a hand on the door, but then looked to her left, to where the tall stone mullion window stood. Through it she could see the Christmas tree, which stood sparkling in the corner of the room. It was a big tree but small in comparison to the one that stood behind her in the garden. Annie looked over to it as the rain trickled down her face. The tree that stood in the garden was at least thirty feet high with what looked to be a million sparkling lights and, for just a few seconds, Annie stared at it through the rain and thought of all the Christmases she'd missed with Lily. How if she'd been a real mother to her, they'd be looking forward to this Christmas together, and how she too might have had a Christmas tree to sit by, a real fire and all the Christmas fayre, and most of all, she thought of how many of those days she'd have got to share with Bastion.

Annie turned back towards the house and stood on her tiptoes to look in through the stone windows, to where the children all stood in a group, dressed in a red and grey uniform. Right beside them, sitting on a red and gold settee, was her Lily, who was singing along with the songs, a huge smile on her face and with Bastion and the other little girl sitting beside her. The whole scene was a picture of innocence, of happiness and a perfect Christmas. She looked back at the door and shook her head. There was no way she could walk in there and take Lily. Bastion would never allow it. She tiptoed around the building looking for another way in, another way of getting to Lily without being seen. Maybe if she could find a way in she could hide, wait for an opportunity to arise to snatch Lily, and at least she would be somewhere dry and out of the rain. She found herself looking in through a kitchen window, at a dark-skinned, rotund woman who was hugging another. The other woman was a grown up duplicate of Lily and Annie knew immediately that this girl was the daughter that Bastion had never spoken of, and the reason he'd come here with Lily.

'Okay, I've got it. Well, at least he isn't in the hospital, that's good news, isn't it?' The sound of a man's voice came from behind her and Annie quickly ducked behind a large rubbish bin, where she crouched down with her eyes closed and held her breath until he'd walked past and entered the Hall by a back door. She sat behind the bin, on the floor in the mud, not caring how wet or dirty she became. After all being in the gutter was what she'd become used to; being socially unacceptable was normal to her and living in fear was a fact of life. Today would be no different. She knew that Griff had already flashed the blade and he wouldn't hesitate to use it, should he decide to. Her eyes went to a greenhouse, to the woods that stood beyond and she wondered how easily she could escape, how far she would get on a cold winter's night in high heels and a soaked wool suit.

She shook her head knowing that she wouldn't get far. Besides, what was the point? Somehow she had to get back to London, somehow she had to get back to her stash of drugs and somehow she had to keep Griff sweet until she did.

Chapter Thirty

Jess sat in the kitchen, waiting. She pursed her lips, tapped her fingernails on the oak table and kept looking at her watch as the minutes slowly ticked by.

'Oh, Nomsa, I can't just sit here, I should be out looking for him,' she said as Nomsa once again turned to the sink, filled the kettle and placed it to boil. It was what Nomsa did. In times of great happiness or sadness, she always put the kettle on, she always made tea and like a proper mother hen, she always looked after everyone around her.

'Now, now, my girl. You know it's best that you're here, you should be waiting for him when he gets back.' Nomsa tried to smile, but the smile didn't quite reach as far as her eyes and her normal sparkle just wasn't there, making Jess realise how frightened for Jack she was. 'I haven't known your daddy that long, but what I do know is that if it was him who was missing, I'd be waiting here for him when he got back.'

Jess smiled at the sentiment. It made her happy that Nomsa and her father seemed to be getting on so well. And she was pleased for Nomsa too, she deserved a little love and it was good that she'd finally met someone to share the buckets full she had to offer in return.

'Besides, the others are out looking and you know they won't come home without him, don't you?' She paused and lifted the steaming hot kettle from the range. 'Now, how about a nice cup of tea?' She poured the water into the teapot and gave it a stir before Jess had time to answer.

Jess held back the tears. She had to believe that Nomsa was right and had to hope that Jack would be home sooner, rather than later. Closing her eyes, she listened to the sound from the grand hall, where the local schoolchildren were once again practising their Christmas carols. It was their final practise before Christmas Eve, when half the village would descend upon the Hall and the Christmas festivities would begin.

'Seriously, Nomsa, I'm sorry, but if I drink another cup of tea, I swear I'll drown in it.' She moved position and turned towards the door. 'I should have known something was wrong. I should have realised he was missing the minute he didn't turn up for the ... appointment. Why ... why didn't I realise?'

'Honey, you really can't blame yourself.' Nomsa pulled open the fridge door. 'Why don't you try and eat something?'

'I can't eat, not yet. If anything has happened to him, I'll never forgive myself.' It was true, she wouldn't. She should have known that Jack wouldn't just disappear. Not like this, not on purpose. She hadn't questioned him when he'd left early that morning and now she wished she had. If only she'd asked what he was doing, where he was going and then, when he hadn't turned up to go to the hospital, she'd have known where to look, rather than just cursing him and going without him.

'Where are the girls?' Jess asked as she fiddled with the cup of tea. 'Do you think Bastion is well enough to keep an eye on them both? I mean, he still isn't well, is he?' She stood up and paced up and down the room. 'Nomsa, I know Bandit put you in charge of keeping me sane, but I'm literally going crazy sitting here. I really need to do something.' She turned and grabbed her coat.

She peered through the crack in the kitchen door into the grand hall to see around twenty children in school uniform singing 'When Santa Got Stuck Up The Chimney', and on the settee beside them were Poppy and Lily, who were both singing along and joining in with the actions. Bastion was watching them both, a huge smile spread across his face.

Jess turned away and pulled on her coat. She walked across the kitchen and went to open the back door, but Nomsa spun around on the spot and shook her head. 'Jess, don't.' She walked to the window and peered out. 'I think …'

'What is it?' Jess asked as she fastened her coat.

'I don't know. I … I … well, I thought I saw someone looking through the window.' She picked up a frying pan, and moved towards the back door, just as it opened and Bandit walked in. They looked at one another, laughed, and Nomsa placed the pan back on its rack.

'What on earth were you going to do, Nomsa? Whack the bad guys with the frying pan?' Jess stopped laughing and sat back down, placing a protective hand on her stomach.

'Maybe I'm being a bit sensitive, but I'd still rather you didn't go out there, my girl. And yes, if I had to protect you, I sure as hell would have whooped them with my pan.' Nomsa placed a loving hand on Jess's shoulder. 'Especially now, especially with you being in the family way.'

They locked eyes and a half-smile crossed Jess's lips. It was obvious that Nomsa had guessed and she wanted to jump up and down, celebrate her baby, but couldn't, not until Jack was found. The tears that had been threatening now filled her eyes and she felt Nomsa pull her into a hug.

'There, there, my girl, you let those tears fall.'

But Jess couldn't cry. Her whole body felt numb and broken. It was as though they were once again reliving the past, but this time it was Jack that was missing, not Madeleine and not her.

'Maddie has been onto the hospitals in Scarborough, Bridlington and Whitby and checked with the A & E departments there,' Bandit told Jess and Nomsa. 'Jack hasn't been admitted to any of them, so that's good news, isn't it?' He smiled.

'At least we know he isn't in the hospital, don't we?' Nomsa replied. 'Now, how long shall we wait before we phone the police?'

'I don't know. I've scoured the woods and there's no sign of him. Maddie said we should wait but, to be honest, this is so out of character for Jack that I think we should phone them soon.' He started to take off his coat. 'They'll be a bit reluctant to do anything. They won't see it as an emergency. Not yet.' He took a mug of steaming hot tea from Nomsa. 'And even if we call them tonight, they probably won't do anything till morning.'

Jess stood up. 'Nomsa, I'm sorry. I know you don't want me to go out there, but I have to. I just have to go and look for him. I have to do something.' She walked to the door. 'I have my phone. I won't go far.'

'Jess ... please, don't,' Nomsa pleaded, but Bandit stepped forward and put a finger to his lips.

'Let her go,' he said and winked at Jess. 'It's too hard for her to just sit around. She needs something to do. Something to concentrate on.'

Chapter Thirty-One

Jack shivered relentlessly in the darkness. He'd lost all feeling in his toes and his arms and his shoulders were in agony as he pulled himself up what was left of the steps, one at a time. He licked his dry lips, and his stomach rumbled fiercely. It had been hours since he'd drank anything, and much longer since he'd eaten. The pain still tore through his leg and he tried to manoeuvre himself, millimetre by millimetre, all the while pulling himself along in an attempt to get up the stairs, and all the while thinking about Lily. He wasn't sure if the parts of the staircase that remained were strong enough to take his weight, or whether by climbing up them he'd end up crashing back down to the floor, causing even more damage to himself than he already had. He thought about the obvious break to his leg, the blood that still oozed out from his ankle and wondered if it should hurt more or less as time went on? Had he severed nerves? Was that why he seemed to feel less and less or was it that his body was blocking out the pain?

Jack knew that he'd been drifting in and out of consciousness for the last couple of hours and feared that with each movement up the staircase he'd once again drift off and fall. He'd been a boy scout, he'd done first-aid courses and had been taught that both blood loss and shock could be fatal, as could falling from a height onto a concrete floor.

He thought of Jess, of how she'd be coping. A tear fell down his face at the thought of what he'd already put her through and he began to hate himself for having come here without her, without telling her and for not being there for her ... again. He let out a huge sigh. 'Damn it ...' He'd failed to attend the scan. Jess would have had to go alone. 'I'm so sorry,' he whispered into the darkness.

'Why did I come here alone? At least if Jess had been here when the accident happened she could have gone for help. That was what I should have done and how it should have been.' He mentally kicked himself with his injured leg. 'I'm so, so, stupid. We should have been doing it all together.' He thought of the scan, how proud he'd have felt and how he and Jess should have been holding hands, smiling and meeting their baby. Had she cried when she'd seen it? Had she hated him for not being there and had she gone shopping without him?

Desperation led to Jack finding a new energy from deep within himself. He found himself taking huge gulps of air. He knew that he had to pull himself up those last few steps, but knew it would be agony. He counted down from ten, and then, using his arms, he pulled himself upwards as hard as he could. One step, then the next. The pain shot through him, he screamed and he stared up at his coat that now hung only millimetres from his face. His hand went downwards in an attempt to assess any further damage to his leg, but all he felt was pain. It was a new, severe, throbbing pain that shot upwards from his foot and into his groin. For a while he couldn't move and a new fear took over him. What if he managed to get to the top of the stairs, and still couldn't get to Jess?

'You've got to keep going,' he told himself. 'For Jess. For the baby and, most importantly, you have to save Lily.' Jess, baby, Lily became his mantra as he managed to drag himself out of the cellar and through into the kitchen. He looked up at the unit where he knew his mobile was and tried to reach for it, but the unit was too high and there was no way he could stand. His only option was to keep dragging himself over the floor and within minutes he was outside and in the farmyard, where the rain poured and a rough, gravel pathway led through the yard and towards the Hall. He grabbed at everything he could to pull himself along, all the while thinking of how a baby would learn to crawl, how it too would feel every piece of gravel under its knees and he made a mental note to lay a proper pathway, something that wouldn't be so cruel to a baby's delicate skin. In fact the whole house would need to be made safe, he couldn't risk either Jess or his baby ever getting hurt.

'Come on, focus,' he screamed as he wiped the rain from his face and launched himself out of the yard and onto the cold, wet, woodland floor, with his body moving in more of a shuffle than a crawl through the ever increasing mud, exposed tree roots and sodden leaves that covered the ground. He'd initially lain on his stomach, but dragging his injured leg behind him through the house had been far too painful and the pain had hindered his speed, so now, after a few practised movements, he was more on his bottom, with his injured leg hooked over his other. This gave his leg just enough support to be able to move and with Lily in danger, he felt that his own pain was secondary and that he had to keep going at all costs.

'Heeeeelp, I need heeeeelp!' he screamed as he grabbed at the undergrowth, which squelched in his hands. He felt around for anything that would help, and ended up pulling at the tree roots and fence posts, all of which were cold and covered in ice. Every inch of Jack's body shivered as he screamed, 'Jess, Bandit!' His throat was dry and painful but he continued to scream, 'Come on, anyone!'

He closed his eyes and took deep breaths in an attempt to focus his pain, which shot through every inch of his back and legs. He swallowed hard. The Hall still seemed to be a long way away, but he could see it in the distance and he concentrated on its shape as it loomed before him. He thought of the Christmas lights that would be twinkling through the windows, and how welcoming they would look once he got closer. 'One, two …' He tried counting out each pull on his arms, military-style, and wished he'd known some of Bandit's old marine songs. He kept counting, pulling and moving towards where Jess would be waiting and where he prayed that Lily would be safe. He hoped the others would have kept her close, prayed that for once she and Poppy had played in their rooms, or had sat in Nomsa's kitchen, baking and eating their wares.

Just the thought of Griff hurting Lily gave him a strength and determination he didn't know he had. He couldn't bear the thought of what the man might do. He'd mentioned selling her and Jack didn't even want to think about what that meant. The only thing he could do was try and raise the alarm.

'One, two, pull … heeeelp! … One, two, pull … heeeeelp! …' He could feel his energy failing; his whole body screamed to stop, his mind went blank and for a few moments he closed his eyes as he felt his breathing become slow and shallow. 'Come on, Jack, don't stop now, come on.' He tried to find the energy he needed; he had to get to the Hall, and to Jess. He looked up. The Hall was there, he could see it, but it was still such a long way from him. But he had to get there, he just had to.

Chapter Thirty-Two

It was the sound that Jess heard first. It was a long drawn out wail, almost animalistic, like a wounded fox, cat, or badger, crying for help. She stopped on the track, spun around and squinted as she stared through the rain and into the woods for what seemed like an eternity. She wasn't quite sure which direction the noise had come from and she cursed the winter, which had left the woodland bare so that every noise echoed and bounced off the trees all at once.

She couldn't decide what to do. Did she move forward, to one side or the other, or did she do what most sensible people would do and run back to the safety of the Hall? After all an injured animal could be dangerous and attack, especially if she came upon it suddenly and frightened it. She was torn, but couldn't bear the thought of leaving it to suffer, not all alone, not in the darkness.

Pulling her anorak tightly around her body, Jess stood as still as she could, and listened again, but heard nothing, not until her ringtone suddenly rang out, filling the woodland ironically with *The Lion King*'s 'Circle Of Life'.

'Hey, Maddie, what is it?' Using her torch, she began inching her way forward along the line of the fence until she reached the end of the track and then turned to walk through the woodland. Some people would be scared of being out there alone in the dark, but this was a path she'd walked often during the daylight, and she felt comfort in the fact that she knew the area well and that the lights of the Hall could easily be seen in the distance.

'Jess, Bandit's just told me you are outside searching. Please come back to the Hall. I don't like you being out there, not alone. Isn't it bad enough that Jack's missing, without you going missing too?' Madeleine spoke in a whisper and Jess held the phone tightly to her ear, her torch shining into the distance. 'The schoolkids are all finished, they're going now, so why don't you come back and help me with the girls?'

'Help do what? Give them a bath, put them to bed?' Jess paused; again a noise came from the distance. 'Jack's missing, Maddie, I'm sure the girls can manage without a bath for one night.'

She heard Maddie sigh. 'Okay, okay, I'll ask your father to see to Lily.'

Again Jess stood still and thought of the words she'd just said, 'your father'. She liked the sound of it, but realised that since Bastion had arrived, she hadn't really allowed herself to get to know him, not that well. She still hadn't asked him to take the DNA test, but didn't really understand why. Was she worried that he really wasn't her father? Was she frightened that he'd leave? She thought for a moment and looked into the darkness where all she could see was the rain coming down. She didn't want Bastion to leave, she really wanted him to be her father and what's more she wanted her baby to have a grandfather.

'Jess,' came Madeleine's voice. 'Are you there?'

'Yes.'

'Jess, I really think you should come back, it isn't safe out there.'

Jess ignored Maddie's words and shone her torch one last time into the distance, paused and squinted. There was something there, she could see something moving. She took a step towards it, but then saw a feral cat run past, a field mouse held firmly in its mouth.

'So, are you coming back?' Madeleine asked again.

'Yeah, sure. I'm on my way.' She clicked the phone off, put it back in her pocket and turned to walk back through the darkness towards the Hall.

It was then she once again heard the strangulated sound. 'Jeeeessssssssssssss, heeeeeelp!'

She stopped, waited, listened. 'J- ... J- ... Jack ... Jack is ... is that you?' She spun on the spot, still unable to distinguish where the sound had come from. 'Where ... where are you? Jack?' She dug in her pocket, dragged out her mobile, punched at the keys and rang Madeleine back.

'Maddie, Maddie ... please, he's here. It's Jack. I can hear him ... I heard him scream, please, Maddie, he's in the woods. Get everyone, bring them all, head towards the farmhouse.' She clicked off the phone and began to scour the woodland floor with her torch. 'Come on, Jack. Where are you?' She ran forward, stopped, listened and then ran a few paces more. 'Jack, come on, please, please make a noise, I know it was you.'

Her foot caught on a tree root, making her trip and she landed heavily on her hands and knees. The torch fell to the ground and there in the torchlight was Jack's contorted, tear-stained face.

'Jess ... Jess ...' His words were laboured; he could barely speak, but somehow he managed to flop onto his back. 'Get back to the Hall. It's Lily ... Lily ... danger. She's here ... her mother ... she's here ... d- ... d- ... danger.'

Jess crawled through the grass until she pulled herself close to him. His whole body felt like ice. She knew he was badly hurt and she quickly pulled her coat off, covered his body and held him close. 'You're so cold, Jack. I ... I need to get you warm.'

'Get ... to Lily,' he once again spat out as his body suddenly began to shake violently with cold and pain, but Jess could now hear a commotion coming from the direction of the Hall. Torches lit up the grounds and headed towards her.

'They're coming, Jack.' Tears rolled down her face. 'Hold on, Jack. They're coming, they're going to help you.'

'Nooooo, go back … Lily … danger.'

It was at that moment that Jack went silent, and Jess screamed. 'Jack … Jack … talk to me … Jack, please, please, you have to talk to me.' A huge sob left her throat as she saw the torches come closer. 'Bandit, quickly, he's over here. Maddie, help him … please God help him!' She rocked his slumped body in her arms. 'Don't do this, Jack. Please don't you dare do this to me, not now!'

She felt herself being dragged away, heard the sound of Bandit screaming instructions and then she felt herself floating. It was like watching everything happening in the distance, almost like a dream with muffled noise and a numbness that didn't happen in reality. She couldn't move, couldn't breathe, couldn't take in what was happening.

'You're okay, Jess. You're okay, I've got you, my darling girl.' She heard Bastion's voice beside her and she sank into his arms. She felt them surround her, strong, meaningful and warm, just like she'd always imagined a father's arms would feel. She closed her eyes in the hope that when they opened, everything would be okay. That it would all have been a dream, one in which she was still being hugged by her father, but in much nicer surroundings. She took in a deep breath and the fog began to clear and then she heard the noise, the screaming of instructions and Bastion was still there, still hugging her … But if he was hugging her, who was with Lily?

'Oh, my God, Lily. We have to get to Lily. I don't know what he meant, but Jack, he was trying to say something … before … before he … he said she was in danger. Said her mother was here.' She felt Bastion's arms let her go, and she watched as he turned and ran back to the hotel. Anchorless, she began to float in a sea of uncertainty while Bandit continued to work on Jack; his body was over his, his hands were on his chest. 'One and two and three and four,' came Bandit's voice as he administered compressions and CPR to her Jack.

She turned to see a crowd in front of the Hall. Staff and guests had all come to help, but now there was nothing they could do, except watch, hug and cry. And there in the middle of them was Nomsa, with Poppy holding one hand and Lily safely holding the other. She saw Bastion run up to them, pull Lily into his arms and take hold of Nomsa's hand.

Jess forced herself to look back at where Bandit continued to work on Jack and again the fog descended, making her drop to the floor. She scrambled over the wet woodland ground on her hands and knees, eager to be by his side. 'Bandit, please ... please, I'm begging you, please don't let him die!' she screamed. Her hand went out to touch Jack's cheek. 'He ... he's so cold.' She looked up and into Bandit's eyes. 'Why is he so cold? I ... I have ... I have to get him warm, that'll help, right?' She didn't wait for an answer, but lay beside Jack and curled herself into the side of his lifeless body. 'I ... I can't lose you now, Jack, I just can't. We need you ... your baby and I, we need you.' She looked up at Bandit. 'Please, please promise me ... he isn't going to die, is he?'

But the measured look that Bandit gave her was one that made no promises. She knew he'd seen this before, knew he'd battled to save lives on more than one occasion when he'd been in the marines and knew that he wouldn't stop until all hope was lost.

'They're here.' She heard a shout from the crowd. 'The ambulance, it's here.'

Jess could see blue flashing lights in the distance. They sped through the grounds and screeched to a halt. She got back on her knees and her hand went to Jack's ice-cold forehead, and she kissed his mud-covered cheek. 'Jack, please, listen to me, I'm begging you, you have to try, you have to stay with me, you have to live, they're coming to help you, Jack. They're … they're coming …'

Chapter Thirty-Three

'Get in there,' Griff bellowed, his voice so loud that Annie was sure half the motel with its paper-thin walls would have heard him. 'I've never known anyone as stupid as you.'

Annie felt Griff throw her against the bed. 'You can't blame me, Griff. When I left you in the car park I saw Lily, she was sitting in that big hall with Bastion and that other little 'un, listening to a load of brats murdering Christmas carols and then I went to have a look around, tried to find another way in. I looked through the kitchen window but a woman, she spotted me and I had to run. I went in the hotel I did, right into the entrance and I waited in the corridor next to the reception, I was waiting for my chance, honest.'

'Spare me the details,' Griff growled, pacing the floor. 'Why the fuck didn't you just grab her?'

'Bastion was with her and I couldn't get near. Then the kids stopped singing and people started leaving and then all hell broke loose. People were shouting and I thought they were coming for me so I bolted and ran into the ladies' loos. When it quietened down, I went out again and there was Lily standing alone by the front door. I called to her and she turned and saw me ... but then the woman from the kitchen grabbed her hand and ran outside with her and I couldn't have predicted what happened next, could I?' She tugged at the over-sized skirt suit. 'I even got changed into this, your idea of looking respectable, and now look, I'm covered in mud. I had no choice but to get out of there, the whole place was surrounded by fucking blues and twos, wasn't it?' She pulled a packet of cigarettes from her bag. 'Give us a light, Griff.'

'Fuck off, Annie, get your own.' His hand lifted in the

air and for a moment Annie thought that he would strike her. He grabbed her collar, lifted her to her feet and then threw her backwards, where she landed on the floor beside the bed.

Annie shook with fear. She knew Griff could get mad, knew he was capable of anything and right now while she lay on the floor, she wasn't sure what was on his mind.

She watched as he paced up and down the threadbare carpet. All the while growling, grumbling and cursing. 'Right, here's what we'll do.' He stopped to think. 'I heard some parents talking as they got into their car and they said there was going to be a big celebration on Christmas Eve, with fucking Santa arriving and all the kids singing round the bloody Christmas tree out the front. That's when we'll grab the little bitch. I've got business in London but I'll be back in a couple of days. Then we go to that hotel and you ... you will get the girl, you got that?' He leaned in so close that Annie held her breath, waiting for the blow to land. 'Till then, you stay here and lie low. Here.' He threw a rolled up piece of cling film towards her. 'That'll tide you over and you can earn the money you need for food.' He pulled the curtain back and looked out at the car park. 'I'll finalise the sale of the bitch for Christmas Eve. She'll make a nice little Christmas present for someone.'

Annie watched as Griff stormed through the door. She then waited until the van disappeared round the corner. She needed help, needed someone to come and get her and she closed her eyes for a moment wondering who she could ask, but shook her head. There was no one. She used to be someone, she used to have friends, important, rich friends. She'd been a high-class escort who they'd all requested for their dates. She'd been at the top of her game and she'd had respect. She sobbed. No one respected her now, no one would be there to help her if she called and there was no one she would class as a true friend, not now, not any more. She stood up and looked in the mirror. 'What happened to you, Annie? How did you turn out this way?' She looked down at her arms and sighed. 'Yeah, that'd be what did it,' she whispered to herself as she walked back to where the cling film-wrapped stash of drugs lay.

Chapter Thirty-Four

Jess drifted in and out of sleep but eventually her eyes flicked open and all her senses kicked in at once. The sound of the constant bleep, bleep, bleep of the monitor, the smell of antiseptic, the bright lights that filled the room and the feel of crisp, white cotton sheets beneath her face made her remember where she was.

She wanted nothing more than to sleep. Sleep was good; at least when she slept the fear went away. But then she felt guilty for relaxing, especially while Jack was hanging onto life by a thread. Right through the night she'd kept snapping her eyes open and, each time she did, she realised where she was and the memory of the night before flooded back: Bandit and the paramedics hovering over Jack's body, Jack fading away and her begging him to live. It all came back, along with the palpitations that relentlessly took over her body.

She looked at where Jack still slept, looked at the green line that jumped up and down on the monitor screen, then back to where his right leg was raised and covered in plaster. She still had no idea how he'd managed to drag himself so far, not with the injuries he'd sustained. The surgeon had said he'd never worked on someone who'd not only snapped his Achilles, but had also broken both his leg and his ankle so badly and in so many places. He'd lost far too much blood, he'd gone into shock and with the added exertion of dragging himself through the woods, his whole body had shut down in the most dramatic way. If Bandit hadn't been there, if he hadn't given him the first aid he'd needed, if he hadn't kept going when others might have stopped, then Jack would have died and the night may well have ended in a very different way.

She took in a deep breath, and then wished she hadn't, as the smell of the hospital antiseptic once again filled her nostrils. Her stomach turned, just as it had most mornings since her pregnancy and she jumped up quickly, ran to the sink and retched. She stared into the mirror and noticed the dark circles around her eyes, and grabbed a glass, ran the water and poured herself a drink.

Gulping down the water, she turned. Jack was looking at her. 'I'm so … so … sorry,' he whispered, making Jess run back to the side of the bed.

'Oh, Jack. You're awake.' The tears that she'd held onto since the night before began flooding down her face. 'I've … I've been so scared.'

His hand reached out to touch her face. 'I'm so sorry, I wasn't … I wasn't there for you … for the scan.'

'Don't … don't you dare be sorry. Oh my God, do you know what you did?' She grabbed his hand and kissed his fingers. 'Shall I get a nurse? Are you okay, do you hurt anywhere?'

Jack shook his head. 'No, don't. I … I just want to … Lily, is she safe?'

Jess smiled. 'Lily is safe, don't worry.' Her eyes searched his face. 'Jack, I love you so much.'

'I tried, I tried to get … Oh, Jess, I didn't get to the Hall, did I?' He tried to lift his head from the pillow, but immediately dropped it back down. 'Ouch!' he yelled. 'Damn, that hurts.'

Jess shook her head. 'Don't, don't move. And, no, you didn't get to the Hall. But I promise you, Nomsa and Bastion haven't let Lily out of their sight, not for a minute since last night.'

'But …' Jack began to cough.

'Wait, I'll get you some water.' Jess returned to the sink, picked up the water and came back to hold it to Jack's lips. 'Not too much,' she said as the water wet his lips.

'I was at the farmhouse, in the cellar, and they were there, Lily's mother Annie and some thug named Griff. I heard what they were going to do, they said … said something about taking her, about selling her …' He coughed and took another sip of water. 'When they left I rushed up the steps … they collapsed … I couldn't move, my leg was trapped and … What if …' It was obvious that Jack was struggling to speak, and Jess picked up the alarm, wondering if she should press it and alert the nurse. 'Jess, what if they'd got Lily?'

Jess didn't know what to say. 'The police, they're looking for them …' She lied with the need to calm Jack down, wanting him to relax, but it occurred to her that no one had known what Jack had meant when he'd said that Lily had been in danger. Jess quickly searched for her phone; she needed to get hold of Bastion, tell him that Jack was awake, and what he'd said and made an excuse to leave the room momentarily. 'I'll be two minutes,' she explained as she lifted the phone to her ear, 'I just need to speak to Maddie.'

Jack looked satisfied with the explanation and closed his eyes. The medication was almost certainly making him tired. 'I'm sorry I didn't make it to the scan.' He sighed. 'I really, really wanted to go to the scan.'

Jess allowed another tear to fall down her face as she completed the call and the quickly made her way back to Jack, where she leaned forward to rummage in her bag. 'Here, it's here, Jack. The scan, it's here.' She held up the picture. 'Meet our baby.' She watched as he opened his eyes and welled up as he fixed on the picture. 'Isn't it just the most beautiful thing?'

Jack once again tried to sit up, but couldn't.

Jess nodded. 'It's so beautiful, Jack. Can you imagine, a tiny little baby, our baby?' She paused and looked thoughtful. 'You'll be the best and most protective daddy, ever,' Jess said as she flicked her hair back from her face and locked eyes with the man she loved. There was no doubt in her mind that she and Jack would be happy, and that they'd have their happy ever after, but what she didn't understand was … 'Jack, what were you doing at the farmhouse?'

Jack shook his head from side to side. 'Oh Jess, it's a long, long story. But in short, it's ours. The farmhouse is ours. Emily left it to us.'

Jess sat back in her chair. 'What? Why … I mean … oh my God, we have a house.' The words were more of a question than a statement. She blinked and stared into Jack's face. 'Are you sure?'

Jack tried to look around the room. 'My trousers, where are they?' He slumped back against the pillows.

'The paramedics, they cut them off.' Jess took hold of his hand. 'Why?'

'The letter, the letter that Emily wrote, it explains it all. You have to read it.' Jack closed his eyes and Jess heard his breathing change as he fell back into a deep sleep.

Letting go of his hand Jess walked across and picked up the clear plastic bag that the paramedics had given her. It contained Jack's other clothes along with the contents of what had been in his pockets. She immediately spotted the letter that Emily had written and pulled it out of the bag and began to read.

Chapter Thirty-Five

Bastion turned the key in the door, then stood in the doorway of Jess's room. 'It feels wrong to come in here without her,' he said as he stood nervously holding the door open while Nomsa moved swiftly around the room, filling a bag.

'We have to be in here. Jess asked us to get things for Jack. Now, go in the bathroom and make yourself useful. Jack needs his shaving things, toothbrush and deodorant. You can see to bathroom stuff, I'll see to his clothes and underwear.'

The room was bright and tidy and his eyes were immediately drawn to the Moses basket that stood in the corner. 'Mmmm, the boy did good, didn't he?' He walked to the basket and stroked the material. 'He told me he was going to do this and I'm sure glad he did. Our Jess will be happy with it, that's for sure.'

Nomsa turned and put her arms around his waist. 'Oh, Bastion, I think she'd be even happier if all else was in place. She's had one hell of a time of it lately and I think she'd like to be certain of the people around her.' She stared into his eyes, reached up and kissed him firmly on the lips. 'You know what I'm saying. She really wants to believe you're her daddy.'

'I am her daddy, Nomsa. I'm one hundred per cent sure of that.' He kissed her back, stepped away and went into the bathroom. 'Shaving things, right. Got them, toothbrush, I'm guessing on the blue one and not the pink.' He glanced over his shoulder, opened the bathroom cabinet and saw the DNA test that stood on a shelf within. He'd known that Jess had been planning on sending for it, she'd asked if he minded doing it, but he hadn't realised it had arrived. 'Now, now, what do we have here?' He held it out to Nomsa. 'Looks like she already did her part of it,' he said as he looked in the box and lifted out the sterile tube that had been sealed in a bag. 'So ...'

Nomsa smiled. 'So ... Are you going to do your part?' She squeezed his hand.

'Do you think I should?' He began turning the box over and over in his hands. 'Why do you think she didn't ask me to do it? I said I would, I'd told her I didn't mind.'

'Well, you two haven't really got to know each other too well yet, so maybe she didn't know how to.' Nomsa stood, folding clothes. 'Now, I've got pyjamas, they look quite new so I don't think our Jack normally wears them, no sir. And I've got him some boxer shorts and I've got socks. He sure won't want cold feet, will he?' She paused. 'Well, maybe I'll only pack one pair as he can only use a sock on his good foot at the moment, right?'

Bastion watched as she pushed the garments into the bag. 'Do you think it would be right to do this, without her knowing? I mean, I'm happy to do it, if you think I should,' he said as he continued to turn the box over and over in his hands.

Nomsa nodded. 'Of course it'd be fine, honey. She only bought it with one thing in mind and, if I'm honest, she wouldn't be the only happy lady around here if it turned out that you really were our Jess's daddy.' She blushed, and moved away.

'And what do you mean by that?'

Nomsa laughed. 'Well, being her daddy would kind of give you a reason to stay, now wouldn't it?'

Bastion sighed. Nomsa was such a good woman, he'd never met anyone like her and he wished he'd met her years before. Maybe if he had, they'd have had their own family;

232

maybe Lily would have had a mother figure in her life from the beginning. He had so wished for that for his daughter. Lily had so many questions, so many needs, and he tried his best to meet them but he knew that he struggled each and every day. He also knew that it would only get more difficult as she grew and turned from child to woman.

He watched Nomsa as she stood by the window, her hand nervously shaking as she waited for his response. 'Nomsa.' He walked up behind her, turned her around and placed a hand on her shoulder. 'You know I want to stay here, right? You've made me the happiest I've been for years and I don't want to throw this away.' He pulled her towards him, and breathed in deep. He could smell the musky depths of her perfume. 'Oh, wow, woman, you don't half smell good,' he said with a laugh. 'Do you know that? You smell far too good. And that alone is enough to make a man want to stay forever.'

Nomsa pushed him away. 'Go on with you, all that mushy talk, you'll have me thinking you're liking me and we don't want that now, do we?' Again she turned away and for a few seconds he stayed quiet.

'You, my good lady, have no idea how much I like you. I more than like you, I'm crazy for you and you know what? I really want to stick around; I really do. I just wish I had more to offer you, but you wait, I will. I'll prove to you that I'm a good man and that I can work and support you.' He walked up behind her and put his arms around her waist, nuzzled in behind her neck and placed a kiss there. 'I know I'm Jess's daddy, but I'll prove that to you too. I'll take the test. I'll even walk down to the post office and post it myself.'

He pulled the tube from the box and began reading the instructions while Nomsa watched with interest. 'Seems like I have to rub this around my mouth, against the cheek for thirty seconds.' He smiled. 'Do you have a stop watch?'

Nomsa nodded. 'I sure do, I have one on my phone.' She pulled the mobile out of her apron pocket and began flicking the buttons.

'Well then, you'd better set it going … now,' he said as he pushed the swab into his mouth and began rubbing it against his cheeks.

Chapter Thirty-Six

Jess stood in the middle of the grand hall and looked out of the window towards the huge outdoor Christmas tree, which sparkled with thousands of lights. Saying that she was happy was an understatement. It was Christmas Eve, five days since Jack had had the accident and already he'd been released from hospital. For the first time in her life, Jess was about to spend Christmas with not only the man she loved, but also the man she truly believed to be her father, as well as her younger sister.

'The villagers will be here soon, are we ready?' she asked as she glanced over her shoulder to where Jack sat in his wheelchair, leg outstretched, clipboard in hand. He'd insisted that he didn't want to go to bed. 'I've done nothing but sleep for days,' he'd said and had immediately gone back into his management role, taking charge of bossing everyone around as he went up and down his tick list.

'Yes, I think we're ready for the villagers,' he said as he ticked the last item. 'Food, tick. Tree, tick. Dance floor, tick. Balloons, champagne and fluted glasses, tick, tickety tick.' He smiled as Jess went to swipe him with her hand. 'Okay, did we organise the DJ?'

Jess realised she'd forgotten to ring the DJ as Madeleine had asked her to do a few days before and quickly ran to the phone.

'See, you were laughing at my tick list earlier,' Jack said as he tapped his pen against the arm of the wheelchair. 'But you're not laughing now, are you?' He pulled a face, making Jess laugh. She'd been so sure that he'd die, so sure that she'd lost him that now any face that he wished to pull would only remind her of how lucky she was that she was able to see it.

'Stop it, or you will be sent back to bed,' she teased. 'Where you should be.' She went to the back of his chair and began to push him through the grand hall. 'Doctor said you needed to rest and only if you rest will you get better. In fact, I really don't think they'd have even let you out if it wasn't almost Christmas and if you hadn't been such a pain in the ass to the nurses. They were probably glad to be rid of you.'

'Jess, I'm alive. And they let me out of hospital because I begged them to let me go. I hated it in there.' Again he gave her a smile. 'And the last thing I want is to be in bed for the whole of Christmas. Besides, there are things to do.' He looked smug. 'I've always organised Christmas at the Hall. It's my job.'

'You still need to do what the doctor said.' Jess tried to sound forceful. 'And what's more, you have to do what I say, oh father of my child.'

A commotion could be heard on the staircase and Jess spun the wheelchair around on the spot to see both Lily and Poppy running down the stairs.

'Aunty Jess, the bus is coming up the drive, all the people, they're coming and do you know what?' shouted Poppy. 'Mummy says that Santa will come too.'

'Ohhh, is that right?' Jess questioned. 'But … Santa only comes to good little girls, isn't that right, Jack?'

Jack had already grabbed hold of Poppy; his fingers were wiggling around in the air and Poppy was jumping on his knee, wrapping her arms around his neck and covering him in kisses, before screaming as Jack's hands got closer and closer to tickling her. 'And you, Lily. You're next,' he shouted as he set to work tormenting Poppy.

Lily ran up the stairs and hid her face behind the balustrade. 'Jess, Santa, he will know where to find me, won't he?' she asked, making both Jack and Jess gasp.

'Oh, Lily. Come here, poppet.' Jess sat on the bottom step of the staircase. 'Of course, he'll know where you are,' she said as she pulled the child into her arms. She knew that Lily was feeling insecure. She'd been withdrawn for the last few days since Annie had shown up, and, after what Jack had overheard, everyone in the Hall had been on edge just in case she came back.

'I wasn't sure, but then, Mummy found me, didn't she?' Lily looked up with her saucer-wide eyes and Jess noticed how her bottom lip quivered.

'Mummy didn't exactly find you, honey.' Jess looked to Jack for support, not knowing what else to say, but then watched as the child physically shrank before her.

'Jess, I … I lied.' A sob left her throat. 'The day me and Poppy got locked in the cellar, it was because I saw Mummy. She was there, in the trees, trying to get me and we ran to the house to hide. Then she came here the night Jack was hurt. I saw her hiding in the corridor near the toilets. Do you think she'll come back, Jess? Do you think the police will catch her?'

Jess spun to look at Jack, before turning back to Lily. 'Oh, Lily, my darling girl, don't you worry about that. She won't come back. Not if I have anything to do with it.' Jess didn't know what else to say. 'If she does, then our Jack here, he'll run her over with his wheelchair, won't you, Jack?' She tried to make light of the situation, knowing that an eight-year-old girl should never have to worry, and her mind went back to that first night she'd slept with Lily, how she'd tossed and turned with nightmares that a child should never have.

'I heard Bandit on the phone,' Lily continued. 'He said Mummy was going to take me away, that Jack had overheard her. That she was going to sell me.' She sighed. 'Why would she do that, Jess? She's never really wanted me before, so I guess it makes sense that she'd sell me to someone who did.'

Lily's voice was full of emotion and Jess felt her heart break for the child. She knew she had to be strong for Lily's sake, but for a moment she didn't know what to do or say and she watched as Lily curled up in a ball and sobbed in her arms.

Jess shook her head. 'Don't cry, princess. Life is hard. But do you know what I do when I get sad? I do something really brave, something positive. Sometimes if I'm alone, I sing a happy song, or I close my eyes and I think of those people who love me the most, does that make sense?'

Lily nodded, just as the front door opened and the promised coachload of people all began to enter the Hall, making Jess wish they'd stayed away for just a few minutes more. She reached out and took Lily's hand. 'Lily, you're my sister and we all love you so much. You're safe here, princess, I promise. Everyone here will look after you, you do know that, don't you?' She pulled her sister towards her and stroked her cheek. 'Now, you and Poppy run and get your lovely new coats. You'll need them when we go outside to wait for Santa. But first, we're going to stand by the tree and sing with the choir.'

Both girls ran back up the stairs and Jess turned to Jack who was happily shaking hands with everyone who walked past. Most had heard of his accident, and had stopped to question him about his ordeal. The grand hall soon became full of children and adults, all waiting for the carol service to begin. All Jess could do was hope she'd reassured Lily enough, hope she felt loved and that after the evidence that Jack had given, the police caught Annie, and soon.

'Right, I really think you should be resting.' Jess placed a hand on Jack's shoulder. 'It's only a few days since you were unconscious in a hospital bed and the last thing I want is for you to overdo it and end up back in hospital for Christmas. Besides, it's our wedding in just over a week, I need you fit and healthy for the wedding night.' They both looked at his leg and burst out laughing. 'That's if you can manage like that?'

Jack smirked. 'Oh, I can manage all right, don't you worry about that.' He pulled her towards him and gently pressed a kiss to her lips.

'Good, now off to bed with you.' Jess allowed her hand to linger on his shoulder and for a moment she wished that she could go to bed with him, curl up by his side and keep hold of him for hours and hours.

Jack relented. 'Okay, okay, take me to bed. I'll open the window and listen from up there.' He smiled, a wide disarming smile that melted Jess's heart.

'I wish I could come to bed with you,' she said as she pushed him through the dining room. 'But you, my darling, are going in the service lift and I'll meet you at the top of the stairs.'

Jack began to laugh. 'Well, that's the best offer I'm likely to get tonight, I guess.' He turned his head and raised an eyebrow. 'Unless of course you want to crawl in and get dirty with me later?' Jess blushed and slapped his shoulder.

'Ouch, careful,' Jack shouted. 'I'm still in pain, you have to be nice to me. It's the law.'

'Well, we'll have to see how fit and wide awake you are later,' she added as she pushed his chair forward and then laughed as the service doors closed behind him.

She watched the lift disappear upwards as the words, 'Oh, I'll be awake,' echoed down the shaft. 'And I'll be waiting.'

Chapter Thirty-Seven

Jess and Madeleine stood together outside. Their arms were linked and they rocked to and fro as the sound of 'We Wish You A Merry Christmas' rang out through the grounds of Wrea Head Hall. A hundred people all stood wrapped in coats, hats and scarves in the darkness, as they surrounded the brightly lit Christmas tree, while listening to the children's school choir. It was the event of the year and even though it was cold and the air felt damp, almost all of Scalby had turned out for the occasion.

Life was complete. Jess had Madeleine, who was not only her sister, but her rock, her support system, the one person who'd always been there for her; with the baby on the way, Jess would need her more than ever before. Jess smiled and thought of Jack up in their bed, waiting for her. The thought made her warm and happy. To top her world off, she had both a little sister and a father and they were both here at Wrea Head Hall for Christmas. Jess looked through the crowd to where Bastion stood, one hand holding Lily's, the other discreetly holding Nomsa's. They exchanged glances and even though it was early days, Jess was pleased that Nomsa had indeed finally found someone to love, a man she'd wished for and dreamed of, but somehow had never met, not until now. It wasn't surprising that she'd never met anyone before, she'd never really had the time. She was always at the Hall, even on her days off she came in and made an excuse that something needed her attention, or that she'd forgotten to do something the day before. These visits often led to her being in the kitchen for most of the day, which had always made Jess wonder how lonely she'd really have been without the Hall.

'Is Jack okay?' Madeleine asked as Poppy ran towards them. 'Do you need to go to him?'

Jess shook her head. 'No, he's fine. I put him to bed. He said he'd leave the window open and listen to the carols, but I doubt he will. He looked really tired and I'm kind of guessing that by now he'll be fast asleep.'

Poppy jumped up into her arms. 'Bandit says we're going to have pie and peas. Bernie made baby pies for me and Lily, with chicken and vegetables in them.' She looked pleased with herself that Bernie had taken the time to create her a special pie, just the right size for her and she leaned into Jess, burying her head in her hair.

The air was crisp, the sound of the carols continued, the smell of the log burners filled the air and the magic of Christmas finally began to fill the Hall. Jess couldn't remember a more perfect day and she hoped it would get better before it ended. Then, from somewhere in the distance, a jingling sound could be heard.

'Poppy, look.' She poked Poppy in the ribs and pointed to the lane, where a brightly lit sleigh appeared being pulled by six reindeer, with a jolly Santa dressed in his traditional red coat sitting at the front.

'Santa!' Poppy squealed. 'Lily, he came! Lily, come see Santa. He found you.'

Jess saw Lily turn, her face lighting up and her eyes wide and full of amazement. 'Daddy, he really came,' Jess heard her whisper as she struggled out of his grasp and together Poppy and Lily ran hand in hand towards the sleigh, along with all the other children who'd suddenly all stopped singing.

'Isn't it magical?' Jess said to Madeleine as they both walked to watch where Santa now stood, handing out gifts to the children that now surrounded him, all squealing with delight. The laughter came as much from the parents as it did from the children and a constant shout of, 'Look, Mummy, Daddy, look,' could be heard.

Jess turned to see how Nomsa had snuggled into Bastion, how they smiled and laughed, and then Bastion lifted a hand to cup her chin, making Jess gasp and prod Madeleine. 'Oh my, do you think he will?' She thought he was about to kiss Nomsa, right there in front of the tree, but Nomsa moved away and slapped his hand, and then like Bambi on ice her legs flew up and she landed heavily on her bottom. 'Oh, no!' Jess squealed as both she and Madeleine rushed to help her. 'Nomsa, are you okay?'

'Oh, I'm fine, I'm fine,' Nomsa replied. 'Nothing but my pride is hurt, though my skirt is dirty, and now look.' She pointed upward as without warning, the heavens opened. Rain began to fall in torrents, the sound of thunder filled the air, and a sudden flash of lightning lit up the sky in huge, dagger-like forks, making everyone turn and run for the Hall.

'Children, come on, please, please go inside. Santa will come to you ...' A schoolteacher's voice shouted out above the children's shrieks and they watched as they all ran to the Hall, some clutching their gifts.

'Poppy, Lily!' Jess shouted. She searched amongst the children. 'Where did they go?' She turned to Madeleine. 'Poppy, Lily, where are you?' The rain fell so fast that she could barely see where the girls had stood. For a moment she panicked, but then breathed a sigh of relief as Poppy emerged from the crowd and ran towards her and Maddie.

'Mummy, my present ... The one Santa gave me,' she sobbed as she jumped into her mother's arms. 'I ... I dropped it ...'

'Oh, honey. It just got a bit dirty that's all. Mummy will wash it for you,' Jess heard Madeleine say, but her eyes still searched for Lily. She looked back at the Hall. Had she gone back inside when Nomsa fell? How could she have lost sight of her? They all ran to the Hall, stopping just inside the entrance.

'Wow, where did that rain come from?' Madeleine shouted as Jess ran and scanned the children who now shook themselves free of the rain. But Lily was nowhere to be seen. 'Lily ... Lily!' she shouted, and she saw both Nomsa and Bastion take up the search.

Jess knelt down. 'Poppy, listen to Aunty Jess, this is important.' She stroked the wet hair out of the child's face. 'When you got your present from Santa, did Lily get one with you? I can't see her, do you know where she went?'

Poppy hugged her doll to herself and nodded. 'It's okay, Aunty Jess. Her mummy came to collect her. I think she's gone to stay at her house for Christmas.'

Chapter Thirty-Eight

Annie leaned back in the van seat and closed her eyes as the effects of the drugs took hold. She'd done it, she'd done what he'd said and she'd felt the excitement hit her when Griff had passed her a bag of crack. It had been like he'd given her a present, a treat for behaving and for doing well. And she'd wasted no time in using the stash. She drifted in and out of sleep, and for a while, her mind was content.

But somewhere in the back of her mind there were annoying sounds. First there was the thunderous weather, the banging of raindrops and the flashes of lightning, but then from somewhere behind her came the sound of a child whimpering. Annie didn't like the noise and found herself opening one eye to stare at where Lily crouched in the back of the van, on an old piece of smelly, wet carpet.

'Stop bloody snivelling,' Griff shouted, making Annie jump. She opened both of her eyes, and realised that they'd now left town and were already on the motorway. She hoped that they'd soon be back in London where she could put these past few days behind her and once again settle into the normality that was her life.

Annie observed her daughter, who stared back at her with wide open eyes. 'Stop doing that,' Annie said. 'You don't want to be annoying him, girl, he's nasty.' She didn't want to look at Lily, didn't want her accusing eyes gawking at her. What's more she certainly didn't want to think about what Griff had planned for her. She didn't care, after all, it wouldn't be her problem. Her problem was handing over the child and that was now done. Her debt was paid and now, now it was time she walked away and found a new patch to work, without a pimp. She thought about Bastion's old flat, wondered whether it was still empty and as easy to break into as it always had been. She nodded. Yes, she'd go there. She'd hide out there until after Christmas, as no one would want her services, not this week and especially now she had some crack, she had no reason to work. She shook the bag and eyed its contents; there was enough in there to last her a few days, and when she got back to London, she'd retrieve the bag of stolen drugs that she had hidden in the cellar and she'd take it with her.

The pouring rain, along with the continuous swish of the windscreen wipers and the drone of the motorway, continued to be annoying. Annie stared at the child, just to kill the boredom. The girl had stopped whimpering and now lay curled up on the van floor where she slept. She was so tiny, so perfect and Annie complimented herself on how amazing she'd been to produce a whole person who could walk and talk so cleverly. It had never really occurred to her what she'd done before. For a few moments it was as though she was thinking in slow motion, moving her mind through mud. She tried to smile, knowing that the drugs were making her lips and mouth move in an odd manner, but she didn't care. For now, she felt warm, happy and just a little content with her life.

The van jolted to a stop, crawled for a while and then quickly sped off as though nothing had happened. The monotony of the journey made her restless. The drugs had made her feel warm and sleepy and although she was now as high as she could get, she knew it wouldn't last. The drugs overwhelmed her and she had the urge to close her eyes, but she didn't dare; Griff was unpredictable, and now he had the child he had no need for her, and she began to wonder what he had in store for her. Would he allow her to walk, to get on with her life, or would he make more demands with the threat of his ever present flick knife?

But then, her body gave up and she drifted into sleep and began to dream. Griff was there with other men. They stood, leering, drool dripping down their chins and she could feel the look of dirty, pure evil in their eyes. It was an evil she'd seen so many times before, an evil that only came from the deprived, the sex-starved and from the ones who liked to inflict pain, but this time they looked at the baby that she held in her arms. She glanced down to see Lily, newborn and smelling of milk and talcum powder. It had been a time when Annie had been happy, when she'd been with Bastion, when she'd felt loved, cared for and full of hope for the future. But then, without warning, Griff grabbed the baby from her. He held her up in the air like a prize trophy that he'd won, his eyes lit up all the while with lust like sparklers on Bonfire Night.

'You're not having her, you bastard,' she screamed out loud, her hands punching out and the dream overtook her mind. 'You can't, you can't do that, she's just a baby.' Her heart had been slowed by the drug, but the dream had stirred her and she felt a sudden rush travel through her. Then the van came to a halt, and she felt Griff's hand push against her shoulder.

'Wake up, and get out, we're here,' he said as the van door opened and a gush of cold air flooded in, rousing Annie with a start. She took in a deep breath, and turned slowly. Lily was still there, curled up on the dirty carpet in her brand new bright red coat. And even though the van was now filled with the coldness of night, she was still sleeping.

'Lily, come on, you've gotta wake up,' Annie shouted as she saw Griff begin to pace around the van, with his mobile in his hand.

'Yes, we're here. We've got the girl. You're gonna love her, she's a real peach of a kid,' she heard him say, as once again Annie closed her eyes, desperate to return to the part of her dream where Lily had been a baby, all smiling and cooing in her arms. 'Nah, we don't need her any more. Don't worry, I'll sort it.' Griff had used the word it, but Annie knew he was referring to her. She'd known that as soon as he had Lily, his interest in her would wane. She wouldn't be needed and it was now more than apparent that she no longer mattered. 'I know, I'll make it quick.' Griff continued to speak into the mobile, while looking at the van and directly at where Annie sat.

'Nah, she's too fucked up, she isn't worth selling.' He spat at the floor, walked away from the van and kept talking. 'No one would pay for that, not now.'

The words went over and over round Annie's mind, and she began to panic, suddenly realising that her time was up, that Griff didn't even see her as worth selling any more and he was going to dispose of her, just as she'd seen him do with so many other girls in the past.

'Mummy,' came Lily's tiny voice. 'I want Daddy. I want to go home. I want to go back to the nice house, to Nomsa.'

Annie looked over her shoulder. She needed to stay focused, needed to be sure of where Griff was at all times and, most of all, she needed to escape. Her eyes landed on Lily; she alone was her security blanket. While she had the child, she was safe. 'Lily, come to Mummy, darling.' She held a hand out to the girl, but Lily moved backwards, her eyes widening, and she shook her head.

'Where are we going?' The question made Annie sit up far too quickly and the feeling of nausea hit. She jumped out of the van and made her way to the wheel arch. Her legs felt weak, her body suddenly bent in two and she began to retch uncontrollably. She grabbed at the side of the van, wobbling in the stilettos; she needed to steady her footing. She couldn't fall, not here, and for the hundredth time that day she wished that she'd worn more suitable shoes. She thought back to the box of footwear in her room at the brothel. All her shoes were high, most were stiletto and none would have been suitable for running in. It was then that she saw a flash of red in the corner of her eye, a scurry of feet and a squeal as Lily jumped down from the van and tried to run. 'Oh, no you don't, you little shit, you get back here, you're my insurance.' She grabbed for Lily's collar, missed and then lurched her whole body forward in a rugby-style tackle. 'You get back here. Do you hear me?' She took hold of Lily's wrist and squeezed.

Lily stared at her with tear-filled eyes.

'Where the hell are we?' Annie looked up to the sky as the torrents of rain fell and landed heavily on her face. She stood there allowing the drops to hit her, all the while knowing that unless she could escape, this was probably the last rain she'd ever see or feel.

She searched her surroundings and saw that the motorway ran adjacent to the motel. There was a huge car park to one side, with a truck stop to the other. Would it be possible to get to one of the trucks? Would one of the men save her, or would they see her as fair game where she could find herself in deeper water than she already was? She took note of the rooms; they were all on one level and there were no windows at the front, just doors, all of which had metal reinforcement and three locks each, a sure sign that this place was not the Ritz. And then there was the office. It stood right at the other end of the complex and Annie could only just see the man who sat behind the counter. He was big and fat and from the way he sat in a comfy chair, his feet up on a stool with a television in the corner, he looked as though he was just settling down for the night; at a guess, he planned on ignoring any trouble that arose. She saw Griff walk in and Annie presumed he'd gone to collect the keys.

Annie began trembling with fear, knowing that even if she made a run for it, even if she managed to hide, Griff would easily find her. No, she had to play the long game, had to wait and find a chance to escape.

'Get off me,' Lily suddenly shouted as her foot kicked out and caught Annie square on the ankle, making her turn. She lifted her hand and swung it in Lily's direction, but pulled back at the last moment when she saw the look of horror in Lily's eyes.

'Next time you kick me, you'll get it, do you understand?' Annie pushed Lily towards the path, all the while searching for an escape route, hoping that a miracle would happen. But they were surrounded by fields, and not just one field, but long expanses of farmland that seemed to go on for miles. She spun around on the spot and squinted. Far in the distance she could see just a few tiny lights dotted across the horizon. It could have been a big farm with quite a lot of windows, or a small hamlet with just a half dozen houses dotted along a road. Whatever it was, the lights meant life, they meant people and they meant potential safety. She looked down at her feet. Would she make it across the fields, would she get there, to the houses?

Annie wished she'd known where she was. She'd never been one for travelling and didn't know many places outside of London, but the one thing she did know was that this place was not London. It didn't sound or smell like London and, what's more, they hadn't travelled far enough to get there. With her limited knowledge of England, she guessed at being somewhere on either the outskirts of York or Leeds.

'Go on, get in there,' Griff's voice unexpectedly bellowed above the sound of the rain and the motorway traffic. 'Get in there, room one, right at the end.' He pushed the first key in the lock, quickly followed by the second and third, before kicking the door open with his foot. 'You,' he said, poking Annie in the ribs, 'don't you get comfy. You've got work to do.'

Annie sighed. 'Come on, Griff, it's pissing it down. I'm not working the street in this.' She looked round the room. 'Where are we?'

'You don't need to know.' He threw a towel at her. 'Now dry yourself off.'

Annie rubbed her hair with the towel as she paced around the room. It was pretty standard as far as motels went – God knows she'd seen enough of them over the years – and she dropped the towel as her hand went across the teak table, the set of drawers and then finally the gold patterned bedspread, which felt grimy but somewhat cleaner than her own in London.

Griff picked up the towel and threw it back at Annie. 'Now, give the kid a bath. She needs to be clean and smelling pretty.' A sick, torturous laugh left his lips. 'And you, it wouldn't hurt you to take a bath for a change, Annie. Manager says there are more clean towels in there.' He pointed to a cupboard, and looked her up and down. 'You stink.'

Annie stood, nervously watching his movements, waiting for his hand to reach for the flick knife, but it didn't. She'd been sure he wouldn't think twice, and had thought it was in his mind, but he'd told her to bathe so he probably wasn't going to kill her, not right away. Still, for peace of mind she pushed Lily to stand in front of her while he hovered around the room.

'Right, I'll be back.' He walked towards the door.

'Where are you going and how long you going to be?' Annie demanded, her eyes continuously looking around the room, searching for a weapon.

'I'll be back later. You've got about an hour, and as I

said, both of you, get a fucking bath.' He pointed to the bathroom, then slammed the door behind him, and the multiple keys turned to lock her and Lily in the room.

Annie stood staring at the door.

'Why did he lock us in?' Lily asked as she ran to the door and tried to open it. She then turned and glared at Annie, before making her way to the corner of the room, where she sat down with her back to the wall.

'It's for our own safety. To keep the bad men out.' Annie didn't know what else to say. She made her way around the room, looking, searching and checking. But the bedroom had no windows and she began to kick at the walls. They were trapped, with no way out. She moved from the bedroom to the bathroom, where she saw a small, two-foot square window. It was high up, above the bath, and Annie stood on its edge while she tried unjamming the catch. Painting over it had sealed it closed and Annie cursed.

'Damn you!' she screamed. 'Not a fucking fire escape then.' She looked around, she needed something to prise open the window, but there was nothing. Which left her with no alternative but to do as she'd been told. She had to bathe the kid and wait until Griff got back in the hope she'd be able to get past him and get some help.

Annie turned on the taps and began to sniff at the bottles of bubble bath that stood on a shelf. 'Urgh.' Yet still she poured it into the bathwater and splashed it around, in the hope that once diluted, the smell wouldn't be quite so bad.

'Come on, get in,' Annie shouted to Lily who still crouched in the corner of the room. Lily shrank deeper into her coat and shook her head, with her eyes permanently fixed on the door as though she too were planning her escape.

Annie knelt on the vinyl tiles while she moved the water around in the grimy bath, testing the temperature. She thought of the last time she'd done this; the last time she'd bathed Lily as a baby. She remembered how Lily had loved the water, how her arms and legs had all begun waving around all at once and how she used to scream and giggle the moment she'd been undressed and could hear the water running. Annie remembered laughing at her, tickling her and kissing her. 'You're a water baby you are,' she would say as she lowered her into the bubbles, where Lily would kick her feet so hard that the water splashed up and over, drenching Annie in the process. It had been a good time in her life, a happy time before the drugs had once again taken their hold on her. She thought of the way things had gone, how one part of her life had been like a complete fog, yet the other part – the part before the drugs and the part where she was clean, and a mother with a man who'd loved her – all seemed crystal clear. She stared into the bubbles, afraid to break the trance and afraid she'd end up back in the real world, back at the truck stop, waiting to die.

Annie held her hand out to Lily. 'You need to get over here. Griff said we had to get a bath and, if I'm honest with you, I'd do what he says, cause he can be a real bastard if you don't.' She couldn't look Lily in the eye and instead stared at the wall above where she now stood, afraid that if she looked at her, she'd melt; she'd begin to hate herself for what she was about to do and she wouldn't be able to get her ready for what was about to happen.

Lily shook with fear, continuously inching her way along the wall. 'Lily, I said get here.' She watched as the child took one step forward. 'That's it, come on. Get your clothes off and get yourself in the water.' Annie paused, sat back and scratched at her legs. 'You're big enough now to bathe yourself, aren't you?' she said as Lily slowly moved towards her, dropped her coat and dress to the floor and slipped into the bath, where she sat, staring at the taps. 'Here, there's a flannel, get that used.' Annie dropped the once white flannel into the water and noticed that Lily was watching her.

'Is it nice?' Annie asked, but Lily returned the question with a look of disgust. Annie's mind went back again to when Lily had been a baby, when she'd looked up at her with smiles and sparkly eyes. There had been the game of fishes, where Annie had continually allowed the sponge to run in trickles down Lily's skin, a sensation that had made her squeal with delight. And for a moment she thought about playing the same game, but Lily was no longer a baby. She didn't squeal, smile or giggle like she had and Annie sat back against the toilet bowl, watching her as she rubbed the flannel on the soap and then onto her face and body.

She thought of all the time she'd lost and wished that Lily would smile, just once, just like she used to. She wished she'd look at her again with loving eyes, with a need for her love, her hugs and most of all her milk. Those times, those days had been precious. They should have been treasured and Annie wondered why she'd chosen the drugs and the street, wondered how much better her life would have been, if only she'd stayed with Bastion and been a mother to Lily. She nodded. If only life had been that simple. If only she'd have done just that, but she'd made so many bad, irreversible choices. The call of the drugs had been strong and her life on the streets had been the only way she knew she could earn the money to pay for it.

'Here you go, wash your face again, make it sparkle.' She picked the flannel up out of the bath water and passed it back to Lily, who once again rubbed it on the soap and screwed up her face before rubbing it with the flannel. 'There, you're all sparkly clean,' Annie said, smiling.

'Mummy,' Lily said. 'Why don't you like me?' The words were cutting but innocent. They were the words of a child who had no idea why she was here or what Griff was about to do with her. All she knew was that her mother had come for her and taken her away from the people she loved, and that she didn't want to be here.

Annie stared into space and her eyes looked back up to the window. Lily was so young. Would she remember her mother as the woman who didn't like her? Would she ever forgive her for what she was about to do? Annie thought about what would happen to Lily that night and then wondered why she was preparing her for the worst ordeal of her life. The reality was that she, Lily's mother, was washing and bathing her daughter in order to sell her to men for sex. She was going to give her to Griff in order to clear her drug induced debts. She was going to allow those monsters to buy her daughter and take her away. And she was doing it all to save her own skin.

Annie stopped and looked up to where Lily now stood, ready to get out. Would she really let them take her? She looked into Lily's big, saucer-like eyes. 'Lily, I do like you, honest I do. Please, don't ever think that I didn't like you.'

'So why did you take me away from my daddy?' The question was fair, and Annie wished she knew how to answer.

'I … I had no choice, baby.' Annie picked up the shower head and held it over her own hand until the temperature became more suitable for a child. 'Here. Let's get you rinsed off.'

Lily did as she was told and Annie rinsed the soap from her skin, before draining the bath water and wrapping her in one of the big off-white towels, where she stood all bundled up.

What was she doing?

Annie gasped for breath. She looked back up at the window and suddenly realised what she had to do.

'Lily, you need to get dried.' Annie caught her eye and stared into their depths and then, for just a moment, she pulled the child into a hug. 'I do like you, Lily. You must always remember that.' She'd wanted to say the word love, the child deserved the word love, but something had stopped her. After all, how could she profess to love Lily, especially after all she'd done to her? 'Get into your clothes, and your boots, be quick, there's my girl.'

Lily did as she was told, and pulled her dress on, along with her thick woollen tights and boots.

'Now, get your coat on.' She tossed the new red coat at Lily and then went to the door, to look out of the peephole. Griff's van had pulled up at the end of the car park. He sat inside, smoking and talking on the phone, and Annie knew he was making contact with the men. Men who would come, and soon. Men who would pay good money and men who wouldn't care how much they hurt a young, innocent child. She watched for a moment as a second car pulled up. Annie squinted to see more clearly as Bella walked towards Griff. She thought of the night she'd taken Bella's money, how Bella had suffered at the end of Griff's flick knife and now how different she looked without the tons of make-up, bright red lipstick and false eyelashes that for so long had been her trademark.

'Lily, you have to listen to me,' she said as she watched Griff talking to Bella. They laughed together and shared a cigarette. An act Annie thought odd, especially after what Griff had done. Annie spun around, she couldn't think of that now. She had to make things right for Lily.

'Lily, Mummy needs to break that catch.' She pointed to the window in the bathroom. 'I need to make the window open. Can you see anything that I could prise it with?' Annie asked and then watched as Lily dug in her coat pocket and pulled out an old penknife.

Nervously she held it out towards Annie. 'It's Daddy's. I stole it and I think he'd be cross with me if he found out.'

'Oh, Lily. Good, that's a good girl.' She turned to the window and with the blade, she cut into the paint, cut around the catch and watched as the old rusty rivets disintegrated beneath her touch. It had only been the paint that had sealed the window to a close and she pushed it open as hard as she could. But elation was followed by desperation. The window opened and then stopped as it hit a wall that had been built behind. The gap wasn't big enough for her to climb through and the drop was much too far. For a moment, she just stared, knowing she was trapped. She took in a deep breath. 'Lily. Come here.' She pointed to the window and then knelt before the child. 'Lily, listen to me. I've always liked you. No, goddamn it, I've always loved you, you might not realise it, but ...' She watched Lily shrug her shoulders, before she pressed the penknife back into her tiny little hand. 'Put this in your pocket, baby girl. Keep it safe, you might need to use it again before this night is over.'

'Why? Are we going somewhere?' She looked at the window. 'Are we running away?'

Annie couldn't answer and for the first time in years, she regretted it all. She regretted her life, the drugs and most of all she regretted ever having been involved with Griff.

'No, little one. We're not going, but you are.' She picked up the biggest of the bath towels and wiped her eyes. 'I want you to climb up and sit on the windowsill. Then you need to hold onto the towel. Mummy will lower you down to the floor.'

'What if I fall?' Lily began shaking her head. 'I can't do it. I don't want to.'

Annie heard a noise and momentarily closed her eyes. 'Listen to me.' Her voice was now stern. 'You have no choice. Now get up and onto that ledge and when you land on the ground, Lily, you need to run. Run as fast as you can towards the houses, the ones that are right across the field and you don't stop until you get there. Do you hear me?'

Lily nodded her head and a sob left her throat. 'But … but it's dark. I don't want to go.' She looked terrified, but Annie knew that this was the right thing to do.

'Honey. Bad men are coming. They're on their way here right now and I really don't want you to meet them.' She didn't know what else to say, but knew she had to get the child to run. 'Honey, if the bad men see you, they'll hurt you.' Tears began to drip down Annie's face. 'Now, go to those houses, look for a house where there are toys, a slide or a swing. Bang on that door, baby, bang on it hard and get that mummy to help you. She'll phone your daddy for you. Okay?'

Lily looked confused. 'But how do you know she'll be nice?'

Tears continued to fall unashamedly down Annie's face. She didn't have time for the explanations, she knew Griff could walk in at any moment, but she knew that this was the last contact she'd ever get with her daughter. 'Because she's a mummy, baby girl. And all mummies should be nice, shouldn't they? You have to trust me, Lily. I promise, she'll help you.' Annie pushed Lily towards the window. 'Now, climb up.' She stood on the side of the bath and hoisted Lily onto the windowsill. 'Lily, whatever happens, run, and, baby girl, please, don't look back.'

Annie watched Lily's contorted face as she began to sob. She was terrified of climbing out of the window, being dropped to the ground and running through the fields alone. But Annie had no idea what else to do. 'Please, Lily, you have to go, here, grab hold.' Annie had tied a knot in the towel and she watched as Lily grabbed at the knot. 'It's not too far down, just like jumping off of a swing … there you go. Are you on the ground?'

Annie saw Lily's saucer eyes as she nodded and she could see Lily staring back at her, not knowing which way to turn. Annie closed her eyes, she could hear Griff's voice outside. 'Cruel to be kind,' she whispered to herself as she waved her hand at Lily. 'Go, go now,' she growled and then climbed down from her position on the bath. She knew that this would be her last night on earth and that she'd never see her daughter again. She just hoped that her final act of kindness would find her just a small place in her daughter's heart, and in years to come she might realise exactly what she'd just done for her.

Chapter Thirty-Nine

The keys began to turn in the motel door. Griff's voice bellowed outside and the door opened. Griff's frame filled the whole doorway like a volcano rising up out of the doormat. He turned on the main light, looked at Annie, around her and then glanced at the bathroom door.

'What's she doing? Where is she?' he said with menace.

'She's in the bath. Like you said,' Annie answered, scratching at her arms and playing for time to give Lily a chance to get away unseen.

'Come on, Griff. Where's the brat? I'm not sitting out there all night.' Bella strutted into the room and spun around as though searching for something, but, in doing so, Annie caught sight of the white bloodstained lint dressing that covered the left side of her face.

'Bella ...' she said. Annie pointed to Bella's cheek. 'Why ... I mean, what the hell are you doing here? Why the hell would you work with him ... after he did that?'

'Oh bejesus, Annie. You're fucking stupid some days.' She turned, looked at Griff with hate in her eyes, and smirked. 'I have to work with him, don't I? I owe him money, thanks to you.' She shook her head. 'So, I'm here to take the kid. Where is she?' She spoke carefully, and held her face in a certain position as she said the words. 'I haven't got all day. Is she here, or not?' A confused look crossed her already distorted face.

Griff looked at the bathroom door, stepped forward and pushed it with his foot. 'Get out here, you little brat.' The door swung open, the bathroom empty.

Annie could feel herself shaking. She knew he'd erupt and every millimetre of her body trembled, making her reverse until her back was pressed hard against the wall. 'Griff, you ... you've got to realise. I ... I—'

'Where the fuck is she, Annie?' Griff's rage was palpable.

'She's gone,' Annie whispered. 'You'll never find her, not now.' Annie needed to get away, needed to get to the door, but to do that she had to get past Griff.

But he had already worked that out and quickly moved towards her, making Annie drop to the floor, her arms lifted above her head. She screamed as Griff grabbed her hair with one hand, as the other swiped out and caught her in the face. 'What the hell have you gone and done, Annie?' he shouted. He then began tearing around the room, searching. 'Where the hell is she? I want to know, now!'

'Get away from me, Griff. I've called for help,' she lied. 'The police, they'll be here any minute.' She began crawling on her hands and knees like a puppy towards the door.

'The buyers are on their way to the meeting point. They'll go fucking mental. We'll all pay for this.' He spoke directly to Bella, his finger wagging in the air. 'You need to head them off, give me some time to find the kid.'

Bella began to laugh. 'Oh, no. Don't you get me all mixed up in this, Griff. I was just the bloody delivery girl, the one who picks her up here and hands her over at the meeting point, all so that you get to keep your hands all nice and clean.' She nodded her head and put her hands on her hips. 'I was doing you a bloody favour, a way of paying back the debts. Debts I wouldn't have if it wasn't for her.' She jangled her car keys and took a step back, and then used her foot to slam the door behind her. 'And, Annie, don't be fucking stupid all your bloody life, you're not going anywhere.'

'Bella, you ... you have to listen to me.' Annie was still on her knees, her hands held out in prayer. 'He's going to kill me. I heard him on the telephone and as soon as he can, he'll kill you too.'

'Annie, you took my money. Maybe I should save Griff the bother and kill you myself.' She smirked with half of a right handed smile, while the left side looked fixed or frozen with pain.

'But, it wasn't me. I didn't take your money. You have to believe me.' The lies spilled out of her mouth naturally, and she looked Bella in the eye and allowed them to continue. 'I … I saw one of the others, coming out of your room that day. I … I—'

Bella leaned over with long unwashed hair, her eyes millimetres from Annie's. 'Don't fucking lie to me, Annie. I know what you are. You're a good for nothing dirty addict. An addict who would sell her own child. What kind of a mother does that? What kind of fucking monster are you?'

'But she isn't here … I … I couldn't go through with it. I didn't sell her. I let her go, didn't I?' Annie scrambled, on her hands and knees, to a position beneath a teak table. She used the chairs to barricade herself in and for just a few moments she wondered if she'd be safe. But in one swift movement the whole table lifted up and Griff threw it to the other side of the room, Bella standing close behind him.

'Give that here,' Bella screamed as she grabbed Griff's flick knife from his back pocket and pointed it at Annie. 'You, you owe me, bitch, and you … you owe your daughter a fucking apology.' The blade swung in front of her face. 'Poor fucking kid having you for a mother. I can't think of anything worse.' Annie could see the fury in Bella's eyes, and knew she was about to strike.

'Go on, Bella, give it to her. After all, we're all fucked now the kid's gone, aren't we?' Griff bellowed and Annie could see him shuffling from foot to foot. 'Bitch took your money, didn't she? And you … you ended up with that disgusting scar 'cause of her … didn't you?' His fingers pressed against

Bella's face, tore the dressing from her and revealed a bright red, ugly, puckered scar.

'Get the hell off of me, you bastard,' Bella suddenly screamed and her whole body spun at once. The flick knife flashed through the air, slicing Griff clean across the throat. Blood sprayed the room and Griff grabbed at his wound as he began to make an odd spluttering sound, before falling backwards and collapsing to the floor.

Bella laughed, long and piercing. 'You damned asshole. See what it's like to be slashed. It's not fucking nice, is it?' She nodded, hovered over his body and stared into his eyes as the last breath left his body. Then she went down on her knees, and began rocking like a child, while stroking his blood-covered face. 'There, there, Griff, does it hurt?'

Annie moved to her side. 'Bella, come away from him. Please, please, come away, he doesn't deserve your pity, not now.' Her arm went around Bella's shoulders. 'You did the right thing, Bella. He had it coming, didn't he? I'll … I'll stand up for you, you know, in court. I'll speak to the police, I promise.' She pulled Bella into a hug. 'Oh, Bella. He's gone. It's over, we're free. We're finally free of him.'

Bella hugged her back, and for a moment a strange peace came over the room.

Annie closed her eyes as her hand stroked Bella's hair and then she leaned back and looked into her tear-filled eyes. 'Do you know what, Bella? For just a minute, I really thought you were coming for me, I sure did. But … but I should have known you'd go for him, especially after what he'd done …' Suddenly she couldn't draw breath. There was a sharpness that made her pull away and she fell backwards to slump against the bed as she felt the knife retract.

Bella leaned forward and kissed her on the cheek. 'That, my dear Annie, was exactly what you deserved … that was for your little Lily and for the monster you've become.'

Chapter Forty

The only noise that could be heard was the clock that ticked away regardless. Jess, Madeleine and Nomsa all sat in silence. All stared at the carpet, holding hands and barely breathing, while Bandit and Bastion stood outside, waiting for the police.

Madeleine glanced over at Poppy, who had been too frightened to go to her bed and now slept soundly curled up in a chair. Madeleine turned back to the CCTV and switched it back on. She'd watched it repeatedly and had initially sobbed relentlessly. But now she watched without emotion. It all happened right there in front of the camera. The white van pulled up, Annie climbed out and Lily stood looking shocked. The woman had held out her hand, but Lily had looked scared and reluctant to go with her. Annie had held onto the hood of Lily's coat, while beckoning to Poppy. Madeleine had felt her blood boil as she watched her do it over and over, until Lily had shouted at Poppy and pointed to the Hall, which is when Poppy had dropped her doll and Annie had tried to grab at her too. But Lily had been fast, she'd grabbed the doll, pushed it into Poppy's arms and then pushed her away, hard.

'She saved my Poppy. She knew Annie was going to take her too, so she pushed her, shouted at her and acted mean to her, just to make Poppy run.' A single tear fell down Madeleine's face, just as the service lift pinged, opened, and Jack emerged, smiling.

'Well, you think you're on a promise and you wait and wait for your good woman to come up, but then you end up waiting so long that you begin to die of hunger.' He looked between Jess, Nomsa and Madeleine whose faces resembled the gargoyles on the Hall's roof. 'What? What's happened?'

Jess stood up and walked over to Jack. 'Jack, it's ... it's Lily. Annie, she snatched her.' The words were the most difficult she'd ever said, especially after what Jack had gone through to try and save the child. 'It was raining, Nomsa fell, and we took our eyes off Lily for just a few seconds and she was gone.' She tried to explain, but didn't have the words. 'The police are on their way.'

A silence fell between them all until Nomsa spat out, 'Well, as far as I'm concerned, Christmas is cancelled. I can't bake cakes, or cook turkey, not while our little Lily is missing. No, I can't.' Nomsa sobbed continuously into her apron. 'Oh, that word, missing, it sounds so wrong.' She pulled a tissue from a box and waved it in the air. ''Cause she isn't missing, is she? She was taken, taken away from all of us who love her and right before Christmas. Oh, lordy, lordy, what is the world coming to?' Nomsa stood up and paced around the room. 'It's all my fault. If I'd just kissed Bastion back like he'd wanted and hadn't fallen on my stupid ass, none of this would have happened.'

Jack sighed and wheeled himself to Nomsa's side. 'Oh, Nomsa. None of this is your fault.' He took her hand. 'These people are evil. I heard them, I heard what they were planning and they were laughing about taking her.' He paused, lifted his fingers and gently wiped away Nomsa's tears. 'Honey, they were determined, and if it hadn't been today, it would have been tomorrow, or the next day. So you see, it wasn't your fault at all, it was them, they are just nasty, depraved people.' He nodded, while acknowledging his thoughts. 'I really don't think any of us could have stopped them.'

The front door opened and Bastion walked in closely followed by Bandit, two policemen and a policewoman.

Introductions were made. Nomsa stood up to make her usual mugs of tea and Jess perched on Jack's knee. Bandit and Bastion took the policeman to view the CCTV footage.

'What do we do?' Jess asked the policewoman.

'We just have to wait. With the registration plate on the CCTV, the vehicle's details will be circulated, so if they're out there on the road system, it'll ping on the ANPR.'

Jess sat forward. 'And what if it doesn't?'

Chapter Forty-One

Lily inched down the alley, all the while looking up at the window. She stood for a moment and looked at the field. It was a long way to the houses beyond and she wasn't sure if she should climb the fence, go across the field and do what her mummy had said, or wait and hope that someone would come, someone nice who might help her.

She hesitated, but then heard a shout, a loud, angry shout, that came from beyond the window. The man was back and Lily was scared. She headed towards the fence and squashed her body between the rungs, and began making her way through the muddy field. She tried to head towards the houses, towards the tiny lights, but it was dark. The houses now looked a long way away and the only light she could see came from the cars that sped past on the motorway.

She began to run but the mud squelched beneath her feet as the rain still poured and she stopped and took in a deep breath. 'What do I do, Daddy?' she whispered in the hope that he'd suddenly appear and hold her hand, make her feel brave and give her the advice that she needed, just as he always had. It was the first time in her whole life that she'd ever been totally alone and the first time she'd had to make a decision for herself, without an adult there to guide her. She crouched down beside the hedgerow. She was at the edge of the field, and for what seemed like forever, she just sat and sobbed. 'Where are you, Daddy? Please come, please help me.'

She looked up at the dark sky and tried to think what her father would say. The rain had now stopped, but the clouds still circled above her. Yet within them, she could see the Hall. She could see Jess and could hear her words.

'Don't cry, princess. Life is hard. But do you know what I do when I get sad? I do something really brave, something positive and I close my eyes and I think of all those who love me the most, does that make sense? You're my sister and we all love you so much. You're safe here, I promise. Everyone here will look after you, you do know that, don't you?'

Lily stood up. Jess had told her to be brave, she'd told her she'd be safe, but she wasn't. And for a moment she tried to decide whether Jess had lied to her.

She began marching towards the houses, but her boot stuck in the mud and she felt her foot come out of it; her new white sock suddenly became wet, covered in brown slushy ice-cold mud. She turned and looked back at the lights, to where the motel had been, now far in the distance. She stared at it for a few moments, wondering why her mother hadn't come with her. Why hadn't she jumped out of the window too?

Tears once again threatened to fill her eyes, but she didn't want to cry. She was determined to be brave and even though she didn't want to, she had to keep moving forward, knowing that she couldn't go back. She pulled her boot from the mud, and slipped over and onto her side. Her new red coat was now dirty and she pulled a tissue from her pocket and began to try and wipe the mud from it. Again Jess came to mind. 'She'll be so annoyed that I got my coat dirty,' Lily whispered to herself. But then she smiled as she remembered the day they'd been at the hospital, the day that Jess had bought her the coat, and had told her how lucky she was to be her sister. That had been the day Jess had put the two one pound coins in the envelope and had written her phone number on the back. It had been the day she'd said the words, 'I'm going to write down my phone number and if ever you feel scared, afraid or if you just need me, you call. Okay?'

Lily pulled the zip down, opened her pocket and pulled the envelope out. There it was, there was Jess's phone number and with it was the money that she'd given her. Her mummy had told her to run, had told her to go to a house where a mummy would live and she'd said that all mummies were nice. But Lily didn't agree. Not all mummies were. So she stepped onto the street, where she began looking for a phone box. If she could find one, she could phone Jess and then, then she could go home.

Chapter Forty-Two

The fire crackled in the hearth, the Christmas tree twinkled in the early morning light and Jess sat on the chesterfield settee and stared into the flames.

She took in a deep breath. Her eyes were tired, but she couldn't sleep. Not until Bandit and her father returned, not until they brought Lily home and all her family were once again safe under the Hall's roof.

'Hey, you okay?' Madeleine asked as she walked into the grand hall, two mugs of tea in one hand, a bag in the other. 'Nomsa sent more tea.' They both laughed. It was the twentieth mug of tea that Nomsa had sent since they'd had the distraught phone call from Lily. 'I don't know where I am,' she'd said. 'I'm in a village, my coat is all dirty and my sock's covered in mud.' Her tiny voice had sobbed and stuttered between the words and Jess had felt her own heart break as she'd told Lily to put the phone down and call 999 and ask for the police. 'When they get to you, give them my number. Be brave, Lily. We love you and we're waiting for you to come home for Christmas.'

Jess had then sat with her heart in her mouth as she'd waited for the police to call her back.

'Thank you,' she said to Madeleine as she took the tea and began to sip. 'What's in the bag?'

Madeleine passed it to her. 'Emily's diaries. I found them.'

Jess sat forward. 'Let me see. Where were they? Where did you find them?'

'Well, think about it. Where did Emily live for a while, with Eddie's mother?'

Jess nodded. 'In the Gatehouse. Is that where you found them?'

Madeleine smiled. 'They were in the loft, where the dust motes are, waiting to be found,' she said, and opened one of the books.

'And …' Jess grabbed her hand. 'Are you going to write her story?'

Madeleine nodded much to Jess's delight, just as Len walked in with Buddy close on his heels. 'Hey, there, boy. Come here,' she called and the springer jumped up on the settee beside her and snuggled in. 'Thanks for walking him, Len. Is everyone else okay?'

'They are, Jess. I'm just going to bring Jack down. I took him up a couple of hours ago, but I think being on the bed is driving him a bit mad.' He turned and headed towards the stairs, just as the front door opened and Lily ran in, making Jess jump up from her seat.

'Oh my God. Thank goodness you're home. I was so frightened. So very, very frightened.' She sank down to her knees. 'You've been on quite an adventure, little one, haven't you?' She pulled Lily into a hug without waiting for an answer. It was one of those hugs that lasted forever. But finally she let go and then stood up to shepherd her sister towards the settee, where Buddy covered her with a shower of kisses.

Then they were surrounded. Both Bastion and Bandit walked in, and Nomsa ran in from the kitchen and without hesitation placed a kiss firmly on Bastion's lips, before scooping Lily up in her arms. 'Don't you ever scare me again, my little one, do you get that?' She buried her face in the youngster's hair. 'I couldn't bear it if anything happened to you.' She looked up with tears streaming down her face, and Bastion patted her on the shoulder and then put his arms around them both, as everyone gasped.

'What the hell, you all know what's going on anyhow,' he said with a shy grin as he continued to pull both Nomsa and Lily into his tall strong frame.

Everyone began to laugh just as Kirsty MacColl and the Pogues' 'Fairy Tale of New York' started playing on the CD player, and Len came into the room pushing Jack in his wheelchair, followed by Bernie and Ann.

Jess wiped away her tears. It was Christmas and everyone was together, everyone was finally safe and under one roof. She placed a hand on her stomach. 'You, little one, you are going to be part of one hell of a family, do you know that?'

The whole room began to laugh. Jack caught her eye and she felt the love travel between them. She nodded; she had everything she'd ever wanted, right here.

She stood up. 'Where's Poppy?' she asked, just as an excited four-year-old ran into the room and straight to the tree. 'Aunty Jess, Aunty Jess, now that Lily's back can we open our presents?' She stopped in her tracks. She had no idea what had happened the night before, but had been told as she had been put to bed that Santa would only come once Lily came home. And now she stood there, with her whole face lit up. She held out a hand to Lily. 'Come on, Lily. Come and look.' They both knelt down and peered beneath the tree.

Jess smiled. 'Go on, Lily.' She pointed to a gift. 'Take a look at that one, can you read out what it says?'

Lily physically shook with excitement and pulled the gift towards her. 'To Lily,' she said. 'One of the most special little girls in the world. Love Santa x.'

'Go on, Lily, open it,' Jess urged her. 'It's all yours, you're allowed.'

Lily pulled open the parcel to reveal a long pale pink dress. Her mouth dropped open and she looked up at Jess. 'It's so beautiful, Jess. It's a fairy princess dress. Are you sure it's all mine?'

Jess nodded. 'It sure is, honey. It's a bridesmaid's dress. I kind of wondered if you'd be one of my bridesmaids next week at our wedding?'

Chapter Forty-Three

Jess stood before the tall, full-length mirror. She looked herself up and down as she admired her appearance. The long, white, fitted wedding dress hugged her body perfectly. Its neckline looked high at the front, but as she turned she took note of how the cowl back hung loosely behind her.

'Oh, Maddie, do I look okay?' Jess turned to face her sister who sat on the bed leaning against the pillows. Maddie was dressed in a long, pink, satin bridesmaid's dress, with sparkling silver shoes that reflected the tears of joy that filled her eyes.

'Jess, you look more than okay. You look stunning.' She stood up and walked over to the dressing table, picked up a diamante necklace and went to place it around her sister's neck, but Jess stopped her. She opened a drawer and took out a long box, which contained the precious necklace that Emily had left her and wanted her to wear on her wedding day and beyond.

'It was Emily's,' was all Jess had to say as Maddie took it and fastened it around her neck.

'There, now you look perfect.' Her hands rested on Jess's shoulders for a few minutes and together they stared into the mirror, just as they'd done so many times before.

'Come on, or I'll be a mess. I don't want to cry and ruin my make-up, not in my state,' Madeleine whispered as she walked towards the door.

'In your state? What do you mean?' Jess's eyes opened wide. She knew exactly what Maddie meant. The signs were all there, she just needed her to say it.

Madeleine nodded. 'Looks like we'll both be mothers together.'

Jess stepped forward and put a hand on Maddie's stomach, just as Maddie had done to her the week before. 'Oh, Maddie. This is the perfect gift. Our babies, our children, will grow up together, just as we did.'

Madeleine smiled. 'They sure will, but right now ...' She took a deep breath. '... right now, one of us needs to go and get married.'

Jess stopped in her tracks. 'Maddie. There's one more thing.' She picked up an envelope and held it up in the air. 'This came and before I get married, I ... I just have to know the truth. It's time for all the secrets to be put to bed and for the truth to come out, once and for all.' She paused. 'Do you think I should open it?'

Jess and Madeleine held each other's gaze, for both knew that whatever was in the envelope would change lives forever. Good or bad, there would be no turning back.

'Whether Bastion is your father or not, you know that he will be sticking around the Hall, don't you? He and Nomsa are so in love and Bandit and I have offered him a job. But if you want my opinion, honey, no, I don't think you should open it. I think you should give it to Bastion and you should open it together.'

Jess gasped. She knew it was a risk, knew it could ruin the day, but Bastion had been so certain that he was her father when he'd come here, and she just felt deep in her heart that he was her daddy and Lily her sister.

Madeleine pulled open the door and held out her hand to Jess, who took it and followed her into the corridor and then slowly down the grand staircase to where the congregation sat waiting, along with a very excited Lily and Poppy who were both dressed in identical bridesmaid's dresses. They bounced around continually and for a moment Jess wondered if they were both attached to pogo sticks.

But then she looked towards the dining room door,

where Nomsa stood, smiling and patting her eyes with a tissue, with Bastion by her side, looking just a little more than nervous.

Jess took the final steps and cuddled into him. 'I'm so pleased that you're here. Honestly, I am.' She held the envelope out to him. 'This came.' She looked up at him.

He took the envelope from her.

'I'm hoping that this … that this envelope holds the news that both of us want.' She looked at Nomsa. 'That all of us want.'

He nodded and took in a deep breath. 'Okay, well …' He looked directly into her eyes. 'I'm ready if you are, my girl.'

Jess smiled. 'I sure am and … and Dad, once this is done …' She placed her hand on his. '… would you mind walking me down the aisle to my future husband?'

Bastion wiped a tear from his eye, nodded, and without hesitation tore open the envelope and read its contents. Then he held out his arm. 'I had no doubt, my girl, no doubt at all. Now …' He passed her the envelope and allowed her to scan its contents. 'Now, it's time for your daddy to do as you asked and walk you down the aisle to your man.'

Jess smiled, her eyes filling with happy tears and she reached up and kissed him on the cheek. She then looked across the room to where Jack sat in his wheelchair beside the Christmas tree. Their eyes locked together and, as the 'Wedding March' began, with just a little assistance Jack stood and turned to the minister in front of him.

Jess linked her arm with her father's and, followed by Madeleine, Poppy and Lily, she walked towards where Jack waited.

'Are you okay? Should you be standing?' Jess whispered.

But Jack just laughed while looking her up and down. 'Oh, Jess, you look amazing. You are so very beautiful. And, no arguments … after the reception, I'm taking you to the farmhouse and like it or not, I'm going to carry you over the threshold of our new home.' He nodded. 'You just see if I don't.' His eyes sparkled and caught hers and she knew that Jack meant exactly what he said.

Jess let go of her father's arm, smiled and then stepped towards Jack. She reached up and kissed him on the cheek. 'You have no idea how much I love you, do you? And yes, you can carry me over the threshold, even if I have to sit on your knee in the wheelchair. But … but could you make me a promise …?' She glanced from Jack to Bastion, and then to Madeleine and Bandit. 'Do you think next year we could all just have a nice, normal, and really boring Christmas?'

Thank You

Dear Reader

Thank you so much for reading *House of Christmas Secrets*, my sequel to *House of Secrets*.

I really enjoyed writing this book and hope that you enjoyed following Jess's story. I'm sure you'll agree that she had quite a journey on her hands before she found her happiness with Jack.

I'd like to think that anyone reading this book would want to go and stay at the beautiful Wrea Head Hall themselves. I can assure you that the trip is worth it for the food alone, where great attention to detail is always paid. I always love to try the different rooms, each one exquisite in its own way and at least once during my stay I hike through the woods to visit the summer house, or on a cold winter's night I tend to sit by the inglenook looking up at the Christmas tree and listening to Christmas carols while watching the logs burn in the fire.

Like all authors, I've been on quite a writing journey and I still find it surreal that I now have three novels published. With that in mind, I'd love to know your thoughts and I'd be delighted if you'd take just a few moments to leave me a review.

Please feel free to contact me anytime. You will find my Twitter, Facebook and website details on my author bio.

Once again, thank you for reading. It was a pleasure to write this novel for you.

With Love, Lynda x

About the Author

Lynda, is a wife, step-mother and grand-mother, she grew up in the mining village of Bentley, Doncaster, in South Yorkshire.

She is currently the Sales Director of a stationery, office supplies and office furniture company in Doncaster, where she has worked for the past 25 years. Prior to this she'd also been a nurse, a model, an emergency first response instructor and a PADI Scuba Diving Instructor … and yes, she was crazy enough to dive in the sea with sharks, without a cage. Following a car accident in 2008, Lynda was left with limited mobility in her right arm. Unable to dive or teach anymore, she turned to her love of writing, a hobby she'd followed avidly since being a teenager.

Her own life story, along with varied career choices helps Lynda to create stories of romantic suspense, with challenging and unpredictable plots, along with (as in all romances) very happy endings.

Lynda joined the Romantic Novelist Association in 2014 under the umbrella of the New Writers Scheme and in 2015, her debut novel *House of Secrets* won Choc Lit's *Search for a Star* competition.

She lives in a small rural hamlet near Doncaster, with her 'hero at home husband', Haydn, whom she's been happily married to for over 20 years.

House of Christmas Secrets is Lynda's third novel.

For more information on Lynda visit:
www.twitter.com/LyndaStacey
www.lyndastacey.co.uk
www.facebook.com/Lyndastaceyauthor

More Choc Lit

From Lynda Stacey

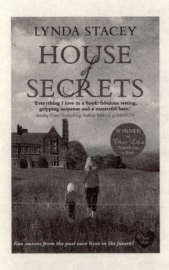

House of Secrets

A woman on the run, a broken man and a house with a shocking secret …

Madeleine Frost has to get away. Her partner Liam has become increasingly controlling to the point that Maddie fears for her safety, and that of her young daughter Poppy.

Desperation leads Maddie to the hotel owned by her estranged father – the extraordinarily beautiful Wrea Head Hall in Yorkshire. There, she meets Christopher 'Bandit' Lawless, an ex-marine and the gamekeeper of the hall, whose brusque manner conceals a painful past.

After discovering a diary belonging to a previous owner, Maddie and Bandit find themselves immersed in the history of the old house, uncovering its secrets, scandals, tragedies – and, all the while, becoming closer.

But Liam still won't let go, he wants Maddie back, and when Liam wants something he gets it, no matter who he hurts …

Winner of Choc Lit's 2015 Search for a Star competition!

Available in paperback from all good bookshops and online stores. Visit www.choc-lit.com for details.

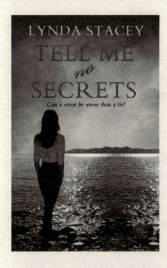

Tell Me No Secrets

What if you couldn't escape your guilt?

Every time Kate Duggan looks in a mirror she is confronted by her guilt; a long, red scar reminding her that she was 'the one to walk away' from the car accident. Not everyone was so lucky …

On the surface her fiancé Rob is supportive – but the reality is different. He's controlling, manipulative and, if the phone call Kate overhears is anything to go by, he has a secret. But just how dangerous is that secret?

When Kate begins work at a Yorkshire-based firm of private investigators, she meets Ben Parker. His strong and silent persona is intriguing but it's also a cover – because something devastating happened to Ben, something he can't get over.

As Kate and Ben begin their first assignment, they realise they have a lot in common. But what they don't realise is that they're about to bring a very dangerous secret home to roost …

Available in paperback from all good bookshops and online stores. Visit www.choc-lit.com for details.

Introducing Choc Lit

We're an independent publisher creating
a delicious selection of fiction.
Where heroes are like chocolate – irresistible!
Quality stories with a romance at the heart.

See our selection here:
www.choc-lit.com

We'd love to hear how you enjoyed *House of Christmas
Secrets*. Please visit **www.choc-lit.com** and give your
feedback or leave a review where you purchased this novel.

Choc Lit novels are selected by genuine readers like yourself.
We only publish stories our Choc Lit Tasting Panel want to
see in print. Our reviews and awards speak for themselves.

**Could you be a Star Selector
and join our Tasting Panel?**
Would you like to play a role in choosing which novels we
decide to publish? Do you enjoy reading women's fiction?
Then you could be perfect for our Choc Lit Tasting Panel.

Visit here for more details…
www.choc-lit.com/join-the-choc-lit-tasting-panel

Keep in touch:
Sign up for our monthly newsletter Spread for all the latest
news and offers: www.spread.choc-lit.com. Follow us
on Twitter: @ChocLituk and Facebook: Choc Lit.

Where heroes are like chocolate – irresistible!